Everything Is Known
The Straight Shooter of the World

I0658970

By
Liza Elliott

E Elliott Studio

Birmingham, Alabama

Liza Elliott/E Elliott Studio
Birmingham, Al/35222
www.everythingelliott.com

Book cover design DeLoach Graphic Design Studio

Everything Is Known/ Liza Elliott. -- 1st ed.
ISBN 978-1-937014-08-7

To my big brother, Ed

"*the state is not a "thing" but a relation – class relations played out as a set of institutionalized social power relations, struggles, and practices.*"

WILLIAM I. ROBINSON, *Global Capitalism and the Crisis of Humanity, 2014*

CONTENTS

SITUATIONAL AWARENESS 1

FLIGHT 9

AFTER HOUR...29

CAP CITY...35

REUNION 47

FIRST WATCH 69

PRIME NUMBER 81

ON THE RUN...85

STRATEGY..95

OUTLIER TOWN...101

BUSINESS 111

SOUTH 117

SOS...129

SITUATION 135

LONGHOUSE 143

CONFUSION...161

RESCUE...169

THE CORE..187

SIBLINGS 199

POPPY 207

EXPOSED 213

GRANDMOTHER................................215

TRAITOR..223

SUSPECTS 227

ROSARIO..239

LOST 245

KISS THE ELDERS..............................249

ALLEGIANCE 257

TIME...267

DELIVERY 277

COMMITTEE...287

DISTRACTION 303

MASSACRE..309

DEPARTURE 315

WAREHOUSE 54 321

BATTLE...335

GOOD BYE...341

RECORD..347

HOME 351

The Fourth Epoch..................................352

CHAPTER ONE

SITUATIONAL AWARENESS

Under the hazy dimming light of another rainy day, Skyla Roseau hopped into the transport hover-van just as the doors slammed shut, unaware it would be her last ride home. She tucked herself into the last open seat. The hem of her charcoal grey trench coat hung just below her knees, above the tassel of beads on her black suede boots. Dense black strands had come loose from the chunky clip holding the bulk of her up-swept hair. They brushed against the red scarf around her neck, a few framing the high cheekbones of her exquisite face.

The overcrowded commuter vans filled with stale air and rigid plastic seats were a drag no workers could escape. The same riders took the same seats every ride like an addiction. Today was no different. The scrawny deaf man always sat on the right aisle in the rear, so he could see all the passengers. The bony, blonde woman who always rocked back and forth in her seat, sat in the middle in front of the ad screen and ignored everyone. Like always, she'd glue her bulging green eyes to the screen of any orange spotless van, which shuttled workers coming on and off shift, twenty-four hours a day. Skyla couldn't wait to get home. Tonight, Jaffa would be there. He had promised to stay.

She leaned into the rush of the van, glad there were only two more stops. She pictured Jaffa opening the door for her before she could unlock it. She hoped he was already there and had fed Jaguar. They both had coal black hair, but unlike hers, theirs were soft to the touch. Jaguar's fur was silky and straight. Jaffa had wild corkscrew curls. When snuggled all together in bed, Skyla would stroke them both as they drifted off to sleep. Contentment would fill her orphan's heart and only then could she relax to welcome her own sleep as a gift.

The van slowed to a stop. The bony woman hesitated. She couldn't pull her nervous face away from the ad screen as it flashed a sale price of some gadget. The deaf man reached over, tapped her arm and pointed to the door. He shook his head and frowned. She pulled up the hood of her jacket before staggering into the drizzle. Skyla wondered if he had acted out of pity, but it really didn't matter. It was rare to see help toward a stranger in public because it broke the policy of "mind your own business" on public behavior. What guts he has, Skyla thought, aware that cameras known as POVs (Points of View) recorded all this. She nodded to him. He lowered his head and smiled. They had only a commuter friendship, just mini bursts of time when they rode the van to work and back, year in and year out. They knew each other's stops, but that was all.

Skyla faced the ad screen flashing one fabulous thing after another. She wished she could mute the grating sound and white out the flashy pictures. The van began to slow as it approached the next stop. She stood up and grabbed the rail overhead for balance. She worked her way by the other passengers toward the middle door. The van came to a stop and the door hissed open. She stepped out into the rain and began a brisk walk steering toward the brown brick building ahead. The deaf man watched her from the window as the van picked up speed, passing her.

Up ahead, Skyla noticed the outline of figures on the corner and slowed her pace to a crawl. Custodians, armed and heavy-booted security agents, half a dozen perhaps, surrounded a man on his knees. She could make out only a vague silhouette from the purple haze of the street lamp against a backdrop of flashing lights from the digital billboards. Even if she knew him, there'd be no point for her to help. There'd be no charges, no trial, and no defense, just guilt for being there. The poor guy could not be saved. So, she hung back in the shadows and waited for him to be carted off to his fate.

Soon enough, the gang of Custodians withdrew. They vanished back to patrol within the shadows of the street while two bulky agents flung the prisoner into an official vehicle and drove away. Skyla watched the drama come to a close and remained still. She was no stranger to street life and knew that running draws attention. Despite the urge to hurry home, she could not be sure the path was clear of Custodians still on the prowl. She paused to take a deep breath and then just as her big brother had once shown her, she moved forward in a quiet pace until she reached the front door of the brown brick building. With a single swipe of her wristband past the outside lock, the door clicked open into an empty foyer. Once inside, she flew up the three flights of stairs to the landing of her door. She paused to pull off her glove. Just as she raised her thumb to the touch sensor lock, the door swung open.

"Love doctor," said Skyla, throwing her arms around Jaffa, just as she had imagined. She inhaled the fresh scent of his black curls, lingered for a moment, then stepped back to kiss him.

He pulled her close and pushed the door shut behind her. He wrapped his solid arms around her. Skyla pushed her curves, full but fit, into his six-pack and found his lips. They stood in each other's embrace and for a few seconds the pressures of work and the hardness of living fell away.

"I hate to move," said Skyla. "Me too, but we can't stand here all night." Jaffa turned and pointed to the couch. "I fed Jaguar. He's waiting for you on his pillow."

"Thanks. You know how he loves his kitty schedule."

"Sure. I got lucky and left early today. My last patient didn't show up," said Jaffa. "He was a crusty old Peripheral type, who lost his job to a new model robot. The rumor mill ran overtime and heaped all the blame on the poor guy."

"What was the Affiliation's reason?" asked Skyla.

"The usual line. He didn't sell enough stuff to make himself valued by his Affiliation."

"That again? Can't the Affiliations come up with a better lie?" Skyla laid her head against his chest.

"You'd think so. The latest round of robots to replace workers is sweeping Cap City. Everyone sees it. But the lie is sweet and easy to digest. Blame the worker, not the owner. Poor guy, he disappeared to save his family from the risk of losing their jobs by association. Now, he's lost to the street. You know how it is."

"Cruel. Community is dead. We're on our own." Skyla pulled his chin to her and kissed his cheek. "You are a good man with a healer's spirit. And I love you." She broke away from him and tossed her trench coat on the iron coat tree in the narrow hall. A shadowy mound on a couch cushion began to move. A long black furry leg extended for a stretch. "Jaguar." He raised his head as she reached to rub his ears. She kissed him on the top of his head. "Jaguar, my little boy." He curled his tail and released it with a soft thump. Skyla stroked Jaguar under his chin and called to Jaffa. "I have it."

Jaffa opened a cabinet and took out a slim bottle of whiskey. He poured two glasses, straight up. "It? What 'it' do you have, my mystery girl?"

"The intro. Finally. I know how to write it." Skyla went over to her computer that sat in the middle of assorted data sticks lined up like rows of corn. She pulled a white one from her pants pocket and plugged it into the data port.

"It's here in a file. I jotted down some key words to use when I write it."

"When did this happen? Yesterday you were ready to quit." Jaffa stretched out on the couch beside the black cat.

"True. But you know I never give up. So, today, at work I looked around the room and there he was, sitting in front of a me all this time." Skyla turned her flirty, sparkling brown eyes on Jaffa.

"Who?"

"Winston. From Orwell's 1984. Winston was just one of countless workers, Peripherals like us." Skyla tapped the keyboard to bring up her file of words. "You know I have to write something flashy for the committee to accept my study. Orwell's book is sort of like tarnished silver, you know, old and dark. His words may be antiques but, with a little polish, they'll have enough shine to get me the degree."

"And the degree will set you up for promotion to the Core," said Jaffa in a flat voice. "And that's what you want."

"Isn't that what all of us want, the chance to get to the top? The Core is the top." Skyla took a sip of whiskey. "I watched this woman in the van on my way home. She sat frozen under POVs, hypnotized by the ad screen. It was like watching Orwell's novel come to life."

"Will your professors even recognize him? I only know about him from you. That guy is from so long ago. It's like me talking about Louis Pasteur and the germ theory of disease." Jaffa toyed with Jaguar's tail.

Skyla turned to Jaffa. "True, but my study is about how three old, taken-for-granted things got together and now rule the world. First, there's the corporations which we have to call by their new name, Affiliations. Then there's the market. Last and hardly noticed anymore, surveillance. What's better than an old Orwellian lens to take a fresh look at how well all this is working for us?"

"That could be risky. The Affiliations' markets love their surveillance and demand adoration. You won't be regarded as an adoring affiliate to them if you whip up the ghost of Orwell and it turns into a horror show."

"I'll be careful. Just jazz it up a little and it's done. It's only a bunch of fancy words strung together." Skyla pulled the data stick from the computer and added it to one of the rows. "Who'd ever read it but my professors? It's just a job to them and the last hoop to jump to finish school." She squeezed in between the man she loved and the cat she cherished.

Jaffa opened the clasp in Skyla's hair letting her thick mane fall to her shoulders. "I have to go to the South tomorrow, my turn at the Outlier clinic. The rats with plague are out of control. Since we are trying to prevent another epidemic, I'll be gone a few days." He tucked a lock of hair behind her ear. "So, I don't think you will be writing this intro tonight."

"Then what shall I be doing tonight?" She sipped at the whiskey and nestled against him. Jaguar yawned and rolled onto his side, stretching out a paw letting it come to rest on her leg.

"We'll think of something." Jaffa glanced at the POVs lens mounted high on the corner of the hallway wall. A tiny white machine sat on a slim shelf below the lens. It projected a time-looped video onto the wall at the exact space monitored by the lens. There were rules against blocking POVs, the ever-present camera lenses. Skyla had insisted to him that a substitution was not the same thing as a block. Privacy was resistance.

CHAPTER TWO

FLIGHT

George Orwell got it wrong. Big Brother did not come from a totalitarian state, but from a totalitarian non-state. And it was Big Data, a relentless, digital spy who with sneaky eyes and listening ears snooped on everything: your clothes, your friends, recording every word you spoke or wrote. It kept account of all this and more to amass the info power it needed to control the market, the heartbeat of the money economy. In time, it took charge of the market by taking absolute control of all surveillance.

Big Data knew how to defeat the market opposition softies for control of all things. With treacherous innocence of face, it spoke outrageous words through any tool with a screen reaching to the most remote hinterlands. It sowed fear while amassing money-power with the soothing balm of market rhetoric. Who doesn't love a market? It loves only a market. Orwell thought state power over people was the prize. Big Data saw the error. It knew power over people is in the money-

power over things. People love to buy things. For Big Data, the state was just one of those things.

Skyla's words flew from her fingertips on the company keyboard to the computer screen, lining up like birds on a wire. She nudged them with care the way one might stroke a baby chick. Perhaps Jaffa had been right. Invoking Orwell was a bit dramatic, but she needed to convince her professors that she could do the heavy lifting of a critical thinker. She had to write them a movie with an all-star cast. She had to ratchet up her words, to show a straight shooter's truth. Only then could she hope to survive the raw competition for the coveted final degree, her ticket to promotion, and the Core. Skyla reread her words, certain she could defend them.

She had staked out the signal, the name Orwell, and the challenge that he was wrong. This would lead to the science, the data, and her findings about their world ruled only by data and markets but not people. She would call her study A Bizarre Bazaar.

With Orwell's lens focusing her thoughts and each keystroke as a dagger, she had cut away the cloak that shielded Big Data, the slick digital spy controlled by corporations that controlled her fate by controlling every transaction she had ever made or could ever make. Big Data controlled her, like everyone else, once they were assigned at birth to one of its five mega corporate Affiliations. By building a super-spy system for Big Data, the five global Affiliations could buy and sell all human activity for profit.

To Skyla, Big Data, the digital spy and the Affiliations were one and the same.

Skyla paused to check her notes for the next key word—abdication. Yes, the head of state who sold it all away, she thought, the Humpty Dumpty. Her words began to fly to the screen again.

He was large of frame and girth but was petit and petty of mind. He could not aspire to rule the world and instead strove to collapse the globe into his provincial homestead. He could feel every aspect of it like his own body. The paunch he could not hide when he sat down formed the hill before him. It served as the border beyond which he had no interest. If he couldn't feel it or touch it, it was of no use to him.

Like people milling about a room, the farther they strayed from his belly-hill, the more they disappeared, out of focus, being unusable to him. Only people close to him mattered. And for them he would pillage it all—the planet, the souls of his fans, the rule of law and nations. But never his own fragile psyche. He did not like to think too deeply.

She sat back in her chair and sensed her big brother's voice in her head. His firm whisper filled her ear, the tune he chanted each morning as he buttoned up her coat and saw her off to school. "The world needs a smart girl. Skyla. Be that girl." In a sea of orphans at the children's home where they had been placed, he was her compass, her North Star. Skyla studied her gutsy words, the words of a smart girl. Her big brother would be proud of them, of her, if only she could show him, but he had vanished one day. His voice remained stowed away deep in her heart, surfacing now and then, like a reminder, like now.

She glanced out the window wall of her office and spotted a drone hovering at eye level. She tapped the keyboard of the computer to restore the screen saver, a confetti style logo of Celebration Wholesale. There was nothing random at Celebration Wholesale, Skyla knew, including the drone outside her window.

This small winged model, sleek and silent, shaped like a robin, watched its target from its breast of smooth tinted glass. No one could ever see where the lens was pointed. Everyone assumed it was pointing at them.

Skyla hoped the glass bird did not see her composing the introduction on the computer. She doubted it mattered what she wrote just now in front of the drone, just the fact that she did. Writing was not part of her job. Filling orders and fielding questions in customer service was her job. So, all in all, breaking rules of Celebration Wholesale did matter enough that a drone was sent to spy on her. She suspected the interior room POVs lens could not detect her screen due to the glare from outside light. As for the telematics embedded in Celebration Wholesale's computer system, it could only recognize the key-stroke pattern of customer service scripts to monitor length of time per call, products sold, and her break time. Robust telematics that could detect and "read" her texts were not the norm for low-value status companies like Celebration Wholesale in Affiliation Green. Still, no companies tolerated personal use of their computers for long. She adjusted her headset, keeping her eyes on the computer even though she had two more minutes left in her break. She stared at her folded hands and listened to the whir of the overhead ceiling fans, letting it spin her thoughts toward a daydream.

In the spare minutes, she dreamed about her words of Mr. Orwell's long forgotten future foretold. She scrolled back through time to knock on his door and alert him to the mistake that existed within his prediction. The state did not survive to be a worldwide "big brother" but was dismantled piece by piece and sold on the scrapheap of outdated tools. Its parts were picked up on the cheap by the new corporate digital spy, aka Big Data, who rose to power with the promise of absolute security in all things.

Orwell underestimated the choice of the people for security above all else. In the end, people did not reject surveillance out of fear of "big brother" like he thought they would. Instead, no government routinely creating generalized fear had to convince the citizens with much effort that they needed to be watched. People welcomed checkpoints, bag searches, and monitors as the routine of daily life. They snatched up the camera with gusto, lured by social media and the chance to take and bare their own pictures. Selfies did more to boost the exposure of all things personal than any Stasi or KGB or CIA of the pre-Collapse world. The personal is public. Social is media. People wanted to be seen, all the time, everywhere. Big Data, the shadowy spy of money power, alive in the five, new, corporate Affiliations, conned the people. Big Data sold the people what they wanted, the lenses, the software, all of it, even as Big Data, itself, took control of everything. Soon, everything was known. Everything is known. Everything will be known.

At the threshold of the office doorway, the scuffs and scrapes of shuffling shoes grew louder and louder. The noise snapped her out of the daydream and jerked her back to the present. The break was over. She glanced around the office. Perhaps it was careless to stay at her desk during break. All other hourly wage Peripheral workers, or "wagers" as Skyla called them in her study, escaped to the cafeteria, the rooftop park, or the lobby. No one hung back at their desk, a wireless coop of earphones and mikes, one of hundreds in a sprawling bland grey room filled with bright, cold light. They were expected to leave during break and doing the unexpected could affect the balance. Celebration Wholesale demanded balance from every wager to better sell every extravagant thing they could to anyone who could buy such a thing for any celebration. Why else would they send a drone? Skyla figured the company might suspect a wager not taking a break was off balance.

"Skyla. Don't you ever relax?" Riff wedged onto his chair at the desk across from her. "They expect you to leave your desk. They want you to go somewhere, anywhere."

"What's it to you?" Skyla squinted her bright brown eyes, framed with delicate full eyebrows so she wouldn't have to absorb a full view of her most detested fellow wager. She watched the rest of the wagers as they returned from break.

They led anxious lives of desire for everything marketed to them in a seamless, vaporous way as if it was in the air they breathed. The perfume of consumption. It could not be turned off any more than you can turn off the air, lest you suffocate.

Their downcast eyes could not hide their anxiety about job security. There was no stopping the poisonous chatter about new customer service robots that they had heard. The worry wore away at them.

The only hope for their Peripheral jobs lay in the irony that the robots might prove incapable of processing the high level of confusion or stupidity of customer calls that made up the bulk of the job. Perhaps only humans can be rational in the face of the irrational. Only human to human interface works in that case. Score one for humans, she thought to herself.

Riff adjusted his headset, smoothing out the thin blonde hair on the top of his head. As if a grand thought occurred to him, he stated with a slow, solemn tone of voice, "You know, Skyla. What you do on your break actually means nothing to me. Do what you want. But don't bring attention to the rest of us."

Riff had clawed up the hourly wage earner ladder to his current job. He gossiped like an old town crier wearing his loyalty to Celebration Wholesale like a Boy Scout badge. Early on, Skyla pegged him for the office stoolie who would sell you out with precision and stealth. It only took him to ask a gutless question like "What is she doing at her desk all day?" in front of the supervisor to initiate someone's rapid, painful job death. Riff was nothing but an organization man, an assassin to take out any threat to Celebration Wholesale.

Skyla had witnessed him in action, his flawless attendance, his devotion to company protocol. She recognized his loyalty as proof of his collusion. She sensed he would attack her soon.

She focused on his slight potbelly and chubby thighs that stretched the seams of his khaki chino pants. She felt sorry for POVs that had to see all that and the rest of him naked during the random healthy body checks. Skyla was no fan of POVs but some things were better left unseen, even though everything is known.

Skyla swiveled her chair so her hands were hidden from the window and saved her intro to the white data stick. She never stored any of her draft work on the caché, which retro fans would still call the cloud. With this tiny act, she fantasized that she could detach from her own Affiliation Blue to create a reality whereby she would know more, and it would know less about her. She answered a phone call now that her break was officially over. The drone pulled back and sped away against a backdrop of haze and brown clouds.

"Celebration Wholesale. How may we celebrate with you?"

"How do I know if something should be celebrated?" said a woman pausing every few words, out of breath.

"Everything can be celebrated. We have items that can meet your every need," replied Skyla. That scripted line annoyed her, but selling products was the purpose of her job. She needed this job. Jobs were hard to get, especially for wagers, for Peripherals, like her.

"I have just been released by my Affiliation. At long last, I am free," the woman said. "But of course, that means I will die soon."

"Ma'am, surely there is a mistake. Why will you die soon?" Skyla knew of the dark ending from being judged unmutual, of losing one's Affiliation with no option to appeal. It was a living death when one's Affiliation struck you from its active list and cataloged your existence into the historical database. You were finished. It was the end of your story, no matter how much you might still be alive.

"There was no mistake," said the woman, "I was declared unmutual. Now I can't buy any medication from any Affiliation. The blood and fluids in my system are already backing up into my lungs. I will drown soon. But that's ok. You see I am free. It's time to celebrate."

Skyla heard a ragged, throaty cough through her headset. "Ma'am, how can I meet your every need?" The scripted line was meant to redirect the conversation and she knew it had to be said. Everything she said was recorded to promote money power, and the unquestioned rule of Big Data, and the Affiliations.

"I think some throw beads, like they use for Mardi Gras would be nice. In green, purple and gold, the Mardi Gras colors. Yes, I'd like to order those," the woman said. "Can I get them by tomorrow?"

"Yes, of course. How many sets would you like? There are a dozen sets in a packet," said Skyla.

"Two, please. Here is my money-unit card." The woman held a card to her phone and the image with number transferred to Skyla's computer screen.

Skyla studied the computer screen then glanced around the room. Her office mates were busy attending to their own calls. No one had seen her face react at the message on the screen, as if someone had taken hold of the skin on her cheeks and yanked it back into her hairline. Mae Carrington, ordering throw beads for an impending death had written an extra message on her card in cursive. *Skyla. Leave now. Great danger.*

"Thank you, very much. Please wait while I send you confirmation of your order." Skyla placed the order with a couple of clicks. She massaged her forehead with her left hand. Her eyes reread the forbidden text, the meaning crystal clear. "Is there anything else we can do for you?"

Skyla heard a deep phlegmy cough followed by silence and then the phone rang off. She kept her eyes on the screen. She knew the room was visible to POVs the ever-present lens, the tool of Big Data, of the Affiliations. Few people could remember life without POVs.

Another call lit up her screen. It rang in her earpiece. She needed this job. She had to answer. She took a deep breath and smiled to no one, knowing POVs would approve.

"Celebration Wholesale. How may we celebrate with you?"

"Why are you still sitting there? You need to leave now. Info will follow." The voice, now muffled by speaking into a cloth gave way to deep coughs.

"I believe you have the wrong number. Please call again for all your celebration needs," said Skyla. She glanced at the clock. Quitting time was hours away. She could not dismiss this message as a prank. Who knew she could read cursive? It was long banned as a threat to Big Data because the writer could conceal secrets in the patterns. Even digital cursive fonts were criminal. Anyone caught using cursive faced deletion, the official word for the death penalty. But if you were dying anyway, the threat no longer held sway. How did Mae Carrington, a complete stranger, know Skyla could read it? Skyla shook away the mystery to act.

She slid her data stick deep into her upswept hair. With one motion, she removed her headset, put her computer on sleep mode, and grabbed her Celebration Wholesale clear plastic satchel. She slid on her trench coat without a sound and walked out. The other wagers focused on their customers. Riff noticed her leave. POVs did too.

Skyla chatted about the crummy weather with Sam, the portly, daytime security guard while she walked through the exit check. She headed toward the door but made a quick pivot toward a service exit on the side. She skidded out behind a deliveryman before the door closed with a lock. She made her way to a small side street leading to a trash alley just as the street alarms began to wail. Grey armored jeeps and urban tanks converged at the main entrance of Celebration Wholesale. A hulky SWAT team, topped in gleaming black helmets stormed the steps, jackboots bounding them two at a time. She watched this shiny display of battle ready police owned by Affiliation Green in the reflection of the glass of a small ice cream shop. She checked herself from looking up toward an POVs lens mounted on the wall of the building beside her. People know never to make eye contact with POVs.

Whiffs of stinking air from rotten fruit emanated from a trash alley, the one place POVs did not monitor with real lenses, but only with data boxes. No Core members or Peripherals stayed for long because of the intolerable stench. Affiliation Orange handled waste removal but paid scant attention to its least profitable sector. None of that mattered to Skyla just now. She smelled her way into the nearby alley. Here, she unclipped her hair and retrieved her prized data stick. She pushed it deep into her inside coat pocket, then zipped it close. After tucking her thick ebony mane inside her collar, she buttoned up her coat to cover her red scarf. She jammed her satchel into her other pocket.

Her silent wrist phone vibrated with a text message showing an image of one word in cursive, *Longhouse*. Then another cursive message: *nix on the glow worm*. Skyla powered down her wrist phone. She slipped it off and smashed it with the heel of her boot to break the nano sim. She scattered the micro splinters into different piles of rotting food at the back of a dumpster, then covered them with other scraps of trash. The brown clouds of morning had given way to swollen grey clouds that darkened the day. They began to rain dirty droplets that pinged off the dumpster and other cans in the alley. Skyla pulled the hood of her coat up over her head. She was grateful for the rain, which gave her cover as now everyone in any street had a hood up. Umbrellas had long been outlawed since the Hong Kong Umbrella Revolution way back before she was born.

She set out to move, shielded by the trash alleys, the highways of the Outliers. Neither members of the Core nor Peripherals, like her, Outliers were the discarded people. If they could not function in the Affiliation run world, they were cast off. Their pitiful lives were their own fault. There would never be sympathy. They scrounged out a life with the dregs and leftovers from the wealthy Core and plain Periphery. Some worked unpredictable day labor jobs while others scrounged in the junk and the trash. Skyla, like most diligent Peripherals plugging away to get by, felt closer to them than the pampered, indulged members of the lavish Core. She would share the Outlier paths and take refuge in their company, knowing they couldn't care less.

The alleys were not parallel to the main streets of the city. Their erratic paths slowed but did not deter the Custodian security agents and the traffic police that kept order for the Affiliations. Outlier residents who knew the alleys well enough could hide deep in the labyrinth and with a twist and turn backtrack through them. Skyla knew them well enough but was unsure of her destination. Longhouse did not have a location. It was everywhere and nowhere. Some people said Longhouse was a hoax, a scam to dupe the people into thinking they could escape the Affiliations. She had made a leap of faith, trusting an unknown message only because it came in cursive, an outlawed tool, but once the venerated medium of poets, teachers, and lovers.

So, she wove her way among the narrow lanes, layered in trash and dingy people huddled in makeshift dwellings. They watched for traffic police on motorbikes in the tight lanes who enforced a merciless slog that went nowhere. The makeshift carts, or bikes, or anything with wheels could only inch along like sludge through a pipe. Meanwhile, the people kept scuffling along, though few had a journey's end. The traffic cops made sure the Outliers knew Big Data's power could reach them too.

On all roadways that skirted the trash alleys, vehicles moved along in a regulated steady pace. Traffic was adjusted to the local conditions from data fed from auto sensors to remote towers. Official Affiliation vehicles could always go offline and speed away. The traffic police had orders to ignore them.

Ahead, an Asian traffic policewoman wearing white gloves gave a ticket to an Outlier for sitting in the alley. Sitting was parking and parking was illegal. Outliers would collect ten tickets that would get them a night in the local traffic jail, where they could shower and get a hot meal. On release, they would submerge into the vast deep of trash alleys and begin to collect tickets again. Traffic police mostly ignored any Outlier's call for help. They did not want to be physically close enough to talk to them or if need be, cuff them. The smell. It was always the smell.

Skyla reached a point where she had to cross a street to find the next trash alley. The weathered Asian traffic cop, wearing a pine green uniform and white gloves, stood on the raised platform, the rain bouncing off its canvas roof.

The traffic police contract, held by an Asian corporation, was part of Affiliation Orange, which operated the remote controlled traffic pace and patterns. Affiliation Orange affiliated most persons of any Asian descent due to its Asian leaders. The white gloves were their hallmark. The traffic cops were there to troubleshoot anything that upset the traffic flow. But, everyone knew they were the traffic spies for the Custodians.

Skyla feared the Custodians. Everyone did. They could forcibly cut anyone from their daily life at any time from any place. Once in custody, the Custodians were free to kill the detainee, then conduct a permanent digital deletion. With this final blow, a life never existed. She tightened her hood and zipped up her collar a bit higher. All she could to do was to keep moving as far as possible from her usual haunts and vanish into the massive anarchy of Outlier towns. She studied the traffic flow, the people walking on sidewalks and the direction the traffic cop faced. A man bumped into her from behind and grabbed her arm, pulling her back from the corner.

"Wait. Stay. It's ok." The whisper was low and deliberate.

"What do you want?" Skyla turned to see his face. "Tangier!"

"Nice to see you, too." They took a few steps back into the shadows. "Give me your satchel. It has a tracker built into it."

"Since when?" Skyla wriggled it out of her pocket and gave it to him.

"Doesn't matter." He squinted large brown eyes similar to his sister's. "Do you know why Mae Carrington contacted you?"

"Mae? Who is she? I don't know her at all."

"You don't remember?" Tangier closed his eyes as if transporting to another dimension, another time. "How could you? You were a baby when everything changed."

"Now, you're scaring me. Tangier, even, this, you dressed like an Outlier. I thought you made Core member. What happened?"

"I did make Core." He pushed opened a metal door to the hallway of a tenement and pulled her in. He glanced around the dank foyer. No POVs here. "Not a word or I won't tell you." Skyla nodded. "I made Core after I finished my degree in value studies. Then it happened. Three Custodians surrounded me on campus and served me with recruitment papers. You can only smile and sign on the spot while your whole existence is being ripped away from you. You can't say no to them. So off I went."

"You're a Custodian? Leave me alone." Skyla started to walk toward the door, but Tangier blocked it.

"Skyla, hear me out. I'm not with them. I'm a double agent. I'm loyal to Longhouse. And Mae Carrington is our grandmother."

"Grandmother? Alive?" Skyla shook her head and stifled a scream. "How do I believe you? My only family, my big brother, who I loved, went away and hasn't been seen or heard from in years. An agent, a Custodian?"

"I'll tell you everything. First we must get you to safety." Tangier placed the plastic satchel on the tile floor. He crouched over it, pulled a small bottle from his pocket and drizzled a viscous liquid over it. Within seconds, the purse melted into a puddle, exposing a microchip. He crushed it with his shoe and stood up.

Skyla ran her hands through her hair and wound a lock into a knot. She tugged on it and calmed herself. "But why? What have I done? I have nothing to hide."

"It's you we need to hide. Something about Orwell? Something about Big Data?"

"I only wrote about Orwell this morning. It was that drone." Skyla hit her head with the palm of her hand. "I didn't think it could see my screen. I was trying to be your smart girl. Remember?"

"You are my smart girl, but it wasn't the drone. They have upgraded the telematics at Celebration Wholesale. They can read anything you type on the keyboard. They watched your words appear and all hell broke loose."

"How did you know?" Skyla squinted her eyes in the dim light.

"I look after you." He put his hands on her shoulders. "There were two alerts about you. Celebration Wholesale today and yesterday one of your idiot professors in the behavior studies department registered your study data as a threat to the Affiliations."

"My study?" Skyla gasped. "How? It's just words. There are no threats to anything. This is ridiculous."

"Doesn't matter now. Opportunists are given a big money prize, a reward for reporting a threat to Affiliation power. If someone needs extra money units, it's an easy way to score. Third level spying makes everyone greedy. You know, those anonymous tips to the Custodians about suspicious behavior is an easy way to score some money units. The Custodians always follow up the tips. They come for you. They will delete you, like any common criminal." He took her hand and tapped "trust me" into the palm of it.

"Why? You're one of them," she tapped back into his hand, while locking her eyes on the cool, calm face she had missed for a very long time. Skyla pulled up her hood and started toward the door.

"Because I am your big brother. I am not Big Data." He spat out the words so hard his cheeks flushed. "Now, let's get you to safety. I have family waiting for you." Tangier opened the door and observed the crowded alley. He motioned for her to follow. She kept close and hoped she was not falling into a trap. Stripped of all gear, she had no choice but to trust Tangier, who sang her to sleep as a little girl, who taught her to read and write cursive, who taught her Morse code, who taught her how to sing and dance, who told her stories of life before the Affiliations, with parents he knew, but she didn't. He had never hurt her. She held on to that and his hand as together they crossed the road under the traffic cop, who waved directions with his white-gloved hands to vehicles that ignored him.

After a few blocks, they disappeared back into the protection of stink and dim light, emerging now and then to cross a road, and then back again into the shadows. The alleys served to move vermin and people, although it was difficult at times to tell the difference.

CHAPTER THREE

AFTER HOUR

Riff waited for his next break like a drooling hyena scoping the next kill. He had completed his last call, selling three boxes of Affiliation Green flags to a small company that sold reefers, scents, and candles. With ten minutes yet to go, he blocked his incoming calls so he could fingerprint his previous customers. It took only a couple of clicks for him to upload notices and ads based on a taste/desire algorithm of their Web use and shopping history. The next time they went online, new product ads fingerprinted to them would appear out of nowhere. He was their connection, their dealer, pushing product they craved to buy. They begged to buy.

When home alone, which was frequent as he didn't have friends or pets, having never managed to keep any, Riff found company by digging into the private lives of customers or fellow wagers. It was a mystery to him why shaving his armpits in order to be clean scared women away. That and his insistence they wash him after sex with a warm washcloth. He thought women wanted clean. He grew to resent them and their putrid ways. For payback, he snooped deep into their email, their financials, their documents, and even phone conversations.

Skyla, his fantasy girl of gorgeous, thick, black hair, with slight feathered bangs that hovered above brown eyes, and smooth chestnut skin was unreachable for him. It cut his enflamed heart to shreds. With the sting of a jilted lover, he stalked Skyla through cyberspace until he came upon her dissertation. It was his biggest find to date and guaranteed a promotion, but not at Celebration Wholesale. "Hello, I am Special Agent Riff," he would practice to his bathroom mirror each morning. Each time he pictured himself in a meeting with the senior agents, the top brass. He would explain how Skyla pissed him off with her arrogant walk, her dismissive smile, as if she were better than he. "Why did she feel so superior?" he would ask them. He would follow with the answer, "She had a deep, dark secret, I figured, which motivated me to spy beyond what is required in my duties." None of his off the clock digs were authorized, but Custodian agents by definition look for dirt and sweep it up, keeping Big Data, the Affiliations, pristine and safe.

Riff arrived early for this evening's daily check in, reviewing the day's events, wondering how he missed whatever set Skyla on the run. He could see a figure through the glass office door, a solid man, with cool blue brown skin and black hair sheared so close it was soft instead of nappy.

"Riff, come in." Senior Agent Stilton leaned back in his chair behind a sleek metal desk.

Monitors, like a checkerboard, covered three sides of the room, seamless as wallpaper, each with a view of a private space. Public space did not exist for all space was owned by an Affiliation—a grocery store checkout line, a street corner, a park, a beauty shop, a hospital, a bedroom, anyplace and anywhere at any time. In this viewing studio, six agents sat at desks in front of them. Stilton studied an agent entering data into a computer. Satisfied that nothing was out of balance, he turned toward Agent Riff. "Got anything more?" He turned an icy look on the grunt.

"No sir. She left in a hurry, just threw off her head set and walked out, calm and cool. I finished my shift, then came here as instructed for new orders."

"We know that. We also know she's gone silent. No wrist phone. No company tracker." Stilton stood up, rolled his huge shoulders back as if standing at attention and walked over to one wall of monitors, one of many walls in secret rooms that comprise the receiving end of POVs. "She fled to the trash alleys."

"That stuck up bitch? God, how could she stand it?"

"Yep. That stuck up bitch is pretty clever. But I have my best man on it. He's already made contact. He'll bring her in." Senior Agent Stilton put his tough, sinewy fingers on Riff's shoulder and squeezed it. "You are our man in Celebration Wholesale. For now, continue in your cover as customer service rep. Let us know if anyone there talks about her or wants to reach out to her. Keep up the good work." Stilton released his grip.

Riff swallowed, having endured the spike of hot pain, the show of rank. He stared at Stilton's lean physique outlined in a fitted, unyielding black uniform shirt. He had already turned away to lean over another agent who was replaying a scene on a monitor. Riff's own flab shamed him. He detested himself.

"There, that's her crossing a street, now turning down a trash alley. She's alone." Stilton stood up and crossed his arms in front of himself. "Not for long."

Riff waited a couple seconds before he spun around and walked out. His face grew red with hot rage. He was just a minion, a petty field agent to them. He brings senior asshole Stilton a big find and all he gets is a paltry, "Keep up the good work." The elevator door opened. He stepped in and slammed the first-floor button with his fist.

Riff replayed his discovery of Skyla's blasphemous study, a clear threat to Affiliations' security. Only last Saturday night, alone as usual in his one bedroom, spanking clean apartment, at two in the morning with a bottle of vodka and a shot glass, he had dug one more time. She was at the top of his list to snoop as payback. No one told him to do this but no one told him not to either. Initially, he couldn't find anything. She had pretty secure firewalls on her documents. Impressive actually. She might be a bitch, but she was smart. Still, with nothing to do with the hours till dawn, he stuck to it. On a hunch, he typed Jaguar, the name of her cat, into a deeply embedded security wall. Her one weak link revealed.

Never use a pet's name, he said out loud as he tapped the return key with a smack. Once he unearthed the files he reported them to Stilton. Although not a final draft, its implications were too disturbing to allow it to be completed, much less published. At least that is what Stilton told him.

Stilton's lack of excitement bothered him. He wondered if someone like a professor had scooped him. His own report would only be considered a confirmation of a threat already known. No prize for that.

Still, what Riff had read made no sense to him. She wrote something about the Affiliations being props for a gang who rules the world. She had highlighted words from a guy named Orwell. Utter nonsense; but if Stilton wanted her gone, so be it. She would become one of "the disappeared." Deleted. It occurred to him that he might well be responsible for sending Skyla to her death. He realized, with sudden great clarity, it was safer for him not to let Stilton know he had read part of it, even if he did not understand it. When the doors of elevator opened, he aimed straight for the bar down the street. Lots of agents met there, but since they were in their alias disguises, Riff never knew exactly who was real or not. He heaved himself onto a barstool and ordered a beer.

CHAPTER FOUR

CAP CITY

Skyla followed close to Tangier, moving in tandem along the way.

"You're slurking," whispered Tangier. He had paused to scan an alley.

"They lurk, then slink. They slurk!" Skyla called back. "I cannot believe you remember that!"

"A long time ago." He waved for her to follow and turned the corner.

Cap City spread out like a web. Thoroughfares jammed with electric cars, trains, and transport vans connected countless identical tiny town centers to each other. Stylish brick or stucco, ivy covered buildings were hidden behind electrified fences. Core members lived in these glamorous oases.

Towns for Peripherals were simple, low-rise no-frills blocks of multi-family units. Checkpoints controlled their access at the main entrance gates that were never locked. Peripherals rarely committed crime, their behavior conditioned over time to avoid risk and the loss of their prized stuff. The mere thought of life as an Outlier was disgusting enough in most cases to keep a Peripheral's behavior in check. Meanwhile, POVs kept watch of it all.

"Skyla, what's wrong?" Tangier stopped when he felt her pull on his arm. He crouched down, forcing her down next to him.

"I have never been to Outlier camps. I only know Outliers in the trash alleys of the Periphery." Skyla stared out over the shapeless camps of makeshift shelters, shacks of plastic and remnant sheets of corrugated steel that went on and on and on. "Look at the squalor. How is this possible?"

"How? You wrote your study on this. You know how!" said Tangier.

"Yeah, I know. The rights of property replaced the rights of people," she replied.

"And, this is what it looks like." He patted her arm. "It's rough."

"But the sheer scale of the misery is beyond imagination. It's cruel," she answered. "Just a rotten beam on which all of the Core and Periphery teeters."

"Still using those fancy words. That's what put you in danger. Do you know why very few people see camp towns? The rules keep us all in our places. The moral rules of Big Data's world are quite clear. Our Faith is in the stuff we buy. We worship at the altar of money power. Prosperity is our salvation."

"You're right. And, you either meet the top requirements for the Core by birth or brains or you end up a Peripheral or Outlier." Skyla stared at the bleak reality in front of her.

"Exactly. And, if you can't be trusted to be a lifelong consumer, then get out of the way. Consuming is the motor of the Affiliations," said Tangier. "It's what makes everything run."

"If you know this, how can you continue as a Custodian, their agent, spying on the rest of us?" Skyla shook her head. "How do you sleep at night?"

Tangier looked up at the brown clouds through air heavy with dust, typical of this time of year when ash from chronic wild fires raging far away gets deposited by winds that blow in circles. "I remember when the sun was bright yellow, the skies blue, the air clear and sweet. And clouds looked like scoops of white ice cream."

"And, I don't." Skyla regarded her big brother, his black hair, thick like hers, the same chestnut skin. Faint creases had begun to frame the corners of his deep set brown eyes, but he was ten years older. "Do you really think you can bring back the past?"

"No. I can only make the present safer for those I love." He stood up. "Let's go."

"Do POVs watch out here?" Skyla scanned the camp for the all-staring lens.

"Yes, but not everything is a fixed lens that you see in the Periphery. Fresh Custodian agents, training in deep cover techniques, do most of the dirty work. I am one of their trainers. No GPS tracking on me. They don't dare question me." Tangier motioned the direction and tapped "code" into her hand. She nodded.

Tangier switched their direction, continuing his zigzag across the grimy camp towns. With each jump across a flooded pathway and shift in direction, Skyla pondered her brother's allegiance to Longhouse. She could only trust the big brother she hadn't seen in years since she knew neither the safe houses nor paths of Longhouse. She cursed the Affiliations for tearing apart her family just for money. They rounded the corner of a trash alley when a short, scruffy man wearing a knit cap stopped them.

"And where do you think you're going?" He pointed a short rifle at them.

"What's it to you, you piece of shit?" Tangier replied.

"It's my business to know. The girl with you, she's on the wanted list." The man stood very erect trying to dominate them.

"Very well done, Knob. You have seen the latest fugitive list. This woman is a look alike for the test." Tangier slapped him on the back in congratulations. "You have passed an important test."

"Sir? A test?" The short man shrank into his boots.

"Yes, of course. I am one of your trainers. That's all I will say. I must keep my own cover. You have been tested on a fugitive watch list protocol. Now, we must continue our work, and you carry on as well. Be assured I will write you a good report." Tangier pulled Skyla along, her face shielded by a cascade of black hair. They left the trainee standing alone, tucking his mini rifle into his pants holster.

"Knob?" tapped Skyla into Tangier's hand.

"All trainees," he tapped back.

Skyla looked up as it darkened overhead and felt the falling temperature despite her coat.

The Outliers scampered about the alleys of the camps, all of them stinking and always slightly wet. Sewage seeped from the shallow septic systems. Water was more or less clean, but one never knew. The Outlier families of true kin or random folk collected in their shelters, the only protection from the cold. The sizzling heat of the daytime air, always dropped with the onset of nighttime. The thin atmosphere let bitter chills coat all zones of Cap City, rich to poor, in frost.

Suddenly, Skyla grabbed Tangier's hand and tapped, "Jaguar?"

"Safe," he tapped back and motioned ahead.

Skyla nodded. Of course, Tangier would know about her beloved cat, which he had never seen. He probably knew everything about her life, even about Jaffa. He was part of the Custodian security and POVs machine, after all.

The shock of seeing her brother had jarred open a memory chest of images buried away long ago. She saw herself as a little girl in a crowded hallway, a noisy household with other kids and adults who were there but not truly present in her life. All the kids were orphans. No one ever spoke of moms or dads. Most like her, never knew them. They were too young to understand the war torn world that wiped out families with little concern for people but with enormous concern for property and profit. Once the Affiliations took complete control, there were fewer orphans, but that was small comfort to her.

Tangier was her comfort. He had a small torn picture of their mother and father, Josephine and Ali, which he hid, like a squirrel hides nuts, deep into the landscape of everyday things. He would reveal the picture to her now and then with a story, usually the same story, but Skyla didn't mind. She loved the brown suede ankle boots with beads her mother wore standing in a garden next to their dad, surrounded by an ocean of colorful flowers, which can no longer grow.

Tangier stood tall, like their dark Moroccan-American father in the picture. He was always there at those growing up milestones—first day of school, the championship track meet when she ran the sprints and relays. An assortment of people was always milling around in the background of her life, but for her, there was only Tangier. She finished high school at the top of her class, raising her award certificate to him in the audience at her commencement exercise. He hugged her tight at the graduation party, his last hug, but she didn't know it then. The next morning, he was gone. An envelope with instructions for applying to the institutes came the next week in the mail, but there was no return address. She was on her own. A small amount of money units was transferred to her account every month, but she never knew from where. She had no way to know. It was not something to share with anyone but Tangier. She thought of him often in the beginning. Not angry. Just sad.

A sharp hiss pulled her from her reverie. Tangier signaled for them to turn left. The narrow path with slippery steps took them down to a sub street door. The shack above it looked like it could blow away at the first heady gust of wind. The unlocked door bounced against its frame. It opened and closed with the vague breeze like breathing.

"CSA! Custodian Service Agency. Stand back." Tangier drew his gun and waved it across the doorway, stomping the door open with his foot.

"Clear," answered a woman's voice. A ripped, towering woman, flashed a scowl as she stood still with an automatic rifle at the ready. "Look who bagged the ferocious little writer? Senior Field Agent Tangier, did you know she writes drivel? Traitorous attacks against our world which we serve to protect?"

"Yep! Here she is, the little vixen." Tangier pushed Skyla toward the soldier and kept his gun drawn on her.

"Tangier! What the hell?" Skyla glanced back at him, tears filling her eyes. "I trusted you, you bastard."

"That's why family is always the weak link. Pet names and relatives." Tangier grabbed a straight chair and slammed it down in front of him. "Sit."

"Did you hurt Jaguar?" Skyla stood motionless.

"Jaguar?" Agent Dee flexed her biceps and shoved Skyla down onto the chair.

"Get me something to drink while I handle her," said Tangier. "Now!"

Tangier leaned close to Skyla and began to tie her to the chair with the dirty rope used many times before. He tapped "trust" on the side of the chair as he wound the rope around her wrists and tied a false knot leaving the ends within her grasp.

She nodded. There was nothing else to do but let this play out. She drew comfort from knowing this jumpy gal-with-guns, Agent Dee, did not know about Jaguar, her cat familiar. Not everything was known at all times by everybody, for once.

Skyla learned in the orphanage how to keep her own secrets, especially her interest in mystics and telepathic power. Tangier had a secret book stash, which she began to read on the sly. She savored the outlawed novels about spies and artists, especially artists who were spies. She devoured the forbidden stories of ancient women who mixed potions and lotions to cast spells. Their stories told her that relationships were possible beyond the limits of the human world. An enchantress could share deep bonds with various beloved animals. They could be more than pets. They were named familiars, that is, members of the family. Skyla had thirsted for a magic potion that could let her fly free from the loneliness of orphanage life. Now she believed with a special animal, she would never be lonely. She studied the ways of familiars and vowed to be worthy to one.

Jaguar arrived in her life as a starving kitten from a trash alley. The tiny cat bestowed her with a familiar's connection that was holy, strong, and real. Even here, now, in this moment of cruel terror, a stranger in a strange place, she sensed his feline power of patience and observation. Stillness, until it was time to strike. Then strike for death. She opened her spirit to his familiar strength, letting it fill her up and sharpen her focus on this screwed up situation where a battle would be fought. That was all she could do, sitting in a chair in a shanty camp town of Outliers with a pumped-up bitch soldier and a high stakes brother. "Sweet, powerful Jaguar, I will find you soon." She said this promise on a sigh as she aimed her eyes on the rope knot, a slip in disguise. Tangier had given her the means to escape. She would trust him. And she would strike the bitch for death.

Agent Dee strode up to the table with two glasses and a bottle of whiskey from the back room. She slammed them down and looked up with a half smile. Grabbing the bottle, she twisted the tight cap off, poured a shot, and pushed it toward Tangier. "Nice work. Where did you find this scum?"

"She's not so smart. A while back, our guy at the grocery store smeared tracker paste on the sleeve of her coat," he replied. He drank the shot and signaled for her to pour another. "Find the sleeve, find her. She has a nose for the trash alleys."

"Where all the crap goes." The smug soldier drank her shot with gusto.

"Since when do you work alone? Where's your back up?" Tangier slid his glass across the tabletop.

"There's no back up. I am on my own. A new assignment." She swung her gun a little closer on her hip.

"You alone? In this hellhole? Why don't I know about it?"

"You tell me. My job is to find a fink, you know, a pathetic poser, someone close to Longhouse. Too close." She poured another shot into his glass. "Mind telling me what brought your sorry ass to this door? A Longhouse hideout?"

"Longhouse is my assignment. With my cover, they trust me." Tangier glanced at Skyla who sat like the Sphinx, seeing all, hearing all, but revealing nothing. He noted the side door behind the soldier, slightly ajar. A trickle of red liquid oozed from beneath it. "And you?" Tangier picked up the glass of whiskey and flung the hooch into her arrogant eyes. Then he shot half his magazine into the chest of the nosy Agent Dee.

Skyla pulled her hands loose and raced to the door that she too, had noticed was ajar. The man was dead, the woman not quite. She opened her eyes to see Tangier and with the barest motion of a nod, slipped away.

"What are we going to do with her, the bitch?" Skyla stared at the vast body sprawled out on top of her rifle. She fought back the urge to kick the bloody heap, a dead relic of Big Data's wicked security network.

"We leave her here. When she doesn't report in, they will come for her. They can't trace the bullets. I only use Outlier guns, you know, Frankenstein guns."

"Frankenstein gun?"

"Made up from parts of different makes and styles of guns. Nothing pure. No numbers. No origin. The bullets are cheap ones that fit any Frankenstein guns. This whole thing will be blamed on Longhouse. This safe house is blown anyway." He took his glass, wiped it clean and smashed it into a thousand shards on the stone floor.

"What about her glass?"

"Leave it. They will see she was drinking and that will count as an error on her part."

"Who were those people she killed?" Skyla took one more look at them, serene and quiet in repose despite their bloody end.

"Longhouse. Resistance fighters against the Affiliations. We never use names. Too risky. I knew him as Salt and her as Pepper." Tangier took one more look around the place. "Come on. We have to go now."

"They suspect you, don't they, the CSA?" Skyla said as she closed the door behind.

"No," he tapped into her hand and moved ahead, hugging the walls and crouching low in the alley of the Outlier town, where every alley was a trash alley. After some minutes, he paused in a corner and whispered, "Agent Dee thought she could out maneuver me. She never wanted to follow procedure and thought she could jump rank with heroics. I warned her that Stilton, the senior agent, doesn't work that way. He hates smart, ambitious women."

"There's plenty of hate to go around. All you have to do is look out beyond your own little space." Skyla waved toward the expanse of the camp town. She moved past a smelly mound, covered in layers of blankets, a wisp of white hair pushing out from the scarf wound about the head.

Steadily she began to see more silhouettes of mounds, the shape the discarded take when they are declared unmutual and tucked into the crevices of the trash.

She felt like crying but could not decide why. The world was a numbers game, grim and humorless. We are nothing but calculations, just percentages that rise or fall below the level of our use value to the Affiliations, she thought. When our ability to buy stuff is so low that the Affiliations lose money units, we are dumped, unmutual, like Mae Carrington. We retreat to grovel in Outlier towns or trash alleys, waiting for death, the ultimate liberator. If old, the wait was short. If young, years of sheer misery and poverty lay ahead.

She looked up at the sky, dark and cloudless, a few faint stars visible. Her breath condensed into droplets, visible for an instant, only to evaporate in the night chill. The silence of the alley, the sound of isolation, distressed her. Loneliness, her own personal torment, worse when Tangier had left, drew strength from silence, but she had fought back, keeping it at bay with her slurky black cat. She cleared her mind and concentrated on Jaguar.

CHAPTER FIVE

REUNION

Tangier motioned with his hand, pointing ahead, signaling a count of one, two, three. Three more alleys to cross and they would reach the top of a hill. Sparse lights flickered from shapeless dwellings, creeping out beyond the edges of tarpaper stuck on most windows. By now Skyla's knees burned from the crouching, slow crawl across dunes of junk and the unlucky, irrelevant people of the Outlier camp towns. She longed to snuggle against Jaffa's chest and Jaguar's fur, to stroke his dense coat.

They crossed a bigger connector street, hidden by the bulky shape of a refuse truck, splitting away as it turned a corner. One more stretch of alley lay ahead. Tangier waved her down. He placed footstep in front of footstep and slid to a window and listened. He tapped SOS with a light touch, once on the glass and waited for a reply. "Ok."

The door opened without sound and they slipped in like ghosts. The small room smelled of mentholated vapor. A tiny kitchen and a bedroom could be seen off of one corner. On the sofa sat a black ball with yellow eyes, aimed like a laser on Skyla.

"Jaguar!" Skyla ran to her familiar and swept him into her arms, kissing his head and stroking his silky black fur. "Where are we?" Only then did she back into a wall and look around. A woman with brown eyes, thick grey hair wound up in a chignon, her skin the color of mocha with a shot of espresso, sat still in a mahogany brown leather club chair. She was wrapped in the faded purple flowers of a well-worn flannel robe trimmed in wilted white lace. Fleece lined, rose colored slippers kept her feet warm. "Mae Carrington?"

"Skyla," she answered in a voice heavy with congestion. "Tangier, thank you for bringing her. I haven't much time." She closed her eyes and calmed her breathing.

"Now, look, you'd best say what needs saying. The clock is ticking down," said Zeinab. "I have been taking care of her for years and this is it. No medicine and poof, she'll be gone." The plump companion adjusted the pillow behind Mae and re-draped the pink blanket across her fragile frame. "Skyla, come closer. Now, don't look shocked. We all know who you are. I am, Zeinab, her best friend." She stood up and smoothed her leopard print blouse over black trousers. Red polish on her toenails peeked out from her black velvet slippers, worn shiny on the edges.

Skyla placed Jaguar in his cat bed on the couch. She took a few steps toward the old woman. "Tangier, a little help here. Please."

"You wondered who put the money units into your account all those years? Your grandmother, Mae." He put his arm around Zeinab and kissed the meadow of grey curls on the top of her head. "Along with this fearless friend."

"Skyla, sit here where I can see you better." Mae patted the straight back chair next to her. "I held you as a very little girl, before the Collapse."

"I'm sorry. I don't remember." Skyla sat, with her hands folded in her lap, next to her grandmother. "My earliest memories are of Tangier and me living in a noisy house with many other kids. I thought that is how everyone lived. Other kids talked about Mom and Dad, but it meant nothing to me. Only brothers made sense because I had one, the best." She nodded toward Tangier.

"Indeed, he is the best!" Mae coughed and took a sip of water from Zeinab. "Without him, we would have lost you. He was but a boy himself when the world broke. The Affiliations' private armies set up checkpoints everywhere. It destroyed communities and split families apart. That's how your parents died, shot after trying to protect you and Tangier, still in your family home. They had been to see me and Zeinab and Jaffa, her grandson, who lived with her."

"Jaffa? My Jaffa?" Skyla felt her heart begin to race. "He never said anything about knowing any of you. He knows you, Tangier?"

"Yes. I swore him to secrecy, to protect you. I could only look after you if you didn't know anything about me." Tangier leaned against the wall. "Be mad at me, not at him."

"I don't know what to think. All my life I wished I had a family and surprise. I did, but it was all a secret? To protect me from what?"

Mae began to cough again, but this time, Skyla stood up and grabbed the glass and helped her sip a bit of water. "Skyla, darling. Let me tell you about your parents. This will all make sense if I start there. Sit." Mae patted Skyla's knee and clasped her hand as Skyla settled on the edge of her chair.

"It was the time of the Collapse. Your parents didn't live too far from me, but they worried about me. They came to make sure I was safe, even though I was fine. I had my garden and wouldn't starve. But, Ali, your father and my son, and Josephine, your mother, arrived with all sorts of provisions. Even batteries, in case I lost power."

"That's true. Your father always worried about electricity," added Zeinab. "He and your mother had those quick analytical minds of engineers, but they misjudged the Affiliations. The private sector had been lapping up all out-sourced work of the government for years. Business ran everything. Your poor parents didn't think that businesses would ever morph into the Affiliations. But, they did."

"But, even if the Affiliations were posing as corporate humans, why would they shoot our parents? They had skills that any Affiliation would want to use," said Skyla. "It wasn't as if there was one epic battle. The Collapse was not a good guy versus bad guy war." She picked up her grandmother's hands and pressed them to her lips. She noticed her own hands were the same as Mae's, long fingers with oval nails.

Mae took a shallow breath. "It was a general's war. One by one, generals replaced the civilians in top government jobs all around the world. They sold out their governments to the Affiliations to get rich. They led new private militaries and rained their brutal battle down on anyone who resisted. Privatizing the world took violence."

"Now, Mae, don't excite yourself. Take your time." Zeinab tossed Mae the quick wink of a longtime close friend.

Mae nodded back and said, "Once you and Tangier were orphaned, I tried to get custody of you. But, the authorities held my own fight with young Custodians against me. You were placed in the orphanage. Without rights, you were lost to me."

"No rights? You are our grandmother," said Skyla.

"Ah, but you forget. There was no government or state anymore. You don't have rights when you are not a citizen of anything. We can't be citizens of a store. Affiliations are giant stores. We are all consumers. Affiliates." Mae coughed and took a sip of water. "There is no rule of law, for there are no laws. What's left are rules alone."

"You couldn't come and visit?" Skyla's eyes welled up with tears.

"Not with the Custodians and POVs watching. The surveillance took control of us all. Those who resisted were executed. The best I could do was set up the money unit accounts thanks to Zeinab and hope Tangier would look after you." Mae glanced at Tangier who nodded to her.

Tangier dragged a stool from the side room toward Mae and sat down, leaning in. "You should tell Skyla about your garden. It will help her understand."

Mae took a shallow breath and closed her eyes as if traveling back on a magic carpet to her garden years before. "On a sunny spring day, early in the twenty-first century, I planted impatiens around my Japanese maple tree. The breeze, warm and slight, felt soft on my face. I loved those kinds of days. My whole yard was my garden. Butterfly bushes, cattails, assorted daisies, foxglove, and snapdragons were my favorites. They fed the butterflies, hummingbirds, and bees. I had a tiny fountain double as a birdbath near the feeder for cardinals, chickadees, and yellow warblers. I loved the flowers and the creatures that loved them too. And, they all loved me back."

"You should have seen it," said Zeinab. "It was like a living quilt with all those patches of color. We spent hours there, trying to make sense of all the ruckus in the world."

Mae laughed. "I actually believed in flower power, peace and love, those old fashion notions, that they had the power to change the world for all, for the better. But, when you live a long time, you see the ugly reality cloud over your dream. Politicians and the lobbyists, who owned them, dismissed peace and love as sentimental and powerless. What they really meant, but wouldn't say, is that they were not profitable. You can't make money with peace and love.

Not big money, anyway. It's not that peace and love don't have power, it's that they are not the right kind of power."

"Flower power is not enough?" Tangier poked Mae's knee and smiled at her.

"No, apparently not," said Mae, "I hope you never lose your sense of humor, my dear Tangier." She sat up straighter in the chair and continued. "I had come in from the garden, into the house when the doorbell rang. How I regret opening the door. That was the day I began to be afraid, for my family and friends, for all of you."

Skyla soaked in the story and noticed in Mae's face, another face, the face of her own father, a face held in a delicate memory, barely perceptible. What can a baby remember? Perhaps nothing. Perhaps a glimmer of belonging to someone who loved you is all there is. "Grandma, what happened next?"

"Two men in black police uniforms with guns stood on my porch. The gangly one with bulging grey eyes said, 'Ma'am, we noticed you do not have the new flags displayed in your yard.' So?" I said. "Then the stocky one said, 'We would be happy to provide you with one if you don't have one.'"

"No thanks. I have never been a flag waving sort, if you know what I mean," I said. Then the first one said, 'We do know what you mean and it is time you deadbeats show some respect for our business leaders who diligently fight for your greatness.' That was it. I told them to leave and that no one comes to my door and insults me. Not even the police. They nodded to each other as if acknowledging something about me they already knew. 'We hope you reconsider,' said the stocky one, 'The next time we may not be so polite.' They said that and left. I called after them, "I can buy my own damn flag if I want to and I don't need you to tell me. Since when do the police shill for a flag company, anyway?"

"You had guts," said Tangier.

Mae gasped for air and nodded. "I closed the door and flopped down in this very chair by my favorite window. A scarlet red cardinal lighted on the Nandina bush by the birdfeeder. Soon his plain brown mate, with just a hint of red on her crown, showed up. I watched him feed her, kind, gentle. Who watches the birds anymore? When did it all go so wrong? That was the moment when the old world passed into memory. Now buying and selling would be the new currency for the new citizenship, but that word would never do."

Skyla stroked Mae's hand and said, "You're right. We can't be citizens of a store."

Mae nodded. "And, those police? They didn't care about safety. They came to sell me a flag. What a useless symbol of allegiance to some global superstore. With corporations in control of our society, faster than hummingbird wings, they reorganized us to suit their god, the market. Those cops who came to my door? Affiliation Red already owned them. The flags they wanted me to buy? Affiliation Red flags."

Mae closed her eyes and leaned back in the chair. Zeinab glanced at Tangier who called, "Grandma, are you alright?"

"She's all right. That memory is like a bruise that never goes away. It breaks her heart into pieces." Zeinab sighed. "So many things began to change. They were already changing."

"What was it like for you, Zeinab?" asked Skyla. You must have stories of your own."

"Plenty, but for another day." Zeinab noticed Mae leaning forward and went to her.

"Tell us something." Skyla help Zeinab adjust the pillows for Mae.

"Ah, Sweetie, the Collapse was like tearing down a monument a brick at a time. Each new rule chipped away at something we took for granted. Without warning, public spaces like city parks were privatized and assigned to an Affiliation. One day you take your baby for a walk in a stroller under the swaying oak trees in the park, and the next day gates appear. Guards with guns stand at attention and a clerk tells you it will cost a day's pay for a half hour walk."

"Really?" Skyla stared at Zeinab. "Did this happen to you?"

"Really. I saw it with my own eyes. I went to take my baby grandson, Jaffa, for a stroll, and found the park locked except to paying people. It was full! All the haughty rich women showed off their fancy workout clothes and jazzed up baby strollers. The guard asked me for a same day's pay to get in."

"I still can't believe Jaffa didn't tell me about you, about any of you," said Skyla, shaking her head. "I'll be angry later. Meantime, what did you do then?"

"I told the guard to bug off!" Zeinab blushed. "I went home and vowed to fight, but I didn't how. Then everything got renamed into geo-regions. What is Panamericanorth? What is Panasia? Who came up with these ridiculous names? Meanwhile, cameras sprouted up everywhere with loads of police on the streets. The new Custodian Service Agency would see everything, everywhere. CSA would do the worrying for you."

"Poor Tangier." said Skyla. "It must have been horrible the day they showed up."

"They stole my life."

"And, Zeinab, for you to think you could fight all this. What did you do?" asked Skyla.

"Nothing, sweetie. Rounding up and splitting people into the Core, the Periphery, and the Outlier towns was sickening and scary. We hunkered down and here we are."

"What could you have done against all that? Easy for me to name it Big Data later on from the safety of my own life," said Skyla. She glanced around the room at her sparse but loyal family. Her gaze rested on Tangier's downcast face. "But, that is my mistake too. I forgot with CSA and POVs no space is private."

"They will kill Skyla," whispered Mae. "What she wrote accuses them all. It's the stuff of revolution." She clutched Tangier's arm, pulling him face to face. "Get her to the Keep. You must go, too. And Jaffa. Leave this hellhole. Don't try to outwit them, like your parents tried. The Affiliations are too strong, POVs are too strong." Mae's color began to drain away, until the warm mocha skin paled to cool violet.

"Quick, let's get her to bed," said Zeinab.

Tangier, Skyla, and Zeinab scooped Mae into their arms and nestled her frail form into a soft bed of pillows and blankets, stacked to keep her sitting upward, the better for her to breathe. Skyla snuggled close to her balanced only on the rim of a chair. She had so many questions, there were so many gaps to fill, but in the end, the quiet closeness of being together meant more.

Mae relaxed, keeping watch on her granddaughter. When a few short bursts of energy surfaced, she talked about meeting Bill Carrington, this nice American fellow, in college while she was an exchange student from Morocco. Although his family was at first shocked at her dark color, she won them over in time. So, Mae could not object when her son Ali fell in love with Josephine Roseau, the pretty, smart exchange student from Montreal, Quebec.

"Skyla, you favor Josephine. She had thick black hair like yours and always wore suede boots with beads. Tangier, you look like your father, Ali, tall with that strong chin and solid cheek bones." Mae pushed herself up from the pillows behind her. "When the Collapse occurred, Ali and Josephine were considered a threat to the growing rearrangement into Affiliations. As engineers, they were drafted into Affiliation Red, the privatized military industrial complex. They would have had to work in weapons development, something they detested."

"They refused to go?" asked Skyla.

"Draft dodgers. That's what the Affiliations called people who refused to recognize their authority." Tangier looked up at Skyla. "My boss called me a 'dodger' the other day, as a joke. It is no joke."

"What the hell? He must know our family history. It's all in the data banks probably under some classified status. Does he suspect you?" asked Skyla.

"No. I am clear. For now, my boss does not know who you are. He ordered the raid at your job, but doesn't know you are my sister. We have to keep it that way," said Tangier.

"But, Tangier, all the more reason for you to go too," whispered Mae. "Jaffa. Where is Jaffa?"

"He is at the clinic in the South. He left this morning. He is fine. Rest," said Skyla. "It is strange to think you all knew about me, but somehow you didn't think I should know you.

"Skyla. Don't be angry. It was my decision, the only way to keep attention from you and Tangier in the early days, said Mae. "When Tangier was stolen by CSA, all the more reason to keep you off their radar.

"As for Jaffa, like I said, I swore him to secrecy. I gave him no choice," said Tangier.

"I have missed all these years with you." Skyla fished out a lock of hair and wove it into a knot. She hung onto it. The pull somehow calmed her. She had done this since she was a toddler.

"Don't be upset, my dear girl. We stayed away out of love to keep you safe. But now that you are wanted by the

Affiliations, we had to bring you in. From today, we will keep you safe by keeping you close. It is a twisted world, indeed." Zeinab paced back and forth, then refilled the water glass near Mae, who was quiet with her eyes closed. "She'll sleep a while now. We should all sleep. Tomorrow will call us soon enough."

"I don't know what to think about all this, but I am sticking with you and Mae forever." Skyla hugged her, letting all the hugs she'd ever wanted to give, wash over Zeinab who hugged right back.

Tangier pulled some blankets from a cupboard. He lobbed them onto a worn sofa. "You take that, Skyla, I'll sleep in Grandma's chair." He closed the door leaving the two old widows to be together, as they had done in the years since losing their husbands long ago.

Skyla folded the blanket lengthwise and opened the top layer, sliding in like a slice of cheese in a sandwich. "Jaguar. Come here little boy." The cat stretched his front paws, then back paws and arched into a Halloween cat pose. He jumped to the floor and walked to the bowl of water. He tested it with his left paw and then gulped it with gusto. He gauged the room and peered at Skyla, propped up on an elbow, waiting for him. He leapt to the sofa and nestled close to her in the bend of her knee. His motor hummed loudly, until she petted his ears and chin, when his purr grew faint. She leaned back, with her head on an arm. "Tangier."

"What?"

"Whose idea was it to teach us cursive and Morse Code?"

"Mae and Zeinab, together."

"Why?"

"Our parents tried to pass a message to them during the Collapse. At the worst time, our father described the plan for our family to go deep cover and escape somewhere. The newly formed Custodian Service Agency for Affiliations listened in. Heard it all."

"How? Where were they?"

"I don't know. Doesn't matter. For years, governments had their spies bug everything: houses, hotels, restaurants, buses, taxis. No one could sweep every room, every place for them. Government spying on citizens was accepted. The fundamental spy infrastructure was all ready for the Affiliations to use."

"So, they never had a chance. I wonder where they were going to take us?" Skyla said while stroking Jaguar.

"Maybe to Mom's family? Who knows? Anyway, I lost track of everyone back then. I was just a kid."

"I know. But, they must have had a plan." Skyla picked up Jaguar's tail and wove it around her fingers.

"Doesn't matter now. They were sitting ducks. Your Big Data got them." Tangier dropped his arms alongside the chair and leaned his head back.

"Looks like you really did read my dissertation. Not bad for a CSA agent. Should I trust him, my little Jaguar?" Skyla placed her hand on his back.

"Skyla, you are in danger. Real danger."

"Me? Danger? A worker bee? A wager? I'm a Peripheral whose only hope to make it to the Core was to get one more boring degree." Skyla held back tears. "Why did you stay away? Why did you make Jaffa lie to me? I don't want to be angry."

"I couldn't contact you in the beginning. CSA kept us new recruits locked down for months as they trained us. I was assigned to the most classified division and by then I couldn't risk it, even for myself. I met Jaffa at a battle test-ing field. Our tours of duty overlapped. I told him about you and that if he ever found you, he could not reveal he knew me."

"But why? What is so dangerous for me?"

"You were a smart little girl. Then, you became the smart woman I hoped you'd be. But, the markets like certainty. Smart women are considered a risk. They ask questions and change things up, which creates market uncertainty. The Affiliations won't tolerate that."

"That's your big reason? I might cause uncertainty for a soulless market? Then what would happen to your precious CSA? You'd be out of a job!" Skyla looked at the closed door to Mae and Zeinab's room. "You denied me contact with my own grandmother because I might upset a damn store? Who gave you that right?"

"Mae. Mae did not want attention drawn to you. She saw that you excelled in school and resisted all the propaganda rammed down our throats in the orphanage. How do you think all those banned books you read got to you? Once I was in CSA and could monitor everything, she'd give me the books from her own hidden collection. She had me drop them into your routine, so you would stumble onto them."

"That's not good enough. What is the real reason?" said Skyla.

Tangier gazed at the floor, then to Jaguar. "You know, the Affiliations are led by men only. Women cannot be the bosses of anything, even at home. These men exist in fear that one smart upstart woman might rise up and demand more than the traditional roles that are allowed. If you and other women start challenging the rules, the surveillance, the markets, and Big Data, revolution will follow."

"Are you kidding? Revolutions need organization. There is no organization of smart women. We live in the age of paranoia. Even a friend can turn third level spy and trade you in to CSA for money. It's all about money. I am on my own. We all are on our own." Skyla shook her head and frowned. She leaned over Jaguar and kissed his head. "I learned to live without you a long time ago, Tangier." She waved her hand toward the closed door. "I am grateful for this visit with Mae and Zeinab. But it, too, will vanish like it wasn't even real."

"I expected you to be angry. But you are wrong about the organization. There is one. Smart women lead it. And you know its name," Tangier replied.

"Longhouse?"

"Yes. We needed to protect you until the time was right to bring you into Longhouse," Tangier said. "Unfortunately, you were noticed. We had to act. You can be important to Longhouse if you choose, but from the Keep."

"Doesn't seem I have any choice now. Death or Longhouse and the Keep." Skyla stared in to space. "Guess Big Data is watching."

"Don't joke," said Tangier. "Big Data is power itself, released from the Rules of Words Committee, given life through the Affiliations, and enforced by CSA. It's the ultimate man's world."

"Yeah, I know that. What makes you think women would lead a revolution and want to be in charge? Plenty of women, especially women in the Core, like things just as they are."

"Longhouse women are not like the women of the Core or anywhere else. They are not part of the Affiliation world, said Tangier. "Starting tomorrow, I'll catch you up on everything you need to know. No more secrets."

"I want to know everything. You can start by explaining the name Longhouse. Really? What sort of name is that? Skyla paused. "And, what about Jaffa? He's in trouble too?"

"He's compromised by your relationship. He'll have to go with you." Tangier closed his eyes and pulled the blanket closer to his chin.

"What have I done? I have wrecked his life." Skyla gazed at Jaguar by her knee. "He warned me to be careful. I didn't listen."

"That doesn't matter now. The priority is to hide your whereabouts from POVs and avoid arrest by CSA. You must trust me on the complicated scam it will take to pull off your escape to the Keep." Tangier ran his hand through his hair and opened his eyes. "Let me handle Jaffa."

"Ok. I trust you. What a horrible mess this is. I wonder what our mother and father would have said about all this? She turned toward Tangier. "What really happened to them, our parents?"

"I have told you for years. Mom and Dad had gone to see Mae to take her provisions and talk about escape. They came home late and went to bed. Nothing seemed wrong. Then the front door burst open and soldiers ran into the house. They grabbed Mom and Dad from their beds. I watched from behind my bedroom door." Tangier's voice softened almost inaudible. "I woke up in the night to Mom screaming, 'No. Don't touch them.' I saw them at the front door, hands cuffed behind their backs, still in their pajamas, still in their slippers. They hit Dad in the face and told Mom not to speak. She looked at me, the last time, tears in her eyes, and sent me a kiss through the air. Then I went and wrapped you in a blanket and held onto you. Some greasy soldier tried to take you from me, but I kicked him. Another soldier, a young black guy with gentle eyes, let me hold you. He put us in a jeep and drove us to the orphanage."

"I know; it is the same story, but it's the only story of our family together in one place that we have. And only you can tell it, and I can only listen, but we both feel it together. After all this happened, how did Mae find you?"

"Someone, I never knew who, let her have one visit. I was 12 years old. You were 2 years old. In the bottom of a basket of clothes, soap, and a random comic book, she had hidden a book on cursive and a pamphlet of Morse code. Learn them, she told me, and teach your sister, or you won't survive." Tangier pulled the footstool nearer and twisted about in the chair. "Tell no one about this visit, not even your sister. It is too dangerous for you both. That's why I never talked about her to you. Later, I saw her every now and then, passing by on a street. She would stop and wink at me. Always random. She set up the money unit account for us. Zeinab worked in a bank and set it up. To this day I don't know how she did it. Jaffa has one too."

"Jaffa. I don't know how he could have lied to me. He's busy seeing patients right now."

"He lied to you because he loves you. He knows the power of POVs and CSA can reach anywhere, even to us on the battlefield. He swore an oath to me, that he would not put you in danger. There were no guarantees you would fall in love with each other, but you did. He will be relieved to know our secret is out."

"I have been living a lie." Skyla rubbed Jaguar's belly as he reached out a paw toward her.

"No. You have been living with partial truths. As of now, everything is known," said Tangier.

"Tangier."

"Now what?"

"Where are Jaffa's parents? He said they were far away. Unreachable. He would never explain."

"You just accepted that?" Tangier shifted around the chair again. "You, who ask so many questions didn't push for details?"

"I guess I didn't think it mattered. Growing up in an orphanage, parents are make believe. They're not ever real."

"His parents are dead. All he knows is Zeinab, who raised him."

"So much loss. What for?" Skyla closed her eyes as if blocking out the dim light in the room could also block out the sinking sadness of it all. "Tangier, what is the Keep?"

"A safe place for you and Jaffa, very far away. I promise tomorrow, no secrets. Now I need to sleep a bit. Our situation is unstable. Fluid." He checked once more that his watch alarm was set for four in the morning. A wave of fatigue from the day's tension broke over Tangier. He closed his eyes and slept.

Skyla stroked Jaguar but remained awake. The day's seismic revelations had opened deep gaps into long slumbering memories, exposing family truths of which she, then an infant, could have had no recollection. These family stories shoved her to the center of her known history, her very identity, her context within a family. She had not been alone, unloved, forgotten. But there was no time left. Mae would be dead within days. And what of Zeinab, Jaffa's grandmother? What else did she not know about Jaffa? Did it matter? Isn't the present enough? She was not sure.

Sleep came and stillness, too. Skyla's last thought was to realize she and Tangier had always used their mother's family name, Roseau. Perhaps it was easier not to be the children of Josephine and Ali Carrington, draft dodgers, the opposition, and enemies of the Affiliations. Mae would have arranged that, or maybe Zeinab. She slept surrounded by her family, her treasured brother and the women who connected her to the past and maybe to the future. And Jaffa. She dreamed of Jaffa.

CHAPTER SIX

FIRST WATCH

Jaguar raised his head and thumped his tail. Skyla opened her eyes and looked toward the door.

Tangier crouched low behind the chair and put his finger to his lips for her to keep quiet.

He checked his watch. Almost four in the morning. A shuffle outside, one, maybe two persons, the muffled sounds of boots like his broke the quiet night. Only Custodian Service Agents were on the prowl at four a.m., the result of intensive training and a belief that much dirty work can be done before dawn. It was neater to snatch someone away from a family still asleep. Moving around was faster before the streets or trash alleys clogged up with traffic.

Tangier had risen in the ranks because he was cool under fire and had a gangster's instinct. It was not unusual for him to go forty-eight hours without reporting in to Stilton. As a Senior Field Agent, no questions were ever asked. His loyalty to the CSA and Affiliations was not in question despite the competition from ego driven lower ranked agents. He always believed it was Stilton who drafted him into CSA. Just now, he had heard a sound he knew too well. He knew they had to get out fast.

He signaled to move. Skyla sat up and wrapped Jaguar into the blanket, which she knotted around her shoulder like a sling. She felt for the data stick in her pocket and with a silent tug of her boots nodded she was ready to move. Tangier rolled back Mae's treasured threadbare Persian carpet, a wedding gift from Bill Carrington, and exposed a trap door. He raised it without a sound and waited for Skyla. She tip-toed in Jaguar like steps, straight and in total balance to the hole in the ground. She braced her arms on each side and lowered herself and Jaguar, calm in the safety of her, to a dirt floor below.

Tangier followed her and pulled the top almost shut, then reached up and pulled the carpet and a chair leg over it all. He wedged the top into place and listened. The spotlight from the small flashlight held in his mouth cast weird shadows on the wall but exposed the tunnel entrance. The longer it was silent the better for Mae and Zeinab, but he couldn't risk waiting any more. Skyla trailed close behind him as he entered the narrow opening, rigged with a few beams over mud clay walls. Jaguar's eyes, like two Topaz gemstones, never took their gaze off of Skyla. Her hand, firmly encasing his shoulders gave them courage.

"What will happen to Mae and Zeinab?" Skyla kept her voice low.

"Nothing." Tangier paused taking a deep breath. His voiced cracked. "Mae is dying." He wiped the threatening tears from his eyes with his sleeve. "She is unmutual and worth nothing. Zeinab is too old to matter to CSA or the Affiliations. She lives as an Outlier by choice, but she is still mutual. She can afford to buy stuff, even if it is cheap stuff. They won't hurt her." He started again, leading through the tunnel. "They know to hide behind the false wall in the closet I built for them."

"We can't leave them. Not now. I just found them. They're all we have." said Skyla, keeping pace with the rapid steps of her brother. "

"We can't go back now. Maybe never. It's just how it is."

"What do you mean it's just how it is? What is?"

"To get you to the Keep. To keep you from being caught by CSA."

"Why do I need to go to the Keep, whatever that is? I am nothing." Skyla's voice stirred Jaguar. She stroked his head to reassure him.

"No, you are someone. You have written the clearest analysis of the Affiliations ever. They want you silenced and your work destroyed. It's that simple. There is no tolerance for opposition despite their hype of free markets that means we are all free. Free, my ass!" Tangier turned left then right. He stopped. "It's about the words. While we have the right of free speech, we don't have the right, you don't have the right to write any speech."

"Since when is writing a study, 'any speech'?"

"Come on, Skyla. Don't be thick. You know as well as I that only 'free speech' is protected because it adheres to the Rules of Words Committee's statutes of free speech. 'Any speech' ignores the rules. If you use outlawed words or arrange approved words in a way that is not allowed by the Committee, it is by default criminal." Tangier took a few more steps. "Come on."

"Criminal? It isn't that good. My work. Why the fuss? My professors have been very critical lately. Besides, who else but the committee even reads it? No one reads studies."

"Affiliations read them. What do Affiliations fear most? Critical thinking. You are a critical thinker, worse yet, a creative, critical thinker. And you must be silenced. If despite all their control of education and media, you write, to use your words, 'that post-postmodern life is a prison of chaos,' then a potential threat to them exists."

"Thinking is a threat? Tossing a few ritzy words around to get a degree is a crime? Who is so threatened?" Skyla stopped to tighten the sling holding Jaguar.

"The Rules of Words Committee. You, if anybody, should know the power of words. Those who create them, those who permit their use, they operate the ultimate machine of control. It is to be feared." Tangier held up for a moment and listened, his ear to the wall of the tunnel. He motioned for them to continue but then pulled up short and turned to her. "CSA monitors everything, even studies. Once your professor gave you up in a deal, CSA stepped up its oversight. They might have let it slide, but you woke the dead with your friend, Orwell" Tangier reached to Jaguar and pet his ears. "You poured on the gas and lit the flame."

"I just wanted to prove I was clever enough to get a degree and make it to Core."

"You know what sealed your fate? Finished it for them? The point that made them have to act?"

"No. What?"

"Big Data. It's brilliant. It says it all. And they know it." Tangier stepped into a small alcove. "And, it is fatal for you if we don't get you to the Keep."

Skyla followed into the alcove and could see a cut out on the area above. "You and Longhouse?"

Tangier nodded. "It's the only way to have any chance to be free of the Affiliations and their world."

"Are you its leader?" Skyla watched her brother search the outline of the opening lid with his fingertips.

"I am appointed by the leaders to protect you."

"What about Jaffa and Jaguar?" asked Skyla.

"Them too. The Longhouse agents, partisans, and covert networks in other sectors of Cap City are all activated." He looked at his watch. Their hour's hike took them deep into the Outlier camp towns. There was little chance this forgotten tunnel held any surveillance value to CSA. "See that lid up there? It could be rusted shut. Maybe junk is piled on top of this."

Skyla moved closer and locked her hands together. "Let me give you a boost. See if you can pop it off."

"Sure?"

"Yes. Let's do this." Skyla braced herself and counted, one, two, three. She held Tangier's foot and added some lift to his jump. He bumped the lid with his hands and it loosened. Bits of dirt fell into their faces. "Come on, one more time. I can do this."

Tangier counted and leapt straight up and dislodged the lid. He grabbed a rope from the edge as he fell back down. The rope held tight to something in the space above. Skyla pulled on it. She nodded at Tangier and readjusted her pet sling with Jaguar tense but staying put. After a jump, she pulled herself along the rope, and rappelled up the side of the wall. When close as she could get, she grabbed onto the rim of the hole with both hands and pulled herself up and out onto the floor. She threw the rope back to Tangier. He scrambled up the rope like a chipmunk.

Tangier tapped "quiet" into her hand. She nodded and stroked Jaguar, trying to wiggle himself free of the sling. The room was empty but for a chair. The windows were covered with tar paper like most of the Outlier dwellings and the sills were covered in a thick sheen of dust. The still air smelled of nothingness. An upright piano sat in a corner. Sheet music from the late twentieth century was piled on the piano bench. A drum set had been pushed next to it.

In the dimness, Jaguar, a restless mini black panther, turned his head. He leaped from Skyla's hip onto the floor and crouched next to the piano. Tangier moved the light along the cat's line of sight. Mouse droppings covered the floor near a chair leg.

"Let's see what else is here," said Skyla. "Don't you think this place is odd? I mean nobody is living here?"

"Very odd. We shouldn't stay. We need to keep moving."

"To where? And don't you need to check in or something? They will think you went over to the dark side. Brother finds sister but doesn't kill her, although that is his mission."

"What are you talking about?"

"This. You and me. After all this time? Maybe you are CSA tried and true. You took me to see Mae and Zeinab. That's a promise you made to them. It assuages your guilt for abandoning me. And, now you will off me and get a promotion. That's how it works. Remember, I studied all this." Skyla opened a cupboard and found three cans of fish. "Wonder who lived here? Only the rich can afford canned fish." She popped open one and sniffed it. "Yep, fishy. Jaguar. Come here." She waved the can and the aroma caught his black nose. He scampered to her as she put a wedge of it on the floor. He gulped it, licking the juice on the floor dry.

Tangier stood still as a statue. "I didn't abandon you. I was taken away. I had no choice." He stepped toward her and grabbed her arm. "But I do now."

"Yeah, and what is it? Am I worth more to you dead or alive?" Skyla squinted her eyes like a sniper drawing a bead on its target. "Your move, big brother."

Tangier dropped her arm. "There's no way to prove anything to you. You know that. All you have are the years I did look after you at the orphanage. If that is not enough, then it isn't. It's your move, Big Data."

"Ok, ok. I am pretty upset, you know. You still haven't told me what in hell is the Keep? A prison? Who runs it?" Skyla turned to face the piano. "What happened to these people? Disappeared? Deleted?" She walked over to a closed door, looked back at Tangier, then swung it open.

"Move! It's a god damned bomb! The door was rigged to start the countdown. We have forty-five seconds to get out of here before it blows." Tangier ran to the hole in the ground as Skyla scooped up Jaguar and sank him in the sling still around her. She grabbed the two other cans of fish, sticking them in her pocket. "Hurry. You first," he said.

Skyla grabbed the rope and rappelled down the hole to the tunnel. Jaguar clawed the sling fabric and held close. Tangier followed and signaled the way forward.

"What was that place?" asked Skyla.

"A leftover booby trap to kill resistors. That bomb was CSA issue used in a previous campaign to sweep the area of Longhouse collaborators," said Tangier.

They ran into darkness, the flashlight providing only enough light to create a foggy haze. They stepped into water for the first time, small puddles, then larger ones. Skyla guessed they were deeper underground, now, perhaps by the river, which ran alongside Cap City on the Outlier side. Rotting houseboats lined the river's edge and disease flourished alongside everything else thrown away here. Even Outliers held to a certain class system and the river dwellers, high from drugs and destitution, held the rank just above death itself.

They felt the bomb blow more than they heard it. The tunnel shook but did not crumble.

Skyla began to gulp for air, her breaths heavy. She realized the grade of the tunnel ran up toward the surface. She had to bend lower and lower not to hit her head on the top of the tunnel. Her boots scuffed the dirt as she worked harder with each step, the tunnel, now very steep, but very shallow.

Tangier, bent almost to ninety degrees, squatted and pushed her to the side and listened. Silence. Skyla pet Jaguar and felt his ears move up and back. "Tangier. Jaguar senses something. Be careful."

"There is a metal manhole cover up there," said Tangier pointing up. "I'll try to move it." He pushed on the rusty rim and it shifted. With another push, the cover lifted just enough for him to slide it a couple inches to the side. Cool air met his face. He pushed again and shoved it aside. He peeked out into a junkyard. A few lights from the river boats flickered, easy to see, for dawn, which came late this time of year, was still hours away. "Come on."

Skyla popped through the hole in one jump and crouched beside him. "Now what?"

"I leave you." Tangier looked at his watch.

Leave me? Here? I don't even know where I am. What am I to do?"

"Give me something that could only come from you. One of your earrings with the Hand of Fatima."

"Not those. You gave me those when we were kids. It's all I have of us then."

"That's why I need one of them. It's the perfect proof," said Tangier. "I know this sucks for you."

She unhooked a silver hoop with a tiny dangling charm in the shape of an open palm from her ear and handed it to him. "I want it back when this is all over."

"I'll do my best. You know, these belonged to Mae. She sent them to you. They were to protect you from the Evil Eye." He stood up and charted a path through the junkyard.

"Then, perhaps it has worked so far." She did not quite believe her own words as she pictured her grandmother, hoping she was still asleep in her bed. "Do you think Mae is dead?"

"Probably. She had little time left." Tangier looked away from his sister toward the sky. "She saved us. Zeinab saved us."

"I know that now," said Skyla. "Zeinab, poor thing, will be lost without Mae."

"Yep. She will. Ok. Enough of this." Tangier stroked the charm and then slipped the earring into his pocket. "Listen. You stay here. Out of sight. No one comes to the river by choice. Longhouse will find you as long as you stay put."

"As if there's anywhere I'd go." Skyla looked at her cat familiar and rubbed her hand against his shoulder.

"Since you never chipped Jaguar, and I killed all your trackers, there is no easy way to find you if you move. So, don't!" Tangier paused to glance around them "I have to check in. I will say you have been helped, moved around. I found your earring as proof. I will implicate Longhouse but that is like saying it's windy. So, what? You can't catch the wind."

"If someone shows up, how will I know they are not CSA?"

"CSA is never polite. They draw blood with the first strike. If you love Jaguar, you will hide him. Don't let them take him." He rubbed Jaguar's head in a cat's favorite spot, just below the ears. He stepped away from them. "They will be in plainclothes to blend in. But their guns are military issue. That's how you tell. Look at their weapons. And, their boots. Steel tips that wrap around to the soles, like a tap shoe. They always shine through."

"Maybe this is all a nightmare, and I will wake up." Skyla backed up deeper under the ledge of wooden slats, stacked like a lean to.

"This is no dream. It is real enough. Now, stay put. Someone from Longhouse or I'll be back for you in the afternoon." Tangier turned back to her. "Trust old Morse. Always trust the code." Then he was gone.

Skyla stared out at the predawn void, no images, no shapes, no shadows. She huddled back under the wood stack until the slats pushed back against her. She loosened the blanket that held Jaguar. He stepped out of it and sat hunched in the shape of a football, his tail brushing Skyla's boot. He took first watch.

CHAPTER SEVEN

PRIME NUMBER

At midnight of the day Riff had been to Agent Stilton's office, his wrist phone buzzed. He was awake and rummaging in some other wager's past. Tonight's victim was a guy at the office who ignored his offer to grab a sandwich together. "Such a dick," said Riff under his breath. He tapped the phone. "Yes."

"I have a prime number for you," said the robotic voice.

"When?" Riff dropped his glass of vodka on the floor.

"In four hours. We will send you coordinates. It must be silent, no gunfire," said the voice.

"Yes. As ordered," said Riff. The phone went dead. He ran to his bathroom and unloaded a nervous, massive diarrhea. "My first one. My first official kill," he said out loud to himself. He ran the shower and soaped up, cleaning himself of any stinky leftovers and readying himself to enforce the rules of the Affiliations. The phone screen lit up

81

with the location. The GPS showed an Outlier town. Damn, he thought, why do I have to go to a shit hole for this? He estimated it would take over an hour to get there, especially at night when hover trains ran less often.

Part of the job, he thought. He put on threadbare and stained loose clothes to blend in with the grime of the Outliers. His regulation boots gleamed with polish, so he took some shoe polish and dulled them, though the steel tip still peeked through. The trim CSA cut of his thin hair could give him away so he pulled out a knit cap and pulled it low, almost to his eyes. He liked this look.

Riff's weapon of choice, a seven inch, double edged blade, stowed in a slim sheath hung next to a mirror in his bedroom. He attached it to a shoulder holster and it rested under his left arm, ready to be plucked by his right hand. He latched his gun into a pocket that functioned as a holster, a design he created. Done. Now, he had to wait a couple hours. But he was ready.

He picked the glass off the floor and put it in the sink. He took a new one, poured a shot and drank it. Settle down, he told himself. He went back to his dig for a little while. When it was time, he took one more shot of vodka and left.

The train made few stops as it passed by the edges of Core towns and Peripheral towns, like his, to the rim of the Outlier's towns. Once off the train, he trekked through the streets, spongy from garbage and slime, toward the address. The smell of the alleys made him retch and he stopped for air. But there was only more stench. The assorted pings and thuds from dripping water off the roofs of the shacks grated on him. He could not let the sound do him in. He had to succeed or be demoted, never to advance in the CSA.

He located the site and paced back and forth a few times, gathering nerve to enter and do the deed. The CSA regulations say never walk back and forth outside a door because it can give the agent away. A sound, a shadow, anything could be detected by the people inside. Riff dismissed it as unnecessary, especially in an Outlier neighborhood like this one, filled with drug addicts, whores, and old people. They would be asleep at four in the morning, the hour for surprise. So, he paced a bit outside the door to collect his guts.

He paused for a moment, rammed the flimsy door, then burst into the room. It was empty. He saw the door to the bedroom ajar. A grey haired lady was slouched over on a stack of pillows. Her arm dangled off the side of the bed. An old flowered robe hung over a chair with rose-colored moccasin slippers tucked underneath. Black velvet slippers tossed on top of each other sat in the corner of the room. He crept toward the motionless figure. "What the hell," he screamed to himself. Death, the ultimate custodian, cheated him from his order to slit her throat.

Where was the other one? There were two. He scrutinized the two bare rooms and pulled open the only closet door. Nothing. He was doomed to everlasting retail as the undercover agent at Celebration Wholesale.

He felt his insides churn. He locked his bowels and would not allow the explosive push he felt. He had to win this or be lost forever to low level operative rank. Where was the other one? He stood on the worn Persian carpet and pounded the table on top of it. With nobody to kill, he left the door open, banging in the damp wind of the Outlier town. He trudged through the muck of outcast living to the hover train stop. He hopped on the first train back to the agency. He only hoped Stilton would not demote him. Something else was in play. If he could find it, he'd be a hero.

CHAPTER EIGHT

ON THE RUN

Skyla wrapped her arms around her knees. Jaguar sat still by her side. She bobbed her head against her forearms, fuming at Tangier. "Jaguar, my little boy, first he shows up out of nowhere and then he drops us in the middle of a scrapheap." She willed herself not to cry over the loss of Mae. Would Mae live long enough to tell her about Josephine and Ali in a way Tangier never could? His were child memories full of a young boy's grief at losing them. Mae could tell her things about her mother that could fill the empty space in her heart where mother/daughter memories should be. This frail woman, coughing with agony, had managed to survive and protect her grandchildren against spirit skilling change. Skyla coveted the chance to hold her pretty hands, to comb her grey hair and listen to her timeworn voice. She held out flickering hope that Mae would tell her about Ali, her father, whose vague face visited her in dreams, the faint trace of his eyes she recognized in her big brother.

She yearned for the chance to hear more of Mae's firsthand stories of the Collapse and the rise of Big Data. "Jaguar, my sweet familiar, I won't ever have a conversation with Mae. I can feel that she is already gone."

Skyla wiped her eyes with her sleeve to stop any tears. "Oh Jaguar, despite all I learned about our miserable world, I missed the point. I can't sell my study for a profit on any market. We are lost. No one buys fancy words for a thrill. I am so sorry, little cat. Here we sit, lost in an Outlier camp town." With a soft voice, Skyla hummed to him and stroked his long tail. He turned his golden eyes to her and blinked.

She watched Jaguar sniff the thick air. "Love is all you need," she sang to him. The classic song played on in her head and she saw Tangier's face, heard his voice singing it to her. She was small then, long before he left to the Custodian Service Agency and she went to the institute. Mae probably taught it to him. She smiled at the thought, but sadness pushed through to her anyway.

As time limped on Skyla filled it with sifted memories of her life. She could hear her own words to Jaffa when they were curled up together on her sofa. "Today, I rushed to class like hordes of other students rushing to their classes. But, what for? The Affiliations don't want us to think. They only want us trained to grind away at jobs that feed the market." Jaffa would console her, shake his head, and brush her lips with his, like a feather. He'd whisper, "You'll get into trouble if you go around saying that sort of thing."

All in all, he was right. Criticizing the market was a traitorous act, but she had never felt loyalty to the Affiliations. She pictured the cramped smoky coffee shop, jammed with students and hustlers, where she confessed a secret to Jaffa. "I have to discover why I feel so apart from all this." She had glanced around the room back to his sympathetic face. "It's all so seamy and grim. But, when I try to purify my mind of this junk, to be calm, and especially when I am brushing Jaguar, I hear voices call to me. They are safe but I don't know them." Skyla loved the memory of Jaffa's heartfelt smile as he said, "Go find them."

"And, I did," she said out loud to Jaguar as if he could hear her thoughts. She continued to talk to the cat who sat very still. "I started to search in the forbidden books from the past, in the stashes guarded by crotchety old librarians. They blocked the horrible antique dealers from raiding secret barns that held the collections. Even if you could find the barn, only those who knew cursive could get access from a librarian. That stopped almost everybody."

She recalled the shadowy shelves of history books in the faint light of the barn. Book by book, she had begun to read everything she could about the pre-Collapse world. She photographed reams of book chapters, old public records, and images to build her own underground collection.

Only Jaffa knew where she kept her prized collection on data sticks, another old technology that she still trusted. She did not trust the data files stored in vast meta servers overseen by CSA and the various Affiliations. The ownership of the data, once uploaded to the caché servers, belonged to the Affiliations. The tech underground despised this policy, which they considered theft. To thwart the caché and protect their own encrypted work, they built high capacity data sticks for saving data. She liked to touch this bit of rebellious technology, to possess it, as if she could hold privacy, itself, in the palm of her hand.

She looked at her hands and remembered Mae's hands. She had held them only a few hours ago. "Jaguar!" He had crawled a few inches away but she could still touch his back paws. "Keep close, little boy."

Skyla played at her hair until she wound a lock into a knot and pulled on it. She had Mae just long enough to physically touch her family history, a recognition that there were people, her people before Tangier and her. She may not have known them but they knew her and interfered directly in her life, because she was their daughter. She belonged to more than just her brother. Loneliness had drained almost any sense of belonging from her heart, over and over again, time over time. For the first time, she could feel she belonged to people, her people. It filled her heart with sympathy and care rather than loneliness.

Skyla watched Jaguar scope out a rustle in some trash, his strong back taut, his paws placed for stability and maximum thrust should he decide to pounce. His tail curled back and forth with a steady hunting beat. She thanked her cat familiar for his steadfastness to her and sent him waves of love. He paused to look at her. He closed and opened topaz eyes then turned back to the hunt.

She watched him and listened to the drops of rain that had begun to fall. A slight buzz flew by her ear, the annoying sound of a mosquito. The junkyard darkened as the brown and blue clouds thickened and blocked any light. She fought the urge to close her eyes. She wondered if POVs had a post out here and somewhere, at some screen, some idiot was watching her. Again, the buzz sound, but this time she saw it. She popped her hands together and caught the insect in her hands. It pricked her palm and felt too rigid for a mosquito. Opening her hands with great care, she picked it up with her fingers. It had a micro red glass eye and wire wings. She placed it on the ground and smashed it with a piece of scrap wood.

POVs had found her. Now what? There was no running for cover. Drones the size of flies, bees, or roaches, along with drone birds extended the reach of POVs to the fringes of camp towns and beyond. She wondered how much they cost. They probably made a tidy profit for someone. Then for some odd reason, she pictured Celebration Wholesale and Riff. He was the type of wager to be working for CSA. What a slimy bastard, she thought. How fragile were the Affiliations if they needed him in CSA?

Skyla began to look for creepy crawlers, stingers, any junkyard bugs hovering too close to Jaguar and her. Blending in, the number one rule of espionage, ruled the pattern used by CSA and POVs in any one location. Even a mouse or a rat could be just another lens. Their eyes, always glassy, gave them away.

Skyla sat back on a board to keep off the wet ground. She debated her next move. What move? Tangier told her to stay or they couldn't find her. But he was CSA so he could flit from insect drone to insect drone and locate her, especially since he knew where he left her. But could he do this without blowing his own cover? And why would she worry about drones when some random satellite heat scanner could find her, as it scanned Outliers for deletion. "Trimming the hedges" a phrase coined by a bigoted newscaster reduced her and all Outliers to nothing more than pesky weeds that needed constant removal by death.

Jaguar poked at something. Skyla heard a moan. She sat up straight, ready to snatch Jaguar and flee. She heard Tangier's words, "Don't move," in her head. Another moan from an exhausted voice, came from the other side of the stack of wood.

"Jaguar," she called. He stayed still. She got to her knees and took a few paces forward.

She peered in the direction Jaguar had faced and tried to sort out any object from shadows for any shape. With the slight light of dawn pushing through the waning drizzle, she could see a figure on its side, curled up under a sheet of corrugated steel. A quivering hand stuck out by his knees, which made the trash around it shake too.

"Are you ok?" Skyla said. "I won't hurt you." The moan sounded again but louder. "I am coming to help you." She moved closer and saw a dilapidated man. His head rested on an empty backpack. His raggedy clothes and scruffy hair were damp from the drizzle.

She rolled him over. He did not resist. His hand continued to shake as if powered on its own. "Longhouse," he whispered as if calling out from a dream.

"Who are you? Why are you here?" Skyla saw a tarnished silver chain around his neck. It had a hand shaped charm dangling from it, not quite the same as the one on her earring.

He lifted his head and lurched to one side. He raised himself with his good arm, just enough to peer at Skyla. She leaned toward him and slid some junk behind his back to support him.

"You are the girl with a Sky name," he whispered.

"Skyla. Yes. I am Skyla. How did you know?"

"We have watched you." He coughed up yellow gunk and spit it away.

"We? Are you CSA?" Skyla crawled closer to him keeping a hand on Jaguar who sniffed his dirt crusted pant leg.

He studied the girl with his sick, wizened eyes. "My name doesn't matter. I am unmutual. I stopped buying anything over a year ago. The Affiliations don't like that. They labeled me crazy because I said I had enough of everything."

"What was your Affiliation?" Skyla thought back to Mae's phone conversation. "Someone else I know was declared unmutual."

"Does it matter?" He coughed from the bottom of his soul, clogged, raspy, and wet.

"I suppose not. Perhaps there's a pattern, but I guess it doesn't help anyway," replied Skyla.

"It won't help me. It won't help anyone."

"How did you get here? Way out here?" Skyla scanned the bleak ghetto scape, the odd rooflines of makeshift dwellings, the shiny wet surfaces, the stench. Alleys or paths hidden by the junk made entry and exit of the place random, unless you knew where to go. "Jaguar! Come here, over here." She tapped her fingertips on the ground next to her. He raised his head and stepped toward her. She noticed the old man's hand no longer shook. He had placed it on his lap as if to keep it safe.

"He is a beautiful familiar. Rare these days. Magic disappeared long ago," the old man whispered over another shallow cough.

Skyla caught Jaguar's front legs and pulled him close. "We are not staying. We are going now." She picked him up and re-swaddled the blanket around him and tied it to herself. The two tins of food were safe in her pocket. The sun inched up over the horizon but the shadows were still dark and long.

"Where are you going? Don't leave an old man to die alone. Please." He coughed again.

Skyla clasped her fingers to her coat sleeve and leaned toward the old man's feet. She rubbed across the toes of his shoes. Silver steel metal shone in the growing light. "You slimy Custodian! You should not have noticed my cat. You should not have known he is a familiar. Pets are always the weak link." She leaned over him and with a sharp tug, snatched the hand charm and chain from his neck. "You don't deserve to wear this."

"Children. Children, too, can be the weak link. It was easy for your father to give up his life to spare yours. He even gave me that hand charm you hold to stop me from killing you. He said it would protect me. Well, it didn't protect me and it won't protect you." The old man shrugged. "I had my orders. There's always a new boss, same as the old boss. The Affiliations are the new boss."

Skyla stood over the dying man. "If you are so important to CSA or the Affiliations, why are you out here alone, left to die? Because, you will die here, in this hell hole where I won't help you."

"It is you who is important. It is you they are tracking. I am dying, yes, but my last act was to find you. And I did. And I am transmitting this all to headquarters. I am a hero." He coughed again, blood seeping from his nose and mouth. His head fell back and being no longer able to sit up, slid against the junk around him. His hand began to shake again. His chest rose and fell with shallow gasps of air.

The man opened his eyes, grey, reddened, but very yellow. "Longhouse." He closed his eyes and heaved a heavy last sigh. Skyla examined the chain and charm in her hand with a keen eye to be sure there were no GPS trackers imbedded. She draped it on the steel tip of one of his boots.

She took one last look at the dead man who claimed he killed her father, who thought himself a hero to the Affiliations, and wondered why he was sent to find her. It made no sense for Longhouse to be the first or last word he said if his final assignment was to snag her for CSA. Perhaps CSA had infiltrated Longhouse.

"Jaguar, we must be extra careful now. Even Longhouse might no longer be safe, for us. Perhaps it never was." She readjusted the sling holding him and took her bearings. The winds blew from the north, so it would stay chilly and dusty, coming across the ruined deforested fields as they do. She would hug the river's edge and go south, away from the city center of Cap City and the tiny towns that surround it.

The night before Skyla went to work at Celebration Wholesale and took the call from Mae Carrington, Jaffa had spent those sweet hours with her. She didn't think he could know how her life had changed in the last forty-eight hours, so she might find him still at the clinic. Outliers there, his loyal patients, would tell her where he was, without the help of POVs. She dreaded the area, squalid, noisy, and rough. She would have to keep Jaguar hidden because the people in the South were so hungry they would eat anything, even a cat. All she could see now was Jaffa's face, his cocoa skin, his green eyes, lush black eyelashes, and his delicious smile, the same smile that adorned the face of his grandmother, Zeinab. There was so much to unwrap now, his secret loyalty to Tangier and a grandmother, all of which he had held from her. She could not summon anger toward him. Instead, she wanted to rest her head against his shoulder and listen. There would be time for explanations later. "Let's go, sweet Jaguar." She glanced around and set out for the south.

CHAPTER NINE

STRATEGY

"Where the hell have you been?" Stilton's snarl invaded the room from the speaker.

"Stuck in the garbage of the world, at your request!" Tangier, towel wrapped across his hips, sat back in the thick cushions of a futon. His hair still dripped from the long hot shower. The plain walls of his sparse one bedroom condo in the Core closed in around him.

"Is she ours?"

"Yep. She has no memory of family so any cast of actors will do."

"She thinks that old hag was actually her grandmother?" Stilton raised his hand in a fist and pumped the air.

"Yep. You should have seen it. I convinced her that she is needed to arrange an account for the care of the long-lost grandmother."

"Fool, she has no known family. People think finding a blood relative will change their life. We are on our own and that's it. When are you going to bring her in? Can't let this drag on. It would be better to have hold of her in case the Committee meeting date changes."

"By the end of the week. The story has to finish or she'll figure out she's being played. We need to wait. She'll reach out to someone for help. Right now, she thinks she found her grandmother, but she was spooked by something at Celebration Wholesale. Something made her run. That was not part of this. She is razor smart, you know."

"Yeah, yeah. The smart ones are the biggest threat. I wanted a quick capture and kill, but then the Rules of Words Committee vetoed that plan. They sent word that they wanted to talk to her first. It is complicated to get all these big shots together on the same time and day from across the world. It takes a few days for them to gather."

"They take a risk talking to her in person. A web chat would be fast and clean. What does the Committee think she will tell them that they don't already know?"

Stilton replied, "They take risks for their egos. It's a luxury, a perk of their position."

"Well said. Hey, gotta go. Next time we talk it will be to hand her off to you in person."

"Alright then, get it done." Stilton vanished. Silence returned.

Tangier tossed his wrist phone onto the side table and closed his eyes. He conjured up playing soccer on the field out back of the orphanage for the kids of parents executed for resisting the Affiliations. There was no hiding the low status of being a draft dodger's orphan. He and Skyla, like other damaged children of draft dodgers and resistance fighters, were forced to memorize stories of heroes towards the Affiliations. Looking back, he saw that to believe in the stories as they must, they had to reject any traditions or beliefs of their parents. The new stories of courage and champions scrubbed away any remaining family traditions, any ethnic customs, or any national character. To survive they had to believe the newly minted folktales of Affiliation glory.

He knew Skyla's suede beaded boots was her personal act of honoring their mother. She tried to be a Roseau by wearing the clothes of their mother, but neither of them knew what that really meant. "You're just wearing a costume," he had told her many times, but she didn't care.

He shifted his memories to the face of one of the boys he knew at the orphanage. Some were known as the lost and found kids. They had no family record at all and so were dumped at the orphanage, too.

Stilton, a few years older, stood out as a tough guy who took delight in scaring the little kids. He gauged success by whether he could make a little boy pee in his pants. Stilton treated Tangier like a pet. He kept young Tangier around all the rowdiness, but not part of it. For his part, Tangier made sure Stilton never knew about his sister, Skyla. Not her name, not her sheer existence, nothing. They were both gone by the time she was a teenager. He watched out for her from afar, like Mae. But she never knew.

Tangier recalled the day at the Institute campus. He had just aced a final in economic models. A Custodian Service Agency guy stopped him. The square-chinned man wore boots with metal tips on the toe, and his neck veins pulsed a slow steady beat. He handed Tangier an envelope and said, "Be there on time." He turned on his heel and left. Tangier never went back to the orphanage. Longhouse helped him send Skyla a set of instructions on how she should apply to the advance studies institutes. He included how the costs would be covered but not by whom. He decided that no contact with her would create a communication dead zone between them. Silence never fueled an CSA investigation.

He stood up from the futon and searched for a bottle of whiskey and a glass. He filled the glass then tossed it back in one gulp. It burned his insides as it made its way to his gut, but it soothed his fury at Stilton. It was Stilton who crashed his plans for a safe career in the production of money power. If it was Stilton who brought him to CSA, it was also Stilton who, unknowingly, led him to Longhouse. Empowered with the hope of the resistance, he could avenge the losses he had suffered on so many levels. He poured another round of whiskey.

A delicate dance lay ahead of him. Tangier considered how he would manage Skyla's safety during the next few days within Stilton's version of events knowing CSA can snatch up anyone at any time. Stilton's slow-motion capture of Skyla made sense only if the goal was to smoke out someone in Longhouse, with the aim of turning the pathetic target into a mole. Stilton to date had no success infiltrating

Longhouse with a deep cover spy. He hoped using Skyla would be his ticket to success.

Tangier drifted back to a memory of the orphanage. The answer was there, in front of him. Right now, it was just like when they were kids. They would lie past each other, talk past each other. They were both lying past each other, now. Tangier knew what to do. He poured another glass and chugged the whiskey. "For you, Mae."

CHAPTER TEN

OUTLIER TOWN

The rhythm of the Outlier town began to beat louder and faster as hungry and grimy people came to life for another daylong hassle of moving around. Day laborers jumped onto flatbed trucks to go work the dirty farms that fed the Outliers. Skyla watched the trucks that used stolen gasoline siphoned off from tanker trucks in the Periphery, creak away to the grubby fields. Potatoes and corn, the Outlier diet, grew in dirt contaminated by poison waste from rusty old industries and old thinking. She heard her stomach growl but dared not eat or drink around here.

Nothing grew or grazed where it did decades ago. Rising tides from long melted polar ice caps had flooded fields. Fracking had split the landscape with earth quakes. A big quake shook her out of bed one night. Amidst the rubble, the dust, and screaming, Tangier found her huddled near her bed. He pulled her away from a damaged wall and a cracked window. Skyla calmed herself with this memory. She once believed Tangier would always rush in and save her, but when he vanished without a word, she learned she could save herself.

She could hear a receiver or tablet stream the morning news, the sound fading in and out from dying batteries. All over the world, even here, cheap dual carbon batteries were used to generate electricity, the juice of the world. The slick underworld battery cartels kept the Outliers supplied with used ones. The trick was to recharge them from sunlight that rarely shined for very long and wind that could not be captured. So, the batteries were crap for the most part. Skyla stroked Jaguar's resting head. She whispered to him, "Obstacles and ineptitude, the Outliers lament."

Buying and selling happened anywhere. The noisy whistles, shouts from hustlers, and yelling back and forth filled the air with a constant hum as the day pushed on. Deals in the Outlier town were paid for by pills, barter, or theft. Money units were useless because they were electronic. No banks in Outlier towns. Coins or paper had disappeared years ago. Pills were the real currency, especially aspirin to treat everything from warts to heart attacks. No one cared if the pills worked. Most didn't. It didn't really matter because they were just a tool for trading and not a remedy for anything.

Skyla watched the penny-ante sellers roll out their tarps on the ground. They stacked eyeglasses, shoes, clothes, toothbrushes, any salvaged objects on them. Everything was for sale. Everything. An intimate moment, "IMs" for short, the street slang for a quick screw, cost twenty aspirin tablets, but could be had in trade for a frying pan. So said the old woman who called out to passers-by. "IMs. IMs for trade." It was not clear to Skyla if the moment of intimacy would be conducted with the old woman, but there was not another woman or man in sight at that moment. She picked up her pace and cut across the path away from the seller.

The messiness of the slum swirled around her with total indifference. She could not walk a straight path to the South but had to side step and quick step her way around scenes of human activity, which ran into each other the way ink lettering does when it gets wet. It was an ugly dance with endless tragedies. Skyla kept a steady hand across Jaguar's back. She only let the very black leather of his nose be exposed. He breathed in and out, calm at her side.

She guessed it must be between eight or nine o'clock in the morning by now. Without a phone or watch she could not know for sure. She wanted to keep track of the days, the journey until she reached Jaffa and home. He was home, their home. He carried the history of a noble city and the home of his ancestors in his name, although long since exiled from it. Skyla loved the city's name and she had found a place to mention it in the pages of her study. For her, the name Jaffa mattered as an important legacy that predicted what was ahead for the world as Big Data's drive for money power confiscates everything and takes no prisoners. Still, on this day, as long as she could get to Jaffa, she did not need to go anywhere else. Together, they carried their fractured pasts along as talismans to remind themselves that the world was not always run by Affiliations.

Skyla felt her chest tighten at the thought of Mae's pre-Collapse stories lost to her. So, she concentrated on Jaffa and his sunny nature, bright, like a sweet orange. She ached to be reunited with his generous heart and old spirit, sinking into his embrace. She took a slow deep breath to clear her mind, to focus on the journey forward.

Skyla looked ahead at the desolation and felt an oily film of despair seep through her pores. It lingered, resistant to being washed away, for there was no escape from the Outlier town. All sins were on display in the faces of the flops, the people who couldn't cut it. One man's stringy red veins on his swollen nose was like a map of his slow boozy path to the camp town for all to see. Another addict's trail of decay, showed in the tattoo of red tracks on her withered arms. That's how she ended up in this dump. The despicable beggar, still wearing a jacket with his company logo, just couldn't keep up the pace. He sat hand extended with an empty cup, condemned because he didn't flood the company coffers fast enough with fresh dazzling sales of stuff.

Big Data forbade any family member helping another through his absolute power as decreed by the Rules of Words Committee. The rule stated no family group should allow the stain of failure from one member to smear the success of the whole family. Weak relatives threw suspicion about Affiliation loyalty on all family members. Big Data had no use for subpar people. Neither did families. No one did. So here they collected together, congealed in a gelatinous mass like the sticky refuse they bought and sold on the street. They were desperate to survive.

Skyla took a few steps back and leaned against a tin wall. A chill crept up her body from feet to shoulders. She shook her shoulders to keep a simmering fear from erupting into panic. Jaguar stirred in his sling. She squatted down and searched for the can of fish. The cat recognized the can and squirmed out of the blanket. He stood attentive, waiting to eat. She scooped a wedge of juicy bits onto a piece of wood she had kept from her earlier shelter. He gulped the wet mound in and looked up at Skyla for more. She obliged with another scoop. "That's all sweet boy. I have to ration this until we get to Jaffa." She scoped out their path through the shanties in a direction toward the South. The wind blew stronger and the smell of decay swirled around her.

She held her contented familiar close and took a few steps. Some people peered at her through squinted eyes as she passed by them. A few reached out silent, empty knotty hands to her but the message of begging was loud. She had nothing to give but also was not used to giving. Asking for something for free could not be more despised than giving someone something for free. She remembered the day she forgot her lunch at elementary school. By noon she was famished but did not ask to share anyone else's lunch. No one offered to share his or hers with her. The young generation schooled in the individualistic, money power culture of Big Data, knew better than to conduct a deal without profit. She never forgot her lunch again. Getting to Jaffa was the only hunger she had now. She centered herself and stroked Jaguar. She pushed on.

The sun climbed higher and Skyla could see the taller buildings of the South in the distance. The building with a tarnished metal spire on the roof had been converted to a health clinic a few years ago. The owner rented the space to the Institutes as a place for any students to practice. He knew no one cared about mistakes made on Outliers. Everyone took their chances, thought Skyla, including me. I will make it there by dusk.

Physicians, like Jaffa, from the Peripheral towns were required to go to the Outlier towns at intervals to keep infectious disease plagues at bay. Skyla had grown use to his trips into the battle against Outlier bacteria and infections, knowing they could travel on wind or rain back to the perfect people of the Periphery and Core.

"What about you, Jaffa," she had asked one day at their favorite coffee shop. She sipped a steamy espresso noir. "Don't you want to work in the Core?"

He paused only for a moment. "Boring. Can you think how awful it would be to give drugs all day to patients who don't need them but think they do? Doctors in the Core just sell medical stuff or procedures like any common business. It's not about care or healing. It is just another shop hawking its merchandise. Come on, you and I are different. For some reason, we are immune to the thrill of buying and selling. We need something more." He picked up her hand

and brushed his fingers across hers. "We want something more."

Skyla broke her reminiscence at the sound of metal crashing up ahead. She could not see anything but she held back for a moment. A foreigner in these parts, she stuck out like a mark. The scavenger sparrows suddenly rose from the tops of trash piles and swooped around in an elliptical path. One of the birds had to be a drone, so she drew up her hood and waited in the shadow. A raven, majestic in full feather, wings spread, lofting on the wind came into view. The black silhouette against the sky dove toward them only to climb high above where he lighted on the edge of a roof. She felt Jaguar's back tighten and his ears twist straight up and forward, alert, but not afraid.

Skyla did feel afraid and scanned the area for another route. Tangier would be furious that she didn't stay put. She wished he would appear like magic the way he did a couple days ago.

For the first time, she cursed herself and the study. "Why couldn't I have written a study on an easy topic that had commercial value, like the relationship of wedding dress style to the fitness habits of brides to be. Think of the money units I could have made in both fitness and fashion industries. I should have written a dissertation that could have been a bestseller, one that could have made money units, lots of money units." The weight of her choice to go highbrow and scholarly crushed down around her. She had doomed herself to a trash alley because she didn't go commercial.

Jaffa, she knew, would disagree. He had called those marketable topics pabulum. For her it meant stagnation. Such a commercial work would only have taken her deeper into the Affiliations money pits where entire sets of human drones, wagers like Riff, worked nonstop in the virtual mine to serve Big Data. She had accepted for a long time that her life's journey lies with Jaffa. Although he did not aspire to life in the Core, she wanted to qualify for it, to prove to herself that she could, even as they chose to stay Peripherals. She cursed her own ambition and blamed herself for drawing out the wrath of the CSA and the Affiliations on a family she didn't know existed. She quickened her pace. Her next steps aimed around the site of the noise but carried her into blackness.

A strong hand grabbed her left arm and pulled it up, close behind her back. "Don't make a sound." With his other free hand, he knocked Skyla's right hand from its usual protective place over Jaguar. "Whoa. A Cat. I love cat meat. It'll be a feast."

Skyla struggled to break free, kicking the attacker in the shin with the heel of her boot, but he only twisted her arm more. She socked him in the side but his solid blubber held firm. She turned toward the left and scooped Jaguar under his belly forcing him to leap out of the sling. A raggedy woman with stringy hair and bony claws for hands, rose up from the ground out of nowhere like a jinn and grabbed him. "He's mine, he's mine." She held him tight by the scruff of his neck. His eyes widened and ears flattened for attack.

The last thing Skyla saw before the world was shut out by a foul smelling black hood was the raven who dive-bombed the wretched woman, and pecked at her head and face. Jaguar watched the raven distract the woman and he leapt away as her hands released him to fight the bird. He paused to hear Skyla scream, "Jaguar, go find Jaffa, go to Jaffa." Then the black hood covered her face. The raven flew back to his perch on a rooftop. She peered at Jaguar who crouched low, his eyes raised to her, two familiars recognizing each other's mystical identity. After a few seconds, Jaguar sprinted away, toward the South, to find Jaffa, invoking the power of the great black panthers from which he descended. Skyla, limp from inhaling the knockout chemical in the cloth, fell into the gnarled hands of the man. He hoisted her on his shoulder and stole away, kicking debris out of the way with his metal tipped boots. They disappeared into the dim creases of the town through a nondescript door that led to hell.

CHAPTER ELEVEN

BUSINESS

Deep under the contours of the Outlier towns by the river, a business operated, making a tidy profit in the best spirit of Big Data. A repulsive industry ran, unregulated, for buying and selling anything overrode any other rule by the Rules of Words Committee of the Affiliations. Among the rooms where this business was conducted, one had been wall papered with paisley red paper. Black velvet paintings of trees and horses hung on the wall. In the middle of the room, behind a massive wooden laminate desk, sat the head guy, the big cheese, the man known as Cheddar.

He surveyed the room, recently decorated with a cherry red leather sofa made of squishy cushions, flanked by brown plastic end tables with little statues of chocolate lab dogs, football players, and a bowling trophy. A red light blinked on an old-fashioned box receiver sitting on the desk. A new product had arrived. Cheddar grunted to himself, secure in his position as boss of the most profitable venture in all of underworld crime.

Life was cheap in the Outlier towns. The hopeless people in infinite supply were just raw material spinning around him. All he had to do was harvest it to feed the "off brand organs markets" needed by both Core members and Peripherals. They asked no questions and paid any price on delivery. To conduct his work in a Core community was unthinkable, but the life-giving organs he supplied made him and the others in his scheme, a fortune in money units.

"Eh, Cheddar. I tossed her in the tank." Grub sank into the soft cushions of the couch. "She's pretty hot."

"Hot? Hot enough?" Cheddar leaned back in his chair and strummed his fingers on the desk. He preferred them young, supple, and untouched. They struggled more, but the high could be immense. Filmed well, a one-off romp might generate enormous profit in the pay per view circuit. Repeat customers fueled the skin flick empire of his patron, Swillian. Cheddar loved the bonus he got for getting the bodies.

"She's primo. Check it out. Bet you'll want to use her for both movie and harvest projects."

"Projects. Yes, sounds better than rape and murder. I'll have to see her. When will she be awake?"

"About an hour. I'll send Ruby in there to wake her up." Grub leaned forward. "She had a cat. A big juicy one."

"Where is it? We haven't had cat meat for a while," said Cheddar. He pulled out a white handkerchief and blew his skinny nose that hung high from the bridge between his tiny eyes. His greasy hair curled at the bottom where it hit his shoulders. His thin lips disappeared when he smiled at the thought of cat stew.

"It got away. Some old bitch grabbed it when it leapt away and then a black bird attacked her and the cat ran off. Pissed me off, the old bitch," said Grub who looked down over his pudgy pale cheeks at his round stomach poking out below the edge of his T-shirt.

"That's too bad." Cheddar shrugged.

"Where's Ramone?"

"Making a delivery. A nice one. Three deliveries at one location. Primo grade. Highly desirable." Cheddar pulled a bottle of whiskey and two glasses from his side drawer. He poured an inch worth in each and shoved one toward Grub. "Here's to good work."

"Hey, boss," Grub picked up the glass, "did you ever think of living in the Core? I mean you got the money for it now."

"And leave all this? Our empire? Never. Out here, no one cares, least of all the Affiliations. They token monitor, that's all. We think they are watching more than they are. I know that from Stilton. We are free out here." He took a swig of the whiskey. "We have everything we want and don't even have to buy it."

"Like that girl in the tank," said Grub.

"Like that girl in the tank." Cheddar turned to the monitor on his desk and hit a button on the keyboard. "Look, there she is, sleeping like a baby. For now."

A knock on the side of the open door interrupted Cheddar's gaze. "It's time for rounds," said Gutter.

Cheddar swallowed the rest of his whiskey in one gulp and slammed the glass on the desk. "Ah! Let's go Doc. What we got?" Grub nodded to his boss, and sat back, watching him follow the doctor out the door.

"We have four losers. All stable. All asleep." Gutter shoved his powder stained hands into his wrinkled white lab coat. He led them down a long hallway to a large green hospital room, lit with scrap florescent bulbs. A whooshing noise from outdated ventilators kept time, breathing in and out for the bodies. IV's dripped into each of their arms and kept them still in a chemical induced coma. Ten bodies meant a full house. Today, only four remained but the census went up and down based on availability.

"We have new one. A girl," said Cheddar.

"I heard. Grub can't keep his mouth shut. You'd better do something about his wagging tongue. There are spies for everything. What if one of those Longhouse types gets wind of his preference for snatching young girls and boys. They can be as nasty as CSA." Gutter crossed his arms like an attending physician who waits for medical students to give the history of a patient.

"True, but we do CSA a favor if and when we take Longhouse types out. In fact, they can be part of the supply chain if we catch one. Who would know where to find them?" Cheddar looked at one bed where a hefty man laid covered with a thin sheet. "Is he next?"

"Yeah. Think so. Some big shot on some corporate board needs a heart-lung combo. This poor loser's lungs are clear and his heart is not too bad for the fatty he is. He's young, so he should be OK." Gutter scanned his notes on the tablet he never let out of his sight.

"What about his liver? I have a new order for a liver and corneas for that matter."

"We can use his. No problem. I'll let Vlad know to prep for the harvest," said Gutter.

"Vlad? Who the hell is Vlad?

Gutter shrugged. "That's his name this week. He changes it to try on identities. He has finally settled on being historic rather than a super hero. He's done being Superman or Batman or Motoman."

"And you trust this guy?" Cheddar waved his hands toward the people lying on beds, doped up from the IV's. "With all this?"

"He's the best damn scrub nurse I ever worked with. So yeah, I trust him." Gutter motioned to move on.

"Ok then, doc. You know, when I still worked at the Mito lab, where we used stem cells from the customer to grow their own matching new organs, I used to think old fashion organ transplants would disappear, you know, because anything can be made new," said Cheddar.

"So? What's your point? Any organ can be manufactured now, that's true. Only, you never own your new organ. You just rent it."

"That's the beauty of it for us. You can't buy your own new organ outright. You have to rent your own for life from the manufacturer. You're screwed if your luck turns and you can't make payments. Someone will rip it right out of you and take it back. That's inspired motivation. Life or death motivation." Cheddar stared at a body as it breathed in and out with the ventilator.

"Well, aren't you the philosophical boss today?" Gutter shoved his hands into his pockets.

Cheddar ignored him. He enjoyed talking shop. It gratified him to know in the long run it was cheaper and safer to get a transplant. Buy it, own it, whether it works or not. No returns ever, but one could always buy another. The cheap anti-rejection drug sales skyrocketed thanks to him. The anti-rejection drug makers loved him so much they supplied whatever he needed as long as he kept the market for anti-rejection drugs high. "It's a sweet deal, doc."

"Whatever." Gutter scrolled down his tablet and entered liver and eyes to the removal list and hit save. "Just be glad, no one asks where these parts come from."

"That's for damn sure."

"It is sort of twisted, I think," said Gutter. "The Core members and Peripherals do have a choice, for what it's worth."

"Either way, when their luck runs out, our luck runs up! Cheddar slapped Gutter on the back and laughed. "As for that girl in the tank, no give backs there. I'll get Swillian to have a look. He knows prize product when he sees it." The boss turned toward his office door. "He likes to be first in line before he tricks her out. Or films her. Whichever comes first."

CHAPTER TWELVE

SOUTH

"Will it leave a scar," asked a reeking scraggy boy who watched Jaffa open a sterile pack on the bedside table. The jagged cut curled across his thigh above the knee.

"Maybe a little one," said Jaffa. "This is going to sting." He drew some anesthetic into a syringe and leaned over the boy. "Hold still."

"OK, doc." The skinny boy gripped the edges of the gurney. "Ow, that stuff burns!"

"Done. Now, tell me how you got this cut?"

"I fell on something."

"Fell? Sure no one cut you on purpose? Dealing? Stealing? It's ok. Not like I'd turn you in to anyone," Jaffa said. "I have to give you a tetanus shot since you won't tell me. Even the knife you won't admit to can be dirty."

"Man, a shot?" The skinny boy squirmed when Jaffa began to sew.

"Does this hurt?" asked Jaffa, pushing on the edges of the cut.

"Naw, just hate watching needles."

"Then don't look. Find something else to look at while I do this. It won't take long."

"Ok. I'll look at that big black cat that just walked in," said the skinny boy. "Man, that cat is staring at you. I mean at you!"

Jaffa tied the knot on the last stitch and leaned back in his chair. He felt the long, solid body of a cat wind between his legs. Its long tail curled around his leg and held fast. His topaz eyes locked onto Jaffa's face.

Jaffa snapped off his gloves. "Jaguar, what are you doing here? Where is Skyla?" He reached down and picked up his silky friend and rested him on his lap. He put his forehead on Jaguar's and stroked him. Jaguar turned his gaze from Jaffa toward the outside. With each stroke from Jaffa, Jaguar turned his head toward the north. "She's not with you, is she? Something is wrong."

"Hey, that is a very black cat. Can I have it?" The skinny boy reached for Jaguar.

"No, he's mine." Jaffa placed Jaguar on the chair. He turned to put a sterile bandage across the stitched cut. "You. Sit still."

"Now what?"

"This is what." Jaffa jabbed him with the tetanus shot. "Now, get out of here. And don't fall into anything."

"Ow! Ok, sure. Bye doc. Sure I can't have that cat? It's good eatin'." The skinny boy jumped to the ground and reached for Jaguar.

Jaguar hissed. He arched his back then fluffed his fur. "On your way. I told you he is my cat." Jaffa grabbed a sheet and folded it into a sling. He tied the ends behind his neck and lifted Jaguar into the sleeve, leaving his arm in it with him, letting his fingers peek out the edge.

Another doctor in a rumpled grey lab coat stopped at the door. Jaffa glanced up at him. "Hey. Gotta go. Something came up."

"You mean I'm alone with all this crap?" he replied. "Damn, Jaffa, did you see how many people are packed into that waiting room?"

"Hey, you know when you sign up it's anarchy out here. Alonzo is the nurse today so you're lucky. He can do anything." Jaffa stood with the sling away from the doctor.

"Hey, you hurt?"

"Just a sprain. Look, gotta go." Jaffa turned away and when out of the other guy's view swung his overstuffed backpack into a corner behind old rusting barrels and out of sight. "Jaguar, my boy, we don't need CSA tracking us from all those supplies." He stroked Jaguar's head and ears and stepped toward the north. He tugged the edge of his grey knit cap low, meeting the top of his sunglasses, and tucked his well known black and white checked scarf inside his jacket out of sight.

He did not want to be recognized by the local folk from the shacks around the clinic most of whom he had treated for this or that. They, with their good hearts and sob stories, would want to talk. But, it would just slow him down. Soon enough, it was the rubble from eroding shanty shelters and the piles of garbage that slowed him down. With the cat in tow, he aimed for the smaller pathways, darker and even more desolate, but also with fewer people.

He took a deep breath to clear the anger seeping into his thoughts as he stared at the ugly cityscape before him. As far as he could see there were no hospitals. Why should there be? According to the Affiliations, Outliers were immune to the prolonged misery. There was no need for hospitals in Outlier towns.

But, he knew better. Death was no friend to the Outlier. Death takes its time and whether it comes early or late, has no concern for the human doing the dying. It is an electrical current turned off by a spent battery, nothing more, nothing less. Death is cold, biological, mechanical, and reliable.

But, Outlier people still needed doctors for when death had yet to arrive. Jaffa had watched over time how a clinic would emerge in an unmarked section of an old warehouse or even in an abandoned boat still floating in a slip on the river. Word would spread through the gossip of the homeless, the crippled, even the squawking children that doctors and nurses had arrived to stay for a few hours.

"Jaffa, why do you do this pitiful work out there," the Affiliation supplier would ask every time he handed Jaffa a set of medical supplies. "You're too good for pest control."

Jaffa would shrug and say nothing. The Affiliations' quest for maximum disinfection of anything dirty extended to all its sprawling work centers, which were sprayed for bugs and rodents. Likewise, mopping up and spraying of dirty, contagious Outlier people kept the Core and Periphery clean. The Affiliations ordered CSA to operate the clinics as part of security under the Bio-threat rule from the Rules of Words Committee.

Jaffa knew as a physician working under the orders of the dreaded CSA, he would be considered "going rogue" if he were tracked heading north, away from the clinic. "Jaguar, we have to find Skyla before CSA finds her or us." He slipped his wrist phone into a Faraday case, a gift from Tangier. "Nothing can get through that mesh, no calls, no text, no CSA tracking, nothing," Tangier had said. "So, when you take it out, it will take a few minutes for the phone to recalibrate and work. And don't ask me where I got it. Can't say."

Jaffa knew Tangier smuggled small gear out with him when he came back from his stint in EME, Enduring Military Enterprise. Their service time as officers overlapped for a few months at a remote post in the eastern frontier of geo-region Panasia, close to the border with geo-region Panamerica-north.

He had shown Skyla the case once. She demanded to know where to get one for herself. That was when his lying about Tangier began. It bothered him then and it bothered him now, at this moment, scouring through the South with her familiar in tow. He had side stepped the answer by redirecting their conversation to his own stint in EME.

"It was so warped," he told her. "Affiliations are pure competition. They don't work as a global collective, even if together they rule the world with money power."

Jaffa could hear Skyla's voice as she probed for understanding. "Then who are they fighting? What is the point?"

There was no point, he remembered telling her. There was no point in testing war machines and weapons except to sell the latest models with trained operators under the pretense of security. Affiliation Red peddled the fear of Outlier riots as a looming threat, which drove sales and prices sky high. Enduring Military Enterprise was nothing more than endless field testing of the latest military gadgets on live subjects with live ammo for the market. The private security militias maintained by every company, small to large, lapped up the latest battle tested, shiny, products.

Skyla wouldn't leave it at that, he recalled. He forced away the hint of a smile on his face at hearing her words in his head. "They will fight each other one day over what little water is left. They will fight each other one day when there is nothing left to sell or buy. What, then, will people do all day?" Jaffa had no answer for her.

He could only bear witness to the madness. He could not reveal to her that he watched Tangier rehearse new fighters even as he would later comfort the same ones, unlucky during battle tests, dying under his care. In EME dying sometimes took hours. No casualties could survive, for no wounded were allowed to return to civilian life. The Affiliations' very own health care industries needed working, paying customers. They held no obligation to fighters in the

EME. Fighters were paid well to fight, no different than any other temporary job. To prevent the creation of a class of workers disabled from the field testing, battle injuries were designed to be fatal.

"It's all pretty messed up." Jaffa remembered saying to Tangier late one night in a damp, cold tent. He leaned over his boots and drew the words, messed up, in cursive on the dirt floor.

"How do you know that?" whispered Tangier. He pointed to the words being erased with Jaffa's boot.

"What? I am just screwing around. Just random designs to pass the time."

"Listen, I know what I saw. Who taught you that?" Tangier kept his voice low but full of authority.

"My grandmother. It's nothing," said Jaffa with a shrug.

"Her name?"

Jaffa drew a "Z" on the floor only for Tangier to reach over and stop his hand.

Tangier motioned for him to be quiet. After some time, they left the tent, walking a short distance in the chill and gusty wind under the guise of going for a pee. Under the noise of the howling wind Tangier said, "Our grandmothers are friends. Tell no one."

On the way back to the tent, Jaffa had marveled at the revelation but dared not pursue it then. How could he and Tangier not have known about each other if their grandmothers were friends? What made these venerable women guard the existence of grandsons so close that they were willing to deny their boys a friendship? He would have to sort this out with Tangier at another time.

Jaffa pulled his thoughts back to the journey ahead, distracted by the crackling sounds from a window in a shack up ahead. A monitor blasted an announcement that a new round of enrollment for enlistees in the EME was now open for Peripherals. Outliers need not apply. He squeezed Jaguar's shoulders and looked ahead.

A few streets over, he saw a thin woman standing against the metal wall of a shack. She was sucking the hell out of a hand rolled cigarette. Her black spiky hair framed a pale face with soot smeared around her eyes like a mask. A black glossy cream covered her lips.

"Poppy, what are you doing here?"

"Eh, Doc. Ah, you know. Gotta keep movin'. Lots of folks to look after." She blew a long wave of smoke up to the sky. "The life of an Auntie, it never ends. Say, what you tryin' to hide in that sling?"

"A cat. Skyla's cat. Jaguar."

"Your girlfriend's cat? Out here?" Poppy peeled back the edge of the cloth and took a peek at him."

"Doesn't make sense, does it? We're heading back to find her. Look, I need you to do something for me," said Jaffa.

"What'd I get in return? Nothin' is free, baby."

Jaffa dug into his pocket for a box of tobacco cigarettes. "How about these. This is real tobacco. Grown the old-fashioned way down South." He offered the box to her.

"How'd you get them? Ok, none of my business." She grabbed the box and smiled. "Ok, what you want me to do?"

"You know a guy. Tangier. Find him or get word to him to meet me up North. Be sure to say 'up North'."

"That's it? For a box of cigs? You are over paying." She shook her head back and forth slowly. "Somethin's not right. I don't want trouble. You wouldn't be puttin' me in trouble?"

"No trouble. Just business. I like you, Poppy. Always have. Can't I treat you nice?" Jaffa felt Jaguar stir in the sling. "Gotta go. Take care of yourself."

"Go." She took another long drag from her rolled cigarette and leaned back against the wall.

Jaffa fell into the lightless edges of the alleyways of the sprawl, moving with speed along routes that led north. He considered stopping to see his grandmother who resolutely stayed in her tiny apartment in the area closest to the Periphery. Many years ago, she had moved there to be near Mae, who preferred to live in the tolerable Outlier camp town edge to save her money units. All that had changed in the last few days. Longhouse operatives had gotten word of Mae's impending death to him, but too late for him to help her and Zeinab. Now, assuming that Mae was gone, he knew Zeinab would fall into deep mourning and stay tucked in her tiny flat. He wondered if she knew Skyla was in trouble.

Hungry faces looked out from broken windows, while skinny children with swollen bellies from rotten food scrambled around the junk heaps for something to do. Young punks, tattooed with gang symbols and letters from alphabets they couldn't read strutted around with knives tucked into their clothes out of sight. Guns littered the alleys, tossed away because bullets were scarce. Scavengers would snatch them, melt them down to make new bullets that were cheap and unsafe, just like life in the Outlier towns.

Jaffa adjusted the sling so Jaguar sat lower and out of sight. The sun's heat bore down as the humidity rose and the air smelled like a cesspool. If prosperity was salvation, then all these destitute Outliers were the accursed. He watched a gang of young kids scurry by, those born into this mayhem of inadequate mothers and fathers, growing up ignorant of any other way. He feared discovery that he was not one of them that he had things they could and would steal—like a cat. They would kill him for the cat without a thought. He held onto Jaguar and picked up his pace.

He spotted a flock of birds, with shiny glass breasts, flying overhead. Jaffa admired the spy birds for the cutting-edge technology that brilliant engineers or scientists invented in their flashy corporate labs. Each innovation was laced with built in obsolescence like a time released drug. They were pushers for new spyware craved by the surveillance industries of the Affiliations. He despised them for living showy lives in the Core even as they were complicit in the death of private life.

"If you describe the Core with one word, what would it be?" asked Skyla once as they sat at a corner table in a small bistro.

"Colorful. So many bright colors that you never see in the Periphery or Outlier towns."

"Like what?"

"Green grass, green trees are everywhere since they control water resources. Flowers everywhere in white pots, pink, red, yellow and every variation. The sidewalks are wide but that is so CSA vehicles can use them too if they ever lock down an area. The streets are smooth. The glass and steel houses reflect the sunlight such that there is any. Streetlights brighten the neighborhoods twenty-four hours a day. There is always a warm glow to the Core."

"Are the people colorful?"

"They are perfect in every way. There is no room for ugly in the Core," said Jaffa.

A "caw caw" sound scattered his thoughts. At least three hours into his trek, Jaguar squirmed in the sling. Jaffa looked up to see a large raven, wings spread wide circling ahead of them. Jaguar tried to stand up in the sling. "Meow," he called. Then another loud meow followed. Jaffa steadied the cat not sure of what to do.

The raven circled around flying closer and closer until his face met Jaffa's dark eyes, letting him see his own dense black eyes were real, that he was not a drone, not a spy. Jaguar stood alert in the sling and meowed to him, being kept stable with Jaffa's hand across his chest. The raven flew north. Jaguar squirmed trying to take steps in the taut cloth that surrounded him. He meowed a low, long whine at Jaffa and turned his head toward the departing raven. "Ok, I get it. You have seen the raven before. We should follow it to find Skyla." Jaffa rubbed the insistent cat's ears, settling him into low profile, with paws flat and tail curled around his side. "Stay close, Jaguar, we are about to go deep into horror zones where it takes but a moment to butcher a rare cat or a foreign man for profit." He raised his eyes toward the raven, its searing caw piercing his ears, imploring him to follow his direction. They slipped forward into the shadows.

CHAPTER THIRTEEN

SOS

"Jaguar. My little boy. Jaguar." Skyla rolled over onto her side and propped herself up with an elbow. The bright white light from chrome rimmed globes bounced around the room off of shiny metal bed rails and a steel door. She squinted at the room surrounding her. Nothing. No windows. No Jaguar. Skyla felt the age-old orphan's torment, being lost and alone, claw its way into her psyche. She had wrestled with it before and broken loose of its clutches. She shut her eyes like the mindful athlete who reviews the moves she takes to win the match.

To start, Skyla took inventory of herself. She did not hurt anywhere. She still wore her own clothes minus her boots, the cat sling, and trench coat. After a deep breath, she opened her eyes and began to rock her legs back and forth in rhythm. The slight, isometric movements energized her muscles and gave her confidence. Skyla refocused only to see darker forces massing on the horizon.

Many appalling tales of revolting perversion swirled about the Outlier underworld where amusement was simple, debased, and cheap. Low budget porn and relentless pimping could make any enterprising thug rich as hell. She tried to shake this thought from her head but in a world of possibilities, it was a big one. This was not a fate she had considered when she struck out to find Jaffa in the South. She cursed her plight but knew she had enough street game to survive.

And so, she, the expert on the system, began the game. Where was the monitor, the camera? Where was it? She scanned the room for the telltale spot, the lens through which someone was watching her. She found one in the ceiling and one at eye level on a wall for close-ups and panorama, stills and video. She enunciated the words, "Really? This is the best you got?" to the wall camera betting that her chances to survive would be better if she showed some fight. No one cared about helplessness in a predator and prey culture. "See me? Are you all watching? Do you know who I am? I am defiance. Pure defiance. I will make your life a nightmare, all of you hideous racketeering losers," she said aiming her face at the ceiling camera. "Got it?"

The door opened. "They got it. That was perfect," said the pinkish plump woman wearing a skin-tight purple knit vest and silver leggings. The purple shiny stilettos matched her lipstick. The heels clicked on the tile floor as she walked to the bedside. "Before you say anything, I am Ruby. Respect me, and I will not hurt you. That's all you need to know."

"Yes, ma'am. May I know where I am?" Skyla used her soft inside voice.

"Well done. That's it. Respectful." Ruby looked Skyla over and took her right hand in hers. "You want to know where you are? That's easy. You are on the stage of every porn loving member of society's favorite live show. You are the newest star. Fresh. They like them scared. Are you scared? You should be."

"I am scared. Are we live now?"

"No. I like to get to know my new star before she makes her debut." Ruby raised her hand to slap Skyla's face.

Skyla grabbed the wrist midair and yanked it down, pulling Ruby's face within inches of her own. Still using her soft, inside voice, she said, "Never hit me. I am nobody's bitch. Got that? Nobody!" She released the arm, knocking Ruby off balance.

Ruby regained her poise, rubbing her wrist. "This is going to fun. The last girl didn't last a day before she crapped out. Slit her own throat with a blade I left in the room. But, not before Swillian had taken his turn first with her. I always leave the girl a way out. But only after Swillian checks out his newest star. That's the plan. You live as long as you let Swillian be the boss of you any way he wants. Become his partner, you live, for a while. Resist, you die. By your own hand. I always leave a blade around. I am not cruel."

"Someone must be paying you a whole lot of money units. Why else would you strut around in that get up?" Skyla could not hold back against the stale, used up accomplice to some gangland pimp, who trafficked the unlucky from the trash alleys. "Have you looked in a mirror lately?

"Shut up." Ruby stomped toward her, beads of sweat framing her eyebrows. "You don't get to talk to me like that."

"You want to get out of here? Help me. I'll double whatever you are getting paid," said Skyla.

"I don't care about the money. I don't get money, you fool," said Ruby. "You think this is about money? I could trick for that on the outside. No, it's not the money."

"Drugs. You get drugs. For someone?" asked Skyla. She saw Ruby flinch just enough to give away the secret. Skyla noted it, the chain that kept Ruby in line.

"You better worry about yourself. Swillian ain't a gentleman. He likes to dress like Mr. Fancypants and pretend he's some famous playboy but he's just a dressed up punk that gets off having an audience. I am warning you, be prepared. He likes it rough. Gives it and takes it, rough." Ruby shook her head. "You are the first girl in months that I have even talked to this long. I will tell you a little story. If you survive Swillian, Cheddar gets you next. Then maybe Gutter. Then it's definitely over."

"Who is Gutter? And Cheddar?" Skyla curved her fingers into fists without a sound.

"Gutter is the doc who will harvest your organs. And you won't even know it's happening. You'll just be gone. Poof!" Ruby waved her hand in the air and looked far away. "Cheddar runs this outfit, the business man. Either way Gutter gets you in the end. If you off yourself early or later, it's up to you. But only after Swillian loses interest. That's the system, here, baby." Ruby began to back up toward the door.

"Ruby. Please. You can stop this." Skyla felt panic begin to suffocate her.

"No, baby, I can't. Consider yourself warned." Ruby pushed the button and the door slid open then closed.

The lights began to dim leaving Skyla alone to wait on a metal bed for Swillian.

CHAPTER FOURTEEN

SITUATION

Cheddar switched the channel of the monitor to get a closer look at the new girl, Grub's new hot one. He knew they were all hot to Grub, who loved to snatch young pretty women traveling alone from the street. Once they had passed out, he would feel up their breasts but only over their clothes. Cheddar caught him in the act once, so now he held total control over him. It was a secret precious to Cheddar who knew if Swillian ever thought Grub had actually touched their skin, Grub would be a dead man. Cheddar pitied Grub, ugly and puffy, copping a feel when he tossed his catches around in the van or onto the bed in the tank. That was all the satisfaction he was ever going to get.

The lights were low in the room, but he could see the girl had thick hair. She sat cross legged on the bed with her eyes closed. She drew something with circles or waves on the mattress with her fingertips. He weighed the consequence if he went against the policy. Swillian was gone for that night. Would Ruby cover for him or would she rat him out for more drugs for that sick little brat of hers? Swillian was the big pharma connection. Cheddar could run the operation, but without Swillian, there was nothing, no money units, no profit.

"Hey, big boss," said Gutter, pushing open the door. "That the new one?"

"Yeah. Thought you were doing something, gutting someone," replied Cheddar still staring at the monitor. "Look at that hair."

"Yeah. Nice hair. We have a situation."

"What situation?" Cheddar spun his chair around to face the doctor.

"Grub."

"What has he done?"

"He's gone. CSA pulled him. I guess it is CSA. There's a new guy." Gutter plopped down on a squishy cushion of the red leather sofa. "I went to the garage to check the stock and there he was, checking out the van."

"This is not good. Not good at all." Cheddar took off his glasses and wiped his nose with a tissue. He slid the glasses back on and peered at Gutter. "What the hell do we do now?"

"Why nothing. What will change? CSA knows what we do here. They don't care. They have someone on the street nosing around, we still get product. They take their cut of profits. Everyone is happy." Gutter pulled a cigarette from his pocket and lit it. He took a long, deep drag from it and blew smoke circles into Cheddar's face.

"You so sure? Did you talk to Grub? Did Stilton communicate with you? He should have talked to me. I don't like it. I don't like it one bit." Cheddar stood up behind his desk. "You forget. CSA watches everything. They know what we are going to do before we do it."

"Calm down. We haven't changed a thing. We have been doing the same things for years. Maybe Grub screwed up with his boss. That's on him, not us. Just wanted you to know." Gutter glanced to the monitor. "She is the only new thing."

"She's just a girl off the street, like any of them. She did have a cat that Grub let get away." Cheddar began to pace back and forth. "What if she is important?"

"She is important to us for her organs, nothing else. Swillian's little side caper, his own private porn industry makes him a little profit but we don't make much from it. He's getting rich off of making snuff films with these girls." Gutter leaned into the back cushions of the sofa.

"Then tell me why we put up with him, again?" Cheddar stopped pacing and turned toward Gutter.

"Why? Because we don't get our hands dirty with the actual killing. The buyers of organs, hypocrites that they are, do not want to feel guilty with murdering someone for their organs. It's all about the marketing. 'Clean organs.' If the organs are harvested because a man or woman have been killed by accident or suicide, they imagine they are giving a second chance of life to the poor soul, albeit, just some of their usable parts." Gutter folded his hands on his lap. "We are very far from ethics here."

"Ah, yes, that's it, Saint Gutter. We have to lie so those rich folks can sleep at night?"

"Cheddar, are you growing a conscience? Since when do you care about lies?" Gutter leaned forward to pull another cigarette from his pocket. He tapped it on the desk. "You have never refused your own chance with the girls after Swillian. Actually, most off themselves after you finish. What does that say about you?"

Cheddar stood still in front of Gutter and said, "Says they hate the thought of Swillian. He is gone tonight, which is strange, too. Since when does he leave when a fresh girl is waiting in the tank?"

Gutter leaned back, nodding his head. "I am telling you, this is a real situation. No Swillian. No Grub. A new CSA agent to procure new product. This is a situation."

"Maybe we should move up the schedule," said Cheddar. "Can't you overdose her and harvest right away? We have long waiting lists for everything. You make it some-one's big day!"

"Which brings us back to the garage, where I went for more fluids. We are running low. Ramone, the idiot, ran late with his deliveries and couldn't get more stock. I wouldn't risk cutting someone up without more backup. If we ruin the organs, we take a loss. Never good. Grub could have picked some up today too, but he's gone. The new guy didn't bring any with him."

"We have to get the new guy up to speed, what to do, from where, when. I'll talk to him tonight."

Gutter slid off the cushion and stood before the massive desk. "You do that. The girl catches a break tonight. You leave her for Swillian as is the arrangement. He will be back, you know."

Cheddar watched Gutter walk out the door letting it slam shut. He wanted the girl. He hated Gutter for acting superior, as if he were the boss. He was nothing but a drug addicted doc who couldn't make it in the Core. It was he who found the doc aimless and hanging around the door of Mito-Lab. It was he who pitched the idea of organ sales to the doc and set up this sweet deal. He opened the side drawer of his desk and pulled out the bottle of bourbon. He drank from the bottle in great gulps. The burn in his throat filled him with power. He felt his title grow, what he called his long, red stub when it went hard. Big and hard like a big cheddar cheese. His title. He wanted the girl more than ever, but he wouldn't risk losing his well fought for empire for her. He believed in money power and his never fail personal rule: business before pleasure.

"Ruby, come to my office, now. Urgent." Cheddar called for his cousin on the undetectable antique inter-com. He did not doubt her loyalty because he rescued her and her sickly boy from the street a few years ago. She had tried to pick him up on a remote corner not far from his own office at dusk in the rain. She did not recognize him and for that matter; he didn't recognize her until almost too late. When she took his hand, he saw the sixth finger, the little remnant on the side, a trait that ran through the women of his family, his sister and mother had one, his aunt, and Ruby, too. He chuckled, pouring himself another glass of bourbon. That was a close call.

The door swung open, "What is so funny?" Ruby looked around the room. "What is so urgent? I am busy looking after the others. Have you lost count? I have two pissed off boys and two other scared shitless girls to look after. Grub was a little too eager, and Gutter can't keep up without more supplies."

"What is funny? The odds you and I would end up working together. What is urgent? That Gutter needs more stuff. But also, that new girl."

He pushed the bottle and a glass toward Ruby. "Help yourself.'

"You must want something." She poured herself a generous glass and took a sip. "Ok, what is it?"

"Where is Swillian? He knew there was a new girl. He likes new girls better than new boys so what would be more important than a show tonight? And tonight, he has many choices to suit his every mood. These first time episodes are the most popular. He charges double for real time viewing and double for replays of them."

"I don't know. He told Ramone he had something to do and said he'd be back tomorrow." Ruby balanced on the edge of the desk corner. "It has bothered me all evening. And, now there is a new guy from CSA. Grub is out."

"You wouldn't have cut a deal or something to get that shit for your kid, something on the side, would you?" asked Cheddar.

"Screw you. Like I ever get away to see anyone much less cut deals. I don't even see the kid that often. His name is Aloysius, in case you forgot. Quit calling him the kid like he was a goat."

"Yeah, yeah, Ruby, you always had illusions of grandeur, just because once you were a Peripheral. Nice job, cutesy apartment, all gone because of pitiful Aloysius and his chronic immune disease. I forget which one." Cheddar's thin long nose floated high in the air, his eyes peering downward at Ruby below. "Which brings us back to our connection. Swillian. Something is wrong."

"You're the boss. What are you going to do about it?" Ruby tossed back the last of her drink. She stood up and took a step back.

"The show makes lots of money. If Swillian doesn't show by airtime, I will star tonight. It will be a treat for the viewers," said Cheddar.

"And, what happens when Swillian comes back? You better be afraid," said Ruby. "I am afraid, already."

"Just do your job and leave the rest for me."

"Ok, boss. One thing."

"What?" He snapped like a box turtle.

"The new girl is strange. She sits there drawing something imaginary on the bed with her finger. Circles and waves. And, then she will start tapping. Damn, she never stops tapping on the bed, her arm, the wall, I mean, it's weird. Never stops." Ruby paused at the door, "I have a bad feeling about all this."

"Is she live on the feed?"

"Sure, like always boss, since a few hours ago, the lights dimmed a bit to create atmosphere, like Swillian likes." Ruby shook her head and walked away.

Cheddar realized he better pay the new CSA guy a visit soon. Grub had grown on him over the past year but because he worked for CSA and they gave him the boot, Cheddar knew he could not interfere. He had no say in the next agent CSA sent, but it never took long to size them up. He wished they would send a woman, but he heard that CSA women agents only worked in the Core. It was plushier in the Core, but the agents had to be super smart as they worked deep cover. They wouldn't waste a CSA woman agent in the Outlier towns where a brute like Grub would do.

He sucked the last bit of bourbon from the bottle. Time to meet the new guy and give him his official club name, the only one to be used when doing his job. Cheddar insisted on naming his minions, the way a mob boss assigns newcomers a special nickname. The names would remind everyone, that Cheddar ruled every aspect of business, even their identity. But first, he swung around to look at the monitor for one more view, only to see the girl, tapping, tapping, tapping.

CHAPTER FIFTEEN

LONGHOUSE

Jaffa crept into a corner hidden by stacks of corrugated metal. He had thrown his lot in with Jaguar, who had directed him here by way of the raven, a route fraught with squawking, ragtag kids, scores of elderly beggars, and a small ensemble of monks. These harmless bearded men wore long brown robes and murmured chants to old saints long replaced by Big Data's prosperity worship. He waited for a few seconds as they passed in front of him.

He could hardly believe that he, a doctor and scientist had followed a cat and bird on the hunch it would lead them to Skyla. Jaguar began to squirm, pacing with his paws in place inside the sling. "There, there, Jaguar. We'll find Skyla. Soon." Jaffa stroked the cat under his chin by the long black whiskers.

Early dusk had covered the alley and shacks with murkiness and chill. Smoke from wood or refuse burning stoves began to float up through cracks in the seam ridden rooflines. The noise of the street gave way to the relentless hum of monitors, some inside and some outside on a table where anyone could watch. It was the nightly time for the reality shows, which drew big Outlier audiences for the chance to snatch a fantasy or two of the unreachable high life. Huge audiences set their routines by the hour for such shows. These shows contained the one unifying thread, the ever-seducing dope that strung the three unequal castes of Cap City together like a clothesline. That thread, that dope, was the stuff.

Reality shows promoted batches of new stuff for sale every day, available from all the companies of all the Affiliations. Even in the squalor of the Outlier wasteland, the people held onto their aspirational prosperity beliefs. Watching endless shows of wealth and luxury felt like a worship service attended by sinners. If they had only tried a bit harder, or only respected money power more, perhaps they would not have fallen from a Core or Peripheral life. Some would dream of ascension into Core, the epitome of heaven.

Show times were, also, the hours of slow motion and stealth favored by the thieves and hookers of the alleys. When people were distracted by the monitors, anything elsewhere could happen and anything elsewhere did. Jaffa hugged tight to the wall and watched a mishmash of people form a huddle around monitors on the street.

Small gangs, huddling elsewhere, concerned him more as they gauged the slightest movement on the street. Two of the gangs began to exchange gunfire. Jaffa pulled back farther out of the line of fire. The silhouette of the raven against the rising moonlight flew into his view, circling overhead. He landed on a roof just two shacks to their left. "Caw, Caw." Jaguar raised his head and tried to stand feeling the pressure of Jaffa's hand across his back.

Jaffa scoped the area once more and began to slither close to the walls, aiming for the shed below the raven. He detected a rim of light around the small window by the door. The raven did not move from his perch. Jaffa paused, unsure what to do. Dropping in to a stranger's place was not done in Outlier neighborhoods where people shot first and asked questions later.

Without warning, the raven flew to the small ledge below the window and pecked at it. The window opened and the black feathered creature hopped in. Jaffa began to mimic the raven tapping the code on the door. SOS. He repeated it three times. Nothing. He slid down, his back against the building, to a squat position. He stroked Jaguar. "We wait a bit more. If nothing, we must move on." Jaguar forced his head into the palm of Jaffa's hand and kept it there. "I know you're hungry. I'll find something for you."

Jaffa glanced back at the window. It began to open a few inches at a time. The raven appeared sitting on the edge. Jaffa tapped SOS one more time. Someone tapped back, RAVEN. Jaffa tapped YES. The door opened a few inches. "We will not hesitate to kill you. Enter if you dare." A women's voice whispered the mysterious instruction with total authority. Jaffa held Jaguar steady and stepped to the door with slow cautious steps to show there was no threat. The door opened in full. He stepped across the threshold.

A woman with radiant, mahogany eyes and long, char black hair, stood ready with a rifle at hand. She wore camouflage trousers, combat boots and a military grade armored vest. She appraised her visitor. "You know the code? Identify yourself. Why have you come here?" The raven flitted from the window to her shoulder and perched without a sound. The woman reached up to the raven and pet his black claws in her shirt. Jaffa recognized the raven's connection to the formidable woman as the same sort of connection he could sense between Jaguar and Skyla.

"I am Jaffa. This is Jaguar. He is very hungry, if you have anything to spare for him."

"You are worried about the cat?" The muscles in her neck flexed as she spoke. She maintained her still posture and gave Jaffa the once over.

"Yes. He is special. He belongs to my girlfriend and is her familiar."

"Then why is he with you?" The woman had not moved but her eyes focused on Jaguar.

"Something has happened to her. They were separated. Jaguar came to me and we set out to find her. The raven, your raven led us here to you. I believe your raven saw where they were attacked and led us to you for help."

"My raven led you here? You expect me to believe this wild story?" The woman took a step toward him. "And the code?"

"I learned the code from my best friend, my girlfriend's brother, Tangier Roseau, when we served together in the EME." Jaffa stepped back and kept a hand on Jaguar.

"Do you always go around tapping on doors?" The woman's eyes moved toward another room, where a light had been turned on.

"No ma'am. But I trusted your raven. I am desperate to find Skyla, so it was worth the risk."

"I would have killed you if your tapping had been random noise. You can trust nothing out here." She stepped back and lowered the gun. "Call me Genesee."

"Genesee," said Jaffa with a nod.

"You can let your cat free." Genesee signaled to the room. A brown stocky woman came to the doorway. The dim light sparkled on the silver strands of her loose layered hair that graced the collar of her blue denim camp shirt. She took her hands out of the pockets of her cargo pants and strode into the room. "This is Grenadine, my sister," said Genesee.

"Jaffa. Let's get that kitty of yours something to eat. It's ok, now. You are with friends." Grenadine put her hand on his shoulder while he unwrapped the sling, helping Jaguar to his feet on the floor. "Your Skyla must be very special to have a familiar. Only people who can open to their higher self can hear the invitation of a familiar. It's a bond grounded in love. Clan Mother Genesee and her raven, Poe, have been linked for years."

"Poe. Yes, of course." Jaffa nodded, but stood still. Jaguar stretched on the wooden floor. "But, Clan Mother Genesee? Am I supposed to be impressed?"

"Yes." Grenadine pulled Jaffa's chin toward her face and shot him a merciless glare. "You should be 'on your knees' impressed! Clan mothers are inherited titled positions in our society. They, together with the chiefs and councils, wield the political and cultural destiny of our people as far as seven generations ahead. She is a fierce leader in our nation," said Grenadine. She shoved Jaffa toward a table and pulled out a chair for him. "Sit here while I get some treats for Jaguar."

Jaffa hesitated, first looking to Clan Mother Genesee. He tried to decipher her next move. She pulled back a chair across the table and hung the rifle on it, positioned so the gun could be grabbed with one motion from her.

"Go ahead. Sit down," said Genesee. "Grenadine, there's some rabbit from yesterday in the fridge. I think Poe finished the last bit of fish. Jaguar could use a little dark meat, and some water." Poe remained perched on her shoulder, but observed Jaguar's every move.

Jaffa dug into his pants pocket for the Faraday case. He put it on the table then sat down. "Clan Mother Genesee, with respect, no one knows I am here. My phone has been in this case since I left the clinic in the South. Jaguar does not have a chip."

"Good. That is excellent, but you cannot stay here. No one stays here. We are just two sisters with a few friends who come and go. You need to call me Genesee. Everyone does."

"Yes, Ma'am, I can do that," said Jaffa. "But, I don't know what my next move should be. Poe brought us this far. I still don't know what happened or where to find Skyla." He leaned back in the chair, grateful to sit for a while even as the urgency of finding her grew more acute.

Genesee tapped her fingers on the table as if she were playing the piano. "You must get her to the Keep. You both go and never come back."

"You know her? You know about her? Why didn't you say something before?" Jaffa tried to tamp down his surprise.

"We wanted to be sure of your intentions. It is pretty clear you love her if you are willing to track her down saddled with a cat following a raven into the bowels of the slum." The lights dimmed then grew brighter. "We always lose a little power when the nighttime shows start. Where is our screen, Grenadine?"

"Here. I'll turn it on now. We can all watch what gruesome gore is in store for us tonight." Grenadine shoved an old computer monitor onto the table and a control box next to it. She pushed a button and the screen lit up. "We always get good intel from these shows, twisted as some of them are. It takes a few minutes to warm up." Jaguar had finished tearing into the rabbit meat. He stepped to his new friend and wrapped his tail around her leg.

Genesee leaned across the table. She folded her hands and stared at the weary young man across from her. "Jaffa, you must be very frustrated. You have traveled a long treacherous path to find Skyla. You want at this very minute to keep searching for her and instead you find yourself sitting with two old biddies about to watch the free drivel. We can't afford subscription channels so we are stuck with it, but as Grenadine says, the intel is useful."

Jaffa said nothing, instead noticing the spartan front room with only straight back chairs and a plain table. It had the atmosphere of an office, a command center, a place where meetings might take place. He realized that despite any social niceties, this meeting was all business, a sizing up of him and his story. He summoned his waning energy and renewed his commitment to finding Skyla at all costs.

"I assure you, Jaffa, we want to find Skyla too. We are not old biddies. And I can tell you this. You are no longer just a medical doctor from the Periphery who works at the clinics now and then. No. The moment you tossed your backpack aside and took off with Jaguar, under the cover of a fake story of hurting your arm, you were marked. You know the risk of going off the grid. That Faraday case of yours helped you in the short term, but it cannot hide you forever. CSA will find you. They always do."

"You know everything. How?" Jaffa leaned in like an earnest student trying to understand a magician. He couldn't figure her or her context out yet. That's what Skyla would tell him to do, understand the context. So, he snatched a couple of seconds to scan the walls of the room, but they were bare.

He returned his gaze to Poe. "I trusted a bird."

"Not just any bird, but my familiar, like Jaguar, who brought you here." Genesee pushed back her chair and took a deep breath the way one does when trying to decide just what to say. "Jaffa, before anything else happens, you must agree to take Skyla to the Keep. Mae, Zeinab, and I all agreed."

"Who are you? How do you know my grandmother and Mae?" Jaffa searched his mind for a clue, something he had missed. "Longhouse?"

"Longhouse." Her bright eyes narrowed as her full lips drew up tight, in a faint smile. Her voice, soft like velvet but tough as iron carried the words, "We are Longhouse. It is a people, a network, a resistance movement, and it has a leader." Genesee slid back to a wall. She tapped a floorboard and the wall receded into itself to reveal a control panel for a myriad of drones, cameras, monitors, and weapons. "I am showing you this so you will understand that what I say is real, and I have the power to back it up. Longhouse is an absolute zero sum game. There are winners and losers. The struggle to regain human dignity from money power and those who glorify it above people is a fight to the death. Humanity is barely alive now. The time will come when scarcity dooms the Affiliations' ability to power the money economy. It will crash amid the wails of its affiliates for more stuff, but it won't be able to deliver. The countdown draws closer to the end. After centuries of repression, we, the People of the Longhouse and steadfast to our ancestors and traditions, hold the path to plenty and peace. Because we live it, we know it works. It is the counterpoint to the Affiliations. It could just save civilization. We must try for all our sakes. No doubt, there will be a battle."

"Wow. I don't know what to say. I don't understand any of this, but you know Zeinab and you know about me. Am I being drafted into Longhouse?" Jaffa shook his head.

"Not drafted. You joined us." Genesee tilted her head and directed a half smile toward Jaffa. "There is much to learn."

"Ok, well, let's start with your orders to take Skyla to the Keep? Isn't it just a safe house somewhere on the outskirts of the slums by the river? That's the urban legend. Are you aware of that?"

"Of course. We launched that rumor years ago and it has been a most effective decoy." Genesee reached up to stroke Poe along his wings. "Let me tell you the real story of the Keep, our home. It is the last geographic area of sovereign indigenous nations, untouched by the Affiliations who simply cannot find it."

"They can find anything and anyone, anywhere. How can it be hidden?" Jaffa shook his head no.

"There are ways. Think Faraday like your case, there." Genesee pointed to the small rectangle on the table in front of Jaffa.

"Who lives there?"

"The Haudenosaunee, the original people of a territory in what we now call geo-region Panamerica-north. They are the People of the Longhouse, the Six Nations of the Haudenosaunee Confederacy.

"Nations? What nations still exist? Jaffa glanced toward Grenadine then back to Genesee

"An alliance of six sovereign nations that have existed for centuries. But, not as the nation states the Affiliations wanted to destroy," said Genesee. "Big difference. The nations never became states."

"So, you could escape them, off the radar and protected by a reservation? All that was left of your original land, in the end, saved you?" Jaffa glanced again at the control panel in the wall.

"Yes. The reservation was all we had to survive for almost three centuries. Who knew it would be a twist of fate? With it we can still survive," said Genesee, "but not without a fight. In the end, outsiders always want our land. After some time, thanks to Big Data, the Affiliations remembered us and took aim. They want it all—land and resources if they can find us."

"I see. But, why would anyone be safe there? You expect me to believe it is safe from Big Data? Its POVs can scope everything and its CSA knows everything."

"For now, it is safe. It is not, however, easy to reach nor is just anyone allowed entry. Security is supreme to safeguard the people there. They are not an experiment. They are leading authentic lives guided by the Haudenosaunee practice of the Good Mind," said Genesee.

"And, what is that?" Jaffa took a slight impatient breath, and hoped it went unnoticed.

"Bear with me," said Genesee, "I can tell you're anxious to get on with things."

"A little," said Jaffa.

"The concept of the Good Mind teaches us to be actively aware of our thoughts and their intent. Goodmindedness, Peacefulness, and Strength. It is using a pure mind in your interactions with the natural world and people. Peacefulness follows. From the combination of Goodmindedness and Peacefulness you get Strength."

"And you think that strength is enough to withstand the world of Big Data and the Affiliations? Look around us here. All we can see for miles is camp town after camp town of desperate people drowning in abject poverty. It's the sick gift from the money economy that rules the world." Jaffa could feel his mind drift to the clinic, where a street kid would dare ask for a cat to eat.

"You're right, of course. It will require enormous strength and courage. But, we are a strong people who have faced the prospect of extinction before. We are prepared. In the Keep, there is plenty and we thrive on a unique but no less rich life."

"Guess it's all in how you define riches," said Jaffa.

"That is the crux of it." Genesee reached down, picked up Jaguar, and put him on the table. He stepped over to Jaffa and gave him a head butt. He sat, hunched down, folding his front paws in under him, wrapping his tail around his side and faced Poe. Genesee rubbed the top of

Jaguar's head to the tip of his tail following the curve around him.

"Genesee, I hope you don't take this the wrong way," said Jaffa. "How do you know the Longhouse way will work any better than the money economy which has driven men since the beginning of time? It is a waste of time for me to discuss this when Skyla is the social scientist. And I need to get back to searching for her."

"Jaffa, you are right. You need to find her and we will help in any way. But, you need to know why it is so essential that you do. Beyond what Skyla means to you, she is vital for the future of the Haudenosaunee people and the Confederacy. Our nations are made up of clans, our family units, and are led by women. These women are leaders in the authority of their nations as fire keepers, faith keepers, and even medical healers."

"Why would Skyla, of all women, be vital to you?" Jaffa shrugged his shoulders. He weaved Jaguar's tail through his fingers. "What does she have to do with all this?"

"According to the calculations of our honored scholars, we are in the beginning of the Fourth Epoch of Time. In the last epoch, we were colonized by settlers that came from Europe who wanted to kill us and steal our land to set up their own new fifty states. We know it takes three hundred years to liberate a people from a colonial settler state," said Genesee. "Using seventeen seventy-six as the start, we're close to three hundred years, now.

"You think now is the time?" asked Jaffa.

"We have been in a process for decades to decolonize our minds by reclaiming our traditions and beliefs, even our system of governance by the Great Law of Peace. We recovered control of part of our original land because we stayed under the political radar since the Collapse. But, things are changing. We need strong, new leaders to stop the Affiliations from taking our land like the states did."

Jaffa shifted his gaze from Jaguar to Genesee and said, "Zeinab use to say it's always about the land."

"She's right. The fight for it will be brutal as all colonial wars are, said Genesee. "We believe Skyla might be one of the women who could earn the honored title of Jigonsaseh. Perhaps she becomes the Head Clan Mother, the chair of the Clan Mothers' Council of the Confederacy." Genesee studied Jaffa's face for a reaction but he gave nothing away. "She's suited for such positions. Skyla has the sharp mind and the poetic words of a leader."

"What are you talking about? Skyla? She is Skyla Roseau, daughter of a Moroccan-American father, using the French last name of her mother from Montreal, Quebec," said Jaffa trying not to shout. "She and her brother have used that name for security since they were kids. She has nothing to do with this."

"No. You are wrong. You see, her grandmother is from the Wolf clan of Seneca and her grandfather was Mohawk. Both are nations of the Haudenosaunee. Her grandparents settled in the Montreal area for work. Roseau is French for Reed, her mother's family name. They used the French version to fit it." Genesee folded her hands and glanced from Jaffa to Grenadine who nodded back to her.

"Does Skyla know this?" Jaffa kept his voice level and dry.

"Tangier knows. I only told him a few months ago," said Genesee, "I admit I have waited too long. He will tell Skyla."

"I cannot believe what I am hearing here. What was the point of secrecy? And, all this goes on at the Keep? This is where you want her to go?" Jaffa stood up and paced back a forth a few steps in the cramped space. "You think she is some heroine to lead you into battle with the Affiliations as if she were a Joan of Arc? What makes you think she'd ever agree to any of this?"

"No one is forced to go to the Keep. It is the safest place for you and Skyla. Staying here she will live the life of a fugitive, always on the run, always scared, always exhausted. So will you. It is no life at all." Genesee reached to pet Jaguar with a slow, deliberate hand, stopping to rub his ears.

"Even if we want to go, CSA will track us. They see everything. They know everything. Why even the kids in the street will turn anyone in if they can make a profit from it. They are the worst, the ones who have grown up here. They are indentured slaves that work for CSA."

"Like the scrappy ones who live next door. Don't you think they have already told CSA that a guy tapped something weird on my door? I don't worry because they are afraid of Poe and think we are witches." Genesee laughed at herself. "Hey, you old witch Grenadine, we need to send this boy with some provisions. He can't stay but we need to feed him."

"Sure, I'll put something together. Is the cat going with him?" Grenadine opened a cupboard and began to pull out bread and peanut butter. "I think Jaguar should stay with us. He is at risk out on the street."

"I agree. The cat stays here."

"You don't mind? Poe won't mind?" Jaffa wanted to pet the bird but didn't dare.

"Poe brought you and Jaguar to us. You will be back for him." Genesee stood up to help Grenadine.

"Of course, I will be back for him and for you. I have questions that need answers. For instance, why are you here in an Outlier town when you could be living in the Keep?" Jaffa began to adjust his scarf and pull up his collar.

"To watch over Tangier and Skyla. And, you. To know our enemy. We don't have time for all this now. You must be on your way. It will all come clear, we will keep nothing from you." Genesee handed him the sandwiches wrapped in brown paper. Grenadine filled a small canteen and stuffed it into his coat pocket. "Find Skyla and Tangier."

"You know I will."

Genesee led him toward the door. She opened it without a sound and watched a few seconds as Jaffa's shape disappeared into darkness.

Grenadine sat back in her chair to watch the show. The monitor had warmed up, showing a grainy but clear picture.

She gasped. "Look on the monitor. A girl. Alone. She is tapping. SOS. SOS!"

CHAPTER SIXTEEN

CONFUSION

Riff looked up from his computer at the frantic pounding on his apartment door. He grabbed his gun. At two in the morning, the unexpected banging filled him with dread. "Who is it?"

"Open up you son of a bitch, before I break this door in," said a voice he remembered from CSA institute days.

Riff opened the door, standing behind it, as his training dictated, gun in hand. He watched Grub charge into the room and stop.

"What the hell is going on?" Grub grabbed Riff's open vodka bottle from the table and drank a long gulp. He handed the bottle to Riff and began to pace around the room. He stopped once or twice, sizing the place up, as if he might have been a new tenant.

"What are you talking about?" Riff wiped the opening of the vodka bottle with his shirt. He hated spit backs. "Let me get you a glass, you pig." He took a glass from the cupboard and slammed it down by Grub.

"Listen, you little prick, this is why no one likes you." Grub pulled the glass over and filled it with more vodka. "Glasses. Dainty little glasses. Like we are old ladies." He inhaled a shot. Some vodka dripped out of the corner of his fatty lips onto his flabby belly. His sweat stained shirt reeked of something rancid or perhaps his deeply scuffed, mud-caked boots did. He pulled the nearest chair closer and sat down on it with a thud.

"What do you want?" Riff sat at the table and poured himself more vodka. He stared at the CSA classmate wishing he could vaporize him like Motoman would. Riff didn't consider Grub a friend. He didn't have friends at all so he suspected that Grub wanted to set him up or worse, force him to do something against the rules. CSA was all he had and he would not let Grub hurt his hard won career.

"I've been kicked off my assignment. Just like that. Just doing my job and all of a sudden that Senior Field Agent T is doing my job."

"Tangier? He's big time. You must have done something. Stilton or someone must have noticed a problem on the show or with the harvests."

"How do you know all that stuff? What clearance do you have?" Grub sat up straight.

"High enough to know pretty much everything. So don't mess with me." Riff's sneering smile hid his lie, that he knew lots of stuff not because of his rank but because of his late night hacking habit. No one escaped his ire and when

Stilton sent him back to Celebration Wholesale rather than promote him, he scoured the depths of CAS files and all projects he ran. The organ harvest plus porn project captivated his imagination, but Grub as the agent, too noisy, too brash, never made sense to him. "Why are you here? You and me? We aren't buddies."

"Ok, Ok. I know. What do I do now that I am kicked off? Stilton left me hanging. He didn't reassign me even to a desk." Grub swirled the vodka in his glass, his fat fingers looked like a paw. "I figured if anyone could tell me what is going on, it's you. You always had a nose for stuff beyond your pay grade. That can be useful, to me."

"Useful? There is no useful, only nothing. You got nothing right now. Stilton never gives a reason for any of his orders. You just bend over and take it. What can you do but wait until he decides your new assignment. Look at it this way; maybe this is your ticket out of that ghetto."

"I still can't figure it out. I did everything I always did by the book. I snatched a random girl, but lost the cat. She had a cat. Who cares about a cat?" said Grub.

"Is that your latest catch? A girl with a cat? A black cat?" Riff checked the excitement he felt in his pants. "Where is she now?"

"Yeah. I caught her in a trash alley, alone, zig-zagging her way through. She knew how to avoid POVs. That I could tell. I watched her for a couple blocks. She had some kind of blanket thing with her. I thought it might be a baby. Scared the shit out of me, but then I saw the cat. It was a big black one with shiny yellow eyes, the kind that casts spells on you. She helped it jump away."

"Where is the cat now?"

"Ran off somewhere. I was busy snatching the girl. She fought like a ninja for a minute, then the drugs wiped her out. She's in the tank now. We were waiting for Swillian to do his show, but he never showed up. Ruby said he'd be gone that night, but she didn't know where or why. No one really knows. Swillian never misses anything. Something is wrong I tell you." Grub wove his fingers together and cracked his knuckles. "Say, turn on the monitor and let's watch. We can see what has been going on for a while. The show should be available at this hour."

Riff switched the monitor over to the porn channel and clicked on the show streaming icon. Grub dragged his chair over to see it better. "Turn up the volume. I like to hear them scream. I bet this one gives Swillian a fight whenever he shows up."

"Shut up, Grub. I don't want to know how you like it." Riff knew only one girl with a black cat and as much as he tried to hate her, he wasn't sure he could watch the on-coming assault whenever it came to pass. Rule one in CSA training is never know your victims, never get close to those you will have to kill someday. Cleaner that way and he believed it.

Riff thought about killing Grub but disposing of an-other CSA agent was no small feat. He could tell Stilton that Grub attacked him, but the surveillance in his own apartment would disprove that. Grub was no dumb-dumb.

Riff wished he could hide from POVs long enough to get rid of this pest. Grub was too clever to be lured to a dark trash alley, where thick shadows and fewer data monitors made slitting his throat more doable. Those newest generation insect and rodent drones that just came online might also give him away. They would transmit all his actions back to base.

The only smart option was to endure his unwelcome presence and watch as the program music grew louder and the lights grew brighter. A banner across the screen flashed "live." The angles and curves of a girl with blonde hair, curled up in fetal position, showed through a white sheet pulled up around her chin as if she were cold. Her eyes were closed.

"Hey, do you think she's drugged? She isn't moving at all now," said Grub. "No shouting about resistance anymore. She's caved."

"What was she doing?"

"Never saw anything like it. She tapped on everything, her head, her legs, and then she'd draw these crazy shapes on the bed. She's mental as they come." Grub smacked Riff's arm and pointed to the monitor. "Hey, Swillian must have come back." The sound of a door opening then closing signaled the start of the show that had a cult following among viewers in all three levels of the society. "Shit, that is not Swillian," shouted Grub.

"Who is it?"

"Cheddar! The boss. The guy that runs the operation. Wow, he has guts. Swillian goes ballistic if he doesn't do these poor suckers first. He can shut the place down in a minute because he owns the camera and the connections for the harvest gig." Grub started to sweat, balls rolling down his pudgy cheeks. "Man, it is hot in here."

"It's just the vodka. Look, he doesn't wait at all. He's going to jump her without any talk or anything. You can see his dick hanging out of his pants.," said Riff as his bowels churned.

"Shut up." Grub leaned closer to the monitor.

Riff barked back. "You shut up. This guy is crazy. Swillian is a real star, he puts on a playboy show. He talks to them, takes his time, really drives them crazy even if he roughs them up later. This guy is in too much of a hurry. The girl is just lying there. Maybe they did drug her. Look, he is getting close to her."

"Oh shit! Did you see that? She just reached out and grabbed Cheddar's woody and snapped it like a twig!" Grub stood up, screaming at Riff. "She broke him. She ruined him for life."

"I can see that for myself, you idiot. He's doubled up on the floor. And, she ran out of the room. Gone." Riff poured another glass of vodka. "God, think of the pain." Then the monitor went dark, the streaming ended.

Grub grabbed the vodka and gulped from the bottle. He paced around the room, his eyes on Riff. "That show was rigged. That can't be the girl I caught. I swear. Something is not right. How could she get through the door? It only opens with an eye scan. Someone is a stinking traitor. This whole thing reeks. Poor Cheddar. He'll never be normal again. Done. Finished. And Swillian is a no show for all of this? He's dead or something big is going down."

"You should go now." Riff stood up and pointed to the door. "Now. I don't want to be anywhere near you or this screw up. Go. Now."

"Why you pompous son of a bitch. You think I am dirty? Not clean and tidy enough for you and your CSA ambitions? You are nothing but a desk man." Grub spat on the shiny tile floor.

"How convenient you got transferred out of there before this big screw up happened for all to see. Yeah, maybe there is a traitor in CSA." Riff grabbed Grub's arm and shoved him toward the door. The vodka bottle crashed to the floor. Shattered glass spread everywhere. Riff picked up the jagged neck of the bottle and waved it back and forth in front of Grub. "Get out."

"You're right. There is a traitor. But it ain't me." Grub stomped off into the hallway.

The door slammed shut, muffling the footsteps leading away. Riff glared at his spotless workspace, his smooth table, his shiny tile floor all contaminated with the spit and sweat of a guy he barely knew. He began to wipe clean the foul mess from the putrid outbursts of a foul man, the type he detested the most. Yes, he was a deskman and glad of it. It kept him pure, for purity of self and purity of allegiance to the Affiliations held him fast to his highest goals: promotion and money power.

He replayed the scene of the assault in his mind over and over, searching for any detail that he knew was unique to

Skyla. The form was correct, the hand strong, the hair color wrong and texture too stiff, long enough but not loose and cascading, a feature he secretly admired. The girl could not have been Skyla. The Skyla he knew, the girl who reads books and never misses a day of work, couldn't be this tough. Whoever had laid in wait for Cheddar, had anticipated what to do. A professional had planned that attack. It was not the action of a terrified girl or boy, kidnapped from the street at the mercy of some porno film director and his minions. The strike on Cheddar was too precise, and oh, was it awful to see.

Riff resented Grub's sudden appearance at his apartment, to force him to wallow in his disgusting muck. He could not ignore Grub or the show and considered his options. POVs had seen it all and by extension, of course, Stilton, his boss. He weighed the pros and cons of self-revealing his encounter with Grub. An act of cowardice or heroism, it could be interpreted either way, but to do nothing meant he might lack self-discipline, a must have quality if he wanted to advance in CSA. He scrolled down the list of other agents in his mind and stopped at T. Tangier, the famous crack senior field agent who, according to Grub, had just been assigned to the operation. Senior enough, but not higher than Stilton, Tangier would want to know anything related to this operation and that included his own suspicions about Grub's strange visit. Very soon, he, Riff, would know what was going on too.

CHAPTER SEVENTEEN

RESCUE

Tangier swung the door wide and caught Skyla as she ran toward him. He shoved her boots and coat into her hands. He grabbed the front of her hair and ripped off the long blonde wig. She shook her black locks free. He threw the wig behind her as the door banged shut. It slammed into Cheddar's face as he rocked on the floor and wailed loud enough to wake the dead. Skyla slid into her coat and zipped up her boots.

Tangier tossed a rifle to Skyla, who shot out any visible lens. It didn't matter if they were broadcast cameras or POVs. They had to go. "Thanks, big brother. I couldn't stand that stupid wig one more minute." Skyla looked up at Tangier. "Swillian must like blondes. There were half a dozen wigs in there on a shelf."

"Come on. We're not out of this yet." Tangier motioned with his hand the direction they would take. "This was a close one. We can't afford any more delays, any more exposure."

"I was trying to get to Jaffa when this piece of shit snatched me. You left me and CSA found me anyway. I had to move." Skyla adjusted the rifle as she followed him.

"I know. It's just not safe for you and maybe not for me, either. We'll work this out later. Let's go."

They ran down a corridor dank from leaking sewage pipes past tiny, empty rooms. Gutter stared through the round glass window of the patients' room door. All electronic doors had locked shut when Skyla destroyed the lenses. He pounded away, shouting, "Let me out." The bodies began to squirm as their electric IV machines stopped delivering the sedatives to keep them asleep. Skyla could only see his eyes, wide like big round cookies, and his lips, cussing up a storm. Only silence came through the soundproof door.

Across from Gutter's line of sight, Tangier stopped to set a mound of light grey plastique with a timer on the wall. Just ahead, Skyla saw the scrub nurse, Vlad, slumped over on the smelly floor. Blood pooled around him from the gunshot wound in his head, the last role he chose to play, the last gift he gave to himself.

Without a glance, Tangier stepped over the bloody mess and signaled to pick up their pace and cut to the right to a shorter, wide hallway where they sprinted toward a double-door. Tangier shot through the electronic locks with the rifle and pushed them open. The white unmarked, skinny van, used for delivering harvested organs to the Core and the Periphery sat before them. Its official CSA emblem on the lower right corner of the windshield was a ticket to everywhere.

"Skyla, you ride shotgun and keep watch. Cover me if we're attacked," said Tangier.

"Will do." Skyla jumped into the van.

Tangier strode around to the back of the van. One back door was open. The closed door shielded his favorite Outlier asset, Poppy, who had taken Ruby prisoner. He stopped to listen.

"My boy, my Aloysius, what will happen to him?" Ruby pleaded to Poppy to let her go. She raised her tied up hands in prayer. She knew Poppy's type, tough, and street hewn. Black or white. Live or die. There was no grey or third choice. Begging was all she had.

"Stupid bitch. Don't you know your little treasure is dead?" Poppy slapped her across the face, then tightened the rope around Ruby's ankles.

"No! That's not true. He sends me webchats. I send his drugs every week. Ramone takes them when he goes on his runs. Where is he? He'll tell you!" Ruby's tears had melted her mascara into inkblots dripping down her cheeks.

"Ramone is dead. Killed by a gang for all the dope, your dope, he carried on him, like a fool. And so is your boy. Gutter used him a year ago when they were low on product. Cheddar wrote those fake webchats to you."

"No. You lie. I saw him on the monitor." Ruby sobbed as she slumped to the floor of the van.

"Swillian faked the pictures you saw. He's a film guy. He knows how to do that shit with pictures. Cheddar and Swillian have been playing you for years. They needed some chump to look after their hostages. You didn't care what they did to those young boys and girls. You knew. You are as guilty as they are for stealing lives away, for their murders. So don't go all holier than thou about your own brat. If you are such a good mother, when's the last time you saw Aloysius?" Poppy turned away to look after her other charges.

"A year. I haven't seen him for a year. Cheddar never let me leave." Ruby gasped for air as her sobs overwhelmed her breaths, choking her with her own spit.

"And you believed all that crap he fed you, you pathetic fake." Poppy pushed her hand downs. "No prayers here. No redemption for you. Not from me."

Poppy focused on the two boys and two girls sitting on boxes in front of her. One boy, a teenager with dirty blond hair told her that he had been held for almost two weeks, but he couldn't be sure. He said the redheaded boy about ten years old had been snatched only three days before. The two girls had been held for close to three weeks according to the one with brown eyes and brown hair. They arrived on the same day but from different areas and did not know each other. "Why do you think Swillian ignored you girls for so long?" asked Poppy.

"Ruby told us that he won't touch us if we have our periods. And we both got them," said the girl with brown hair. She put her arm around the other girl and pulled her close.

"We made them last for a long time, over a week. That's what we told him. Ruby told us to lie and she backed us up," said the girl with auburn hair. "Ruby made up more lies, like we were sick with the flu, and that helped to keep him away. Ruby talked about her boy all the time."

"Yeah. I don't think she knew he was dead," added the girl with brown hair.

"Yes, well all the same, Ruby knew what was going on. Instead of stopping it, she participated. She wore the gloves, even if they were velvet gloves. She thought it would keep her from being dirty. Doesn't work like that. She is a filthy, lying snake like the rest of them." Poppy smoothed the girls' hair and squeezed their hands. She patted the red haired boy's shoulder. "I am taking you to a safe place. There are many Aunties there who will help you."

"What is an Auntie?" asked the teenage boy with a frown.

"An Auntie is any woman who declares herself a 'safe zone.' You can tell an Auntie your deepest secret or wishes and she will keep them in the vault. You can ask an Auntie for help and she will help however she can. Aunties make no judgment. They help, they heal, they try to make our harsh world a little kinder for you."

"Why would they want to do that? Where's the profit?" The auburn haired girl shook her head and shrugged. "This sounds like something from the old days."

"Yes. I suppose it is an old fashioned thing," said Poppy, "but we do it because it makes us feel happy. I'll tell you a little secret. Sometimes you don't make a profit but you can still be happy without it."

"I am happy you saved us," said the red headed boy. He stood up and hugged Poppy's skinny frame.

"Me too. And this hug is my profit." Poppy hugged him back and kissed the top of his red mop of hair.

Ruby propped herself up, leaning against the wall of the van. "Where are you taking me, Filthy Auntie?"

"I am not taking you anywhere. You belong to Tangier now. Your pitiful pleas and whining won't cut through his hard shell. You will be lucky if he drops you down South by the river to get lost in the mist. Those purple shoes of yours should keep you in business. You are finished up North here."

Tangier had heard enough and swung open the door. He jumped into the van and stood still with his rifle at hand. He studied Ruby, tied up in the corner.

"I should leave her here. It would be safer to shut her up," he said to Poppy.

"True, but they played her. She hates them now for killing her kid. You could drop her down South. She cannot stay up North."

"She will never be trustworthy. She is a rat once, she is a rat always." Tangier stepped over toward Ruby. He bent down in front of her mascara smeared, flushed face. "Listen you little whore. I don't give a damn about you. You would have let all these kids and my sister die because you were too stupid to know you were being played. And they would all be dead if you didn't get caught. By me. So, listen hard. I own you. Got it?"

Ruby winced but said nothing. She shifted her gaze from him down to the floor.

Tangier reached over and grabbed her hair, forcing the swollen eyes to look at his. "Answer me. I own you. And you say, yes sir, you own me."

"Up yours." Ruby's eyes glowed like hot daggers waiting to be thrown.

Tangier pulled Ruby to her feet and shoved her to the back of the van. He cut the rope at her ankles so she could jump. "Go. You have made your choice." She stood there, inert, until he shoved her forward. She landed on the floor of the garage in a heap but turned around.

"No. Take me. I want to go," she screamed raising her hands to Tangier.

"Too late. Poppy, you ride back here with the kids. Keep them quiet till I, and only I, open the door. Got it?"

"Got it."

Tangier jumped down and secured the doors. Ruby stood sobbing for her life, for another chance. He ran to the van front and slid in behind the wheel. Skyla, her hood up, had the garage door remote box in her hand.

"Tracker disabled?" He started the engine.

"Of course. And as back up I hacked into the van computer and reset the past itineraries to coordinates of a year ago. They will match up but be out of date. Unless someone bothers to look that hard, it will buy us additional cover."

"Let's go." Tangier set the van in motion. Skyla pressed the remote and the door to the alley opened.

The door creaked with each pull on the tracks inside of the garage. The alley was empty ahead. The night's darkness spread out over the decrepit terrain. He stopped the van a few feet from the garage door and watched it close again. He pulled a small box with a single red button from his pocket. With a glance in a review side mirror, he pushed the button.

After a three second delay, a gigantic explosion sounded sending a fireball high into the sky, lighting up the Outlier world for miles for a brief few seconds before the darkness fell again. The ground shook, the dogs barked, and the people who never came out at night opened their doors to view the red glow that lingered above the site where dealers of health had traded in death and debauchery.

"The people around here have no idea what just blew up," said Skyla staring at the falling ash visible in the barest light of the night sky. "They don't know anything about what goes on in their very neighborhoods. Why would they? They have learned to look away from each other. They leave looking and knowing to POVs and CSA."

"They will guess it was Swillian's porn studio when they can't get the channel. When the broadcast is dead, rumors will grow." Tangier wove the van through alleys with a slow, deliberate hand. Agents preferred an unhurried ride to avoid ruts in the alleys. There was never a rush to catch a suspect. Sooner or later they'd be caught as there was no escape.

"It's a gruesome thought, Ruby and Gutter blown to bits," said Skyla, "not to mention Cheddar and the poor bodies already drugged up for harvest. They were waking up."

"Not as gruesome as the thought of Swillian and you," Tangier replied, swerving the van to avoid a hole. "I had to save you even if I couldn't save the rest. At least we got the kids out."

"Those poor kids are lucky. I am so grateful that you are my big brother. What made you check Swillian's show?"

"Once you were kidnapped, I scanned all the channels that show porn. It's a huge industry, with most watchers in the Core. They have the time and their relentless appetite for sick, cheap thrills knows no end. They love Swillian's show because he looks like them. Handsome, well dressed, well spoken. He does what none of them dare risk to do."

"I never did see him. After Ruby told me what to expect from that pig, I figured I would have to kill him. Who knew some other guy would try first. Either way, who ever tried to touch me would get his manhood broken first. Then his neck." Skyla pointed to a crowd up ahead then motioned to turn left.

"You are tough." Tangier cracked a tiny smile.

"Yes, I am." Skyla nodded toward her brother.

Tangier guided the van into the short side alley still clear. "CSA will have checkpoints up soon enough. We have to get to get out of here soon."

"Then hurry. But, tell me, how did you get assigned to that harvest porno operation? CSA must have green lighted it, which is even more twisted. They had their own guy, Grub, working there?" asked Skyla.

"Big Data gathers all kinds of info from such CSA operations. The identities of the victims are irrelevant since they are Outliers. The prized intel reveals who are buying the products. Who wants to own a stranger's kidney rather than rent their own? Affiliations want renters of organs, not buyers."

"So, CSA serves this intel right up to the Affiliations to monitor the organ markets?" Skyla shivered and blew warm breath on her hands. "Yuck. It just goes one and on."

"I ran a search on the harvest business and it was way too good. Too much product being sold. Grub was too aggressive snatching people, but then he had made a fatal mistake."

"Which was what?"

"He enjoyed it too much. Every snatch meant he would get favors on the side from Cheddar, whether money units or sex, none of which he reported of course. He began to upset the balance and balance is everything for the Affiliations and CSA." Tangier eased the van over a pile of trash that had spilled out into the alley. "I showed the spread sheets to Stilton. I told him I could get rid of the whole operation with no links back to CSA, not that it matters to anyone but Stilton. He likes things neat, including disposals of any type. He agreed since he was under pressure to reduce product for sale. He removed Grub, and I went in. Neat, clean, simple. Poof! And the whole operation is gone."

"Stilton or any other CSA watchers didn't see me?"

"Once I saw you, I reprogramed the feed to his main console to loop the view of the room before you got there, when it was still empty. So, he did not see you and anyone who did, thinks the random new girl was moved. The average viewer, including CSA watchers, know porn reality shows change scenes all the time. So, it bought me time to come up with a reason to go in. I timed it to go live again when I was there. I knew Cheddar would pay you a visit. So, I watched and planned to impersonate Swillian killing Cheddar before he touched you. But then you tore him up. I admit I didn't see that coming. When I heard his screams, I blasted open the door."

"Wow. That's gutsy," said Skyla. "You are the bargain CSA agent. You save me, the other kids, and, 'poof', kill off the bottom feeders who ran this operation, too!"

"Yep. That's me. It does leave the orders for organs unfulfilled. Sucks for them, "replied Tangier.

"And, no one at the top is held accountable for the pain of the people snatched up against their will. Theft, murder, and sex trafficking are rolled into one neat operation." Skyla looked out of the window at the dusty shacks and defenseless grimy people in and around them. "But there is no top, is there? That is the point. No one and everyone are complicit. And the dead are dead."

"You know, CSA is almost a total Affiliation itself. It holds vast influence on every aspect of Big Data. He thrives and grows bigger on a diet of their surveillance," Tangier added and steered the van to a side path, then stopped. "We let Poppy and the kids go here."

"What is this place?" Skyla watched him jump down and go to the back of the van.

"A safe house run by the Aunties."

Tangier tapped on the back door and called to Poppy. He opened the door to find Poppy sitting on the floor with all four kids asleep against her and each other.

"Don't worry; they are fine. I said, 'group hug' and they did. They wouldn't let go." She laughed as she extricated herself from their sleepy bunch. "This is the first time in weeks for some of them to feel safe."

"Fine, but we have to hustle. Let's go, kids. Rise and shine." Tangier stepped away and tapped on the door of a dingy shack. A tap came back from inside. The door opened inches at a time.

Poppy led the kids, one by one to jump toward Tangier who handed them off to a smiling, puffy cheeked Auntie waiting in the doorway. With a final jump, Poppy reached for Tangier who caught her slight frame like catching a butterfly, careful not to break anything. "We'll be fine."

"I know." Tangier waved her away.

"Jaffa is searching for you. Find him. Go see the Clan Mother. Longhouse is standing by for your requests."

Poppy stepped into the doorway and turned. "Tangier. Things are getting worse. Much worse. You must decide soon where you will be, here or there. I fear for your life. We all do."

Tangier nodded and gave her a half smile. "Go," he said in a whisper. He jumped back in the van, backed up, then drove at a snail's pace down another alley. "I'm sorry I had to leave you on your own. That old guy, with the Khamsa? He's a fake. A CSA plant. Paid his family big money units for him to die out there. I was supposed to set a trap for you, so I fed him a few talking points. Some stupid rookie agent dumped him in the wrong place. You finding him was not part of my plan."

"I saw his boots. Metal tips. That's when I knew to go south to find Jaffa."

"Didn't you believe that I would return for you?"

"What am I to believe about you?" Skyla looked away from him and stared out the window.

"You have to understand, I can't get you to safety without playing their game. I can't seem like I sold out to Longhouse. So, yes, I let their lies play out, and then I tweak them in return with more lies. To keep you safe, to get you to safety, I am playing the highest stakes game of lies ever with my superior officer. He's a guy I have hated ever since the orphanage."

"He was at the orphanage? Who is he?" asked Skyla.

"Stilton. I kept him away from you. You don't know him. We are going to keep it that way. If I get caught, and there is growing suspicion about me, then you and me, we are both done. And I mean finished, deleted. Jaffa, Zeinab, and anyone connected to us."

"Poppy?"

"All the Aunties. Retribution's a bitch. It'll be massive." Tangier picked his way through more rubble in the path, the van swerving close to the shacks. "You must trust me. Remember the opposites game we used to play as kids? I'd say, 'turn right' but you'd know to turn left?"

"Yes. We outsmarted the others because we had our secret game on."

"Well, it's sort of like that right now for us. I could keep you under the radar until you wrote that study. Now, I am under orders to deliver you to the Rules of Words Committee. I have to. It is my primary assignment. And, time to get you out of here is running out."

"This is all my fault." Skyla slapped the dashboard of the van and let out a deep breath.

"Are you kidding me? Of course, it's not your fault for putting into words what any thinking person can see. But most people have forgotten how to put words together the way you did. And if you have done it, you might teach others how to use common, everyday words in a new way, how to think for themselves. Waking up opposition to the Affiliations is dangerous to them."

"It's not that hard if you just open your eyes and look around." Skyla waved her hand towards the stench soaked structures around them. The cloaked dirty people kept moving in a steady rhythm back and forth to nowhere.

"Longhouse has grown stronger. The Affiliations are worried. Outlier towns are immense. What if they are mobilized? The fear in the Core and Periphery is palpable. CSA grows stronger because of it." Tangier tapped the steering wheel with his fingers.

"War between CSA and Longhouse? Is that what you think?"

"I know it is coming and soon. Which is why we must get you to the Keep. You and the others must lead in the future." Tangier peered down an alley, chose not to turn, and kept straight on.

"Keep? Lead what? Enough! You promised you'd explain the Keep when we were with Mae. What the hell is it? And, why does it have anything to do with me?" Skyla paused for a moment. "And, why is the resistance called Longhouse. What is that supposed to mean?"

"OK. You are right. Here goes. It's a lot to take in," replied Tangier in the kindest voice he could muster. "Our mother was Josephine Roseau. Her relatives are in the Keep. She was from the Haudenosaunee nation," replied Tangier. "The People of the Longhouse."

"I thought she was French from Montreal and her family was killed during the Collapse. Are you saying this is a lie?" Skyla ran her hand through her hair and shook her head.

"She spoke French, yes, being from the area around Montreal. Her last name was the French version of Reed, a family name taken up by native people somewhere along the line, way, way back. So, we are Haudenosaunee. The early French colonial settlers called them, the Iroquois."

"This, in addition to the Moroccan-American mix? Does this even matter?" Skyla looked up toward the clouds. "And so, this Keep means what?"

"The Keep is the old reservation and what's left of the historic territory of the original people, the Haudenosaunee. They have kept it hidden since the Collapse. So, seems we have family, there, but I don't know them. I only learned about this a couple months ago from the Longhouse leader, Genesee."

"So, Longhouse, the resistance, comes from the Keep?" Skyla leaned back in her seat and took in a slow deep breath. She held it until her face turned pink then let it out with a soft puff. "I never took Longhouse for more than a brave effort by diehard idealists. Even the name struck me as nothing but a cruel joke, suggesting we are all in the same big boat—or house. This is all too much."

"I know. A whole heritage kept under wraps until now." said Tangier. "But the Haudenosaunee connection did make sense to me. Mom always told me she liked to wear suede boots with beads so she could feel close to home, close to her mother and grandmother. But, it's also the stories of Sky Woman and Lynx, her beloved daughter, who returns as the Jigonsaseh and brings peace."

"Weren't those just stories you made up to tease me about my name?" asked Skyla looking at her suede boots with a tassel of beads on the side.

"Guess not. I think those are creation stories of the Haudenosaunee. What do I know? I was a kid. I do re-member our mom and dad trying to name you. Mom wanted Sky and Dad wanted Lila, so they created Skyla, your name, just for you." Tangier peered out the side window at the two men standing on the next corner. He waited to see their next move. He kept the van crawling along, which scared them back into a shuffle, stopping being against the rules.

"You never knew anything about Mom's past? Didn't you talk to her? You had ten years ahead of me," said Skyla, "I feel so empty. Lost. Is anything true?"

Tangier did not reply but stared at the drone birds flying overhead. He motioned for her to sit back, lower in the seat. "Everything is true. We are just filling in the gaps later rather than sooner." He studied the paths ahead and ambled a turn onto another alley, creeping in a direction away from them. "I was a little kid and nobody cares or remembers about that stuff when they are little. When mom and dad were murdered, it hurt to think about them. If I knew anything, I buried it a long time ago. I had to look after you. In the orphanage, any past was scrapped."

"I know. You're right. None of this is your fault. It's just that so much has happened in the last two days. You expect too much of me." Skyla wrung her hands that sat on the rifle across her lap.

"I believe in you. You are strong. And you always have your big brother." Tangier turned down a wider lane with light in the far distance towards its end. "Remember, our immediate problem is the Affiliations. If CSA is afraid of a few words, then Big Data is terrified. Taking you to the Rules of Words Committee is the only way for me to protect you." Tangier stole a glance as Skyla sat still as her beloved Sphinx, the greatest cat of all. He felt a long buried memory of his mother's voice pushing through to correct him. Her voice chided him that a Lynx was the most sacred of cats, for it is a living homage to Sky Woman's daughter, buried on Turtle Island, who became Mother Earth. "We can reclaim our family together, I promise. We must. But, not today. Now, the real escape begins."

She nodded. A tear rolled down her cheek. "Tangier. I lost Jaguar. And, will I ever see Jaffa again?"

CHAPTER EIGHTEEN

THE CORE

Senior Agent Stilton swiped a long taut piece of orange flannel cloth back and forth at lightning speed over his boots. He polished the steel tips to a shine so bright he could see his own reflection in them. In the glass screen of the monitor on his desk, he checked his look. He adjusted his shirt and buttoned the top button of the black neckband on his scarlet red shirt, worn only for special occasions. Today was a special occasion. He would travel to the Core to pay a professional visit to an extremely sensitive asset.

Today he would pay a call to the home of a high ranking executive of Affiliation Yellow. CSA did not pay social calls or business calls to the elite Core members because they never strayed from the righteous path of profit making. If CSA were to visit, it meant CSA was furious about something.

Stilton left his office by a side door, one known only to senior agents and senior field agents. He went to the garage and selected a matte black car, with iridescent blue windows and jet pack accelerators with visible exhaust hatches in the back. Intimidation was the first step of control. He slid into the front seat and disengaged the automatic remote driver gauge. Only senior agents and senior field agents had the authority to pilot a car manually. Exclusivity was the second step of control. Stilton savored his status, unmatched, above and apart from Core members, Peripherals, and Outliers.

They all feared CSA and thus feared his omniscient power. He could live anywhere he chose, so he chose them all, a villa in the Core, an apartment in the Periphery, a shack in an Outlier camp town. He never slept at the same place two nights in a row and kept no regular pattern of his nighttime excursions.

The midday sun failed to break through the brown puffs of clouds, so the bleak greyness of dull humid air hung over the city. Stilton caressed the steering wheel of the Phantom, his chosen name for his favorite vehicle. He eased into the flow of traffic. The traffic monitor nodded to him as she waved her white gloved hands to guide the automated flow as she was required to do. From the CSA building, Stilton crossed the edges of a Peripheral neighborhood to a grand boulevard that led to a series of exclusive gated communities, the neighborhoods of the members.

Old time city centers had been replaced by small shopping areas located in the center of each gated community. The trendy boutiques, smoky bars, coffee shops, and the ever present fitness centers were all lined up one after the other. Everyone in the Core worked to stay trim, to be flawless. It all served to remind the dwellers of these tiny kingdoms that they were special people. Each home, designed by an architect, was built of glass and steel with wood accents. A few communities still clung to old fashion styles, claiming to be Victorian, but in reality, they were just boxes with some extra ornate carved wood trim tacked on along a front porch, both painted in showy colors. POVs lenses were everywhere, but to keep up the swanky Core look, they were hidden in garden sculptures. Stilton turned off the boulevard into his intended neighborhood and stopped the Phantom in front of the gate. He flashed his lights and showed his ID to the tubby neighborhood guard, leaning out of the gatehouse window. He activated the heavy iron gate. Stilton powered through.

His destination was not far, and he passed several blocks of glass and steel houses with small yards, planted with pink and yellow flowers. Core neighborhoods could afford bright colored plants that made the area showy in contrast to the bleak landscape of the world outside. Peripherals, thought Stilton, grew only edible plants in their gardens. For most it helped to supplement their diets and gave them product to sell in farmers' markets. Some of his agents worked the farmers' markets, as farmer spies, too. It was an excellent cover he had developed during his early days at CSA. His superiors liked the ingenuity. Information and profit, efficiency and ruthlessness, were Stilton's pride.

The Phantom cruised through the shopping district until Stilton slowed it to peer at the window of a large fitness center. The women wore skintight bodysuits as they pedaled cycles, stepped on stairs, and jogged on treadmills. A few could be seen lifting weights or doing squats. Their blond or black ponytails hung limp from sweat. Redheads were rare, but pale white skin was still the first choice made by parents who could tailor make their babies' genetics. The inescapable white skin color of the Core members was a long tradition by now. Stilton knew his Core membership was faultless and lifelong, but his own black skin gave away that his membership was earned, not inherited. These prickly Affiliation rules made him detest the Core all the more, even as he loved it.

He saw the flashy house up ahead, on the corner of a cul de sac. A low profile yellow racer with extra wide performance tires and a spoiler filled the driveway in front. Stilton parked the Phantom in the racer's path, preventing an easy escape in any direction. A young blonde woman dressed in red leggings and a black t-shirt strutted by pushing a blue baby carriage but neither spoke. No one volunteers a word to a CSA agent. People especially feared a CSA agent in dress uniform.

Senior Agent Stilton raised his face to the lens on the side of the door of the four-story building and scowled. Swillian would see his enraged face and make out the words "Open up you son of a bitch" that he said to him. Grub had blamed Swillian for driving the operation into oblivion. It was Swillian who ordered the increase in product, to create new porn episodes to be shown on a more frequent schedule. He of course, relished every moment of the faster pace of production. Gutter had urged Grub to ease up because he had to work overtime to make room for all the new bodies. It didn't help that Cheddar paid Grub extra to feed Swillian's appetite. Grub was a fool to be on the take like that. It was the surest way to end up sidelined at CSA, doomed to assignments in offices like Riff. Stilton milled these facts around in his head while he cracked the knuckles of his hands, and tapped his foot. The polished steel tip reflected flashes of light like a mirror used to signal across long distances.

Stilton did not know the old Morse code, although he knew it existed. CSA dismissed it as a gag used by a few wannabes, low level types trying to be important. With POVs to surpass all else, he could afford to ignore the obscure fantasy game played by the losers in life. He tapped his foot faster. The unsnapping of electronic locks on the door began and it opened slowly.

Swillian stood in a shadow behind the door. He wore blue plaid boxer shorts and a blue dress shirt with sleeves rolled up. His bloodshot eyes above a drippy nose scanned Stilton, the intruder. "What the hell do you want?" He ran a hand through a thick mass of longish, movie star hair.

"Look at yourself, the big superstar." Stilton closed the door behind him and the locks snapped back into place. "Not looking too good." He noticed a syringe sticking out from Stilton's waistband. "That will take you down, way down." He ripped the syringe away and cracked it in two. "Here. This ends here and now. Or the deal is off."

"What do you mean off? I am the boss. I make or break you," said Swillian, walking towards a big room with high ceilings, white walls, and steel blue leather sofas with rare cotton pillows strewn about.

"Do you? CSA can bring down anyone it wants. Even the CEO of an Affiliation." Stilton followed him, his boots clicking on the travertine marble floors. "Pretty nice place you have here. You want to keep it? You quit the porn."

"Now why would I do that? I am every loser's fantasy. They wish they were me." Swillian flopped into a mass of downy pillows on a sofa. He smoothed the front of his shirt and arranged the tails flat across his lap, in symmetry. "See? Neat and clean. That's your job, Stilton, not mine."

"Yes. That is my job, idiot. I am here to clean up your mess. And you know who sent me?" Stilton kept his voice level. "Your daddy. Your daddy, the top, the chairman of the ruling committee of Affiliation Yellow. He says you are risking everything."

Swillian stared out into space. He flicked an imaginary speck off his sleeve. "Dear old Dad. I know. Affiliation Yellow, the favored one, handles pest control, the old medical-industrial complex, big Pharma, and those disgusting robot nurses. What is his complaint this time?"

Stilton eased into a white recliner but kept his feet on the floor. The tinted glass wall behind Swillian distorted the color of the trees outside that listed back and forth in the wind. The blues were darker and the greens seemed almost black in the shadows. Only a trace of sunlight made its way through the brown cloud cover. He watched storm clouds gather. "Your dad's complaint is that you are creating doubt about your ability to fulfill your CEO job obligations. Everyone at the top of all the Affiliations knows you as the porn star. And you are good at it. They give that to you."

"Then what's the big deal? No one gives a shit about porn. They all watch it. Big Pharma is making a killing on anti-rejection drugs. Organ buyers are happy." Swillian sat forward, aiming his zombie eyes at Stilton. "The only ones not happy are the companies who manufacture body specific, tailor-made organs rented for life. Who cares what they want?"

"The ruling committee and your dad care. They crunch the numbers. Your little organ harvest market is undercutting the lucrative renters' market. And the other Affiliations smell blood, like crocodiles in a pond. Any of the other Affiliations would kill to take over Affiliation Yellow's markets. Some think five Affiliations are too many. All the parts of Big Data are jealous of each other."

"Big Data. Yea, I've heard about this little nickname. But you are the eyes of Big Data and you think you can boss us all. But you can't. You can't boss me." Swillian stood up and strolled over to a wet bar. He poured golden whiskey from a cut glass decanter into an etched crystal wine glass. He angled around to face Stilton. "Want a drink?"

"Pass." Stilton folded his hands and bent his fingers backward until the knuckles cracked. "The porn show ends today. That's an order. Ignore it, you will end up in an

Outlier camp, and crawl like vermin on all fours for the rest of your life."

"And if I do, what do I get?" Swillian tossed back the whiskey in one gulp.

"You live. You don't die. POVs is powerful. You cannot hide. You couldn't hide, even in your scummy little studio."

"You sit at your desk and watch everything on a monitor. You couldn't find my studio if you tried, POVs or no POVs." Swillian sat back down on the sofa and put his pedicured bare feet up on a teak coffee table. He smoothed out the front of his shirt, again.

"You are a fool. Your studio was blown up a couple of hours ago. Anyone in there is dead." Stilton stood up. "Don't mess with me. Time to be the little corporate shit that you are and do business the way your father and the committee say."

Swillian jumped up and marched toward the front door. He hit a keypad with his fist and the locks began to unsnap. "Get out."

Stilton walked out the door into the breeze. The tall pine trees lined the walkway away from the house. He hated rich boys like Swillian who never lost a chance to parade their wealth in front of boys like him, boys from an orphanage, boys with no pedigree. Rich boys of the Core believed their inherited status was a natural entitlement, their money power a birthright and invincible from attack. The rot within is what usually did them in, Stilton thought, the rot within. He had developed a keen an eye for the peculiar sexual habits and oblique thinking so rampant in the Core members conduct. Their insatiable hunger for novelty grew as destructive boredom, leisure time, and consumption filled most of their waking hours. Stilton kept abreast of it all, year after year.

There were many Swillians across all the Affiliations and with POVs Stilton knew them all and knew all about them. They naively believed they were invincible and no one could see them despite all the surveillance. And this one, Affiliation Yellow's trust fund baby, would have his day. Stilton knew it would not be pretty, and he knew how to make sure it wasn't pretty. A lesson for all, a reminder that Big Data was to be feared. Every keystroke made was information, every phone call, every broadcast program viewed, Big Data assembled it all and knew you. Your desires, your size, your age, your secrets, even your thoughts, for all of it folded into an algorithm that was you, predictable and known. Stilton relished the logic of it all. He opened the car door and glanced back at the house. Swillian's silhouette showed through the curtains covering the windows.

He sped back to the border lane, the vague land of Cap City territory that was neither Core nor Periphery where the CSA building covered a vast square of land. The Core might be prosperous and more sedate, but he had more fun watching the Affiliation minions in the Periphery.

They never smiled and never looked at an POVs lens. They rode black or white bikes in two rows as was the traffic rule. On the street, small kids were leashed to their parents or babysitters by digital bracelets that would shock them if they drifted too far away. Teenagers, Stilton's favorite recruiting pool, scowled all the time and wore wireless ear buds all the time. With hands jammed into pockets as they walked, they carved their way through any crowd. They were rude all the time, everywhere. Workers of all ages ebbed and flowed into the streets at the designated shift changes like the tides, twice every twenty-four hours. The pressure to maintain enough income to stay mutual with one's Affiliation organized any Peripheral's life. The Peripherals' uneasy watch on the edges between their lives and a fall into poverty made them easier to keep in line than the cocky Core members.

He cracked a half smile, knowing that he could administer fear with bigger or less doses of POVs as he desired. Surveillance, the bad feel good of Big Data, produced, sold, and pushed by all the Affiliations was the power of fear that he controlled. Now, having warned Swillian only as a favor to his father and Affiliation Yellow, Stilton could turn his attention to Skyla, a genuine threat to global order, the witch of Big Data for all to see.

Stilton drove the Phantom into its parking spot in the garage. He sat still, seething about how this girl who grew up in the same orphanage as he, somehow escaped his notice until now. She had to have had a shield, someone high up in the Affiliations who created a cover. But, she overstepped a boundary with her study. Only CSA had the power and right to collect intel and to reveal it about

Affiliations, money power, and people. There were no rights for people, only rules, and Skyla broke the rules.

He took a deep breath and checked his look in the rearview mirror. A silent, yellow low profile racer pulled up behind the Phantom. Swillian swung himself out, one leg at a time, until he stood beside the car. He staggered toward Stilton, whose face he could see in the side mirror of the official vehicle. Before he could raise the gun he held in his hand, Stilton leaped out of the Phantom and stood, weapon raised to Swillian.

"What do you want?" Stilton kept his gun pointed at Swillian's head.

"You piece of shit cop think you can come to my house and tell me what to do?" Swillian tightened his grip on the gun, aimed at the ground, close to his thigh.

"Listen you moron, CSA can do anything it likes. I am CSA. Get it?"

"I get it. Now you get it."

Swillian raised his gun in one grand motion, like they did in the old westerns that he watched on the antique movie channel.

Stilton, did not speculate or hesitate and shot him dead, straight through the heart. He readjusted his shirt and jammed his gun back into his pants pocket. He spat on the body oozing blood onto the cement floor. "The work just keeps on coming," said Stilton under his breath. He turned to call the elevator and seconds later rode it up to his office.

In the corner of the garage, in the dark crack by a pillar, Riff stood frozen from the shock of witnessing the execution of a Core member, an executive of Affiliation Yellow by the hand of CSA. The car tag on the racer told him all he needed to know. He stopped the video from his wrist phone that recorded the murder, the car tag and the dead body. He knelt down on one knee, leaned into the shadow and linked into the main CSA monitor database and located the POVs lens data from the last ten minutes. With a couple of taps, he downloaded a copy of the video and audio clip of it all and sent it with his own, deep into distant network files. He deleted all digital trail of them from his wrist phone.

Riff felt the floor for the trap door that would lead to a tunnel ending in a trash alley. As much as he detested trash alleys, they today, right now, could give him the escape he needed. He could avoid POVs for the moment. For once he felt strong, even powerful, for he alone possessed the truth about an event. Stilton without a doubt would edit out that little scene from the main computer, perhaps doing it now. Perhaps already done, Riff considered. Someday, his small video records could save him. Insurance. He could sell it for big profit, one day.

Riff pushed open a door, easing it outward in typical quiet CSA style with as little sound as possible. The rush of cool air bathed over his face. He opened his eyes. His bowels began to churn. Senior Agent Stilton sat on the edge of a rusty, brown electric transformer box. He bent forward, dissecting him with scalpel eyes.

"Riff. Got something to show me?"

SIBLINGS

Skyla studied the people around the shacks, as Tangier drove the van along the rough alleys in the Outlier neighborhoods. She didn't know where he was taking her, but Tangier always had a plan. At that moment, she felt lucky to be with him because for most people there was no return from Outlier camp towns.

Skyla thought about her study in a new light. It had taken on a life of its own, like Godzilla. The CSA observers of the new creature feared not only its existence, but that it could not be controlled. Her study, a monster of long buried, but still worthy ideas, could resurrect a new rival to challenge the Affiliations. It had to be silenced. It had to be killed. Ideas, being resistant to killing, were a palpable, ever-present danger to Big Data, the vain, selfish, digital spy. It would always defend itself by launching a detailed search and destroy for any opposition ideas. Skyla finally admitted to herself that when she walked out of Celebration Wholesale, she had chosen a side.

She, the simple new recruit, armed with nothing more than mighty words had kicked Big Data in the face. If not for Tangier, she would already be arrested, sentenced, and killed. Who would comfort Jaffa? Who would look after Jaguar? Pangs of guilt pricked her heart, little cuts that reminded her that she did not keep him safe. He was more than a pet. He was her familiar. He awarded that to her and she lost him in the sinister streets of an Outlier camp town. She glanced at her big brother gripping the steering wheel and despite his presence sensed the soft chill of aloneness.

The van swerved close to a huddle of kids playing a game with stones in the dirt. For a moment, they paused and reached out hands to her, empty hands. In the rearview mirror, she could see them return to their game, tussling each other, oblivious to her. She struggled against a sense of defeat. Her search to understand how anyone could have thought a profit driven world would be a just world had led her to creeping around in a van trying to escape POVs. That same profit driven world had cost her own parents their lives. It had made orphans of Tangier and her.

The van pitched as it edged a pothole and sent her swaying back and forth in her seat. She noticed Tangier digging into a pants pocket.

"It's sort of smashed, but it's still good. You must be hungry." He handed her a bent, squished protein bar. "We can't eat anything around here, you know. Can't afford to get sick."

"Thanks." Skyla took the bar, peeled back the wrapping, and took a bite. She offered a bite to Tangier.

"No, it's for you. Not hungry now anyway."

"You have to let me fight, you know. I have skills," she said.

"You think you are going to wrestle someone? Hand to hand combat? Shoot someone? With that gun?" Tangier laughed.

"I showed you back there I can break things. And this gun? My aim is true and my shots can kill. But, isn't it time to tell me what is going to happen after the meeting with the committee? Where are we going, right now?" Skyla stopped for a moment. "Will I ever find Jaguar? Ever?"

"That's a lot of questions. Jaguar, don't know about him. Jaffa, hope so, but not sure. The end game is to get you to safety. That means the Keep."

"The Keep? If you expect me to go there and leave everything and everyone I know behind, no questions asked, you do not know me anymore." Skyla pounded the door with her fist. "I am the driver in my life. I will decide what happens to me."

Tangier's eyes grew round and full. He thrust his face toward her. "Oh, like you decided back there what was going to happen? I told you to stay put, but no, you moved. Then, the lowest disgusting piece of vomit in the galaxy snatched you. And then what do you do?" He pulled away and sat back in his seat. "You tap SOS in the code. Cursive.

You are seen all over the globe and now everyone knows you exist. Not just CSA and Big Data, but every boring idiot on this planet! Point of Views. POVs! Did you forget?"

Skyla did not move. Words came to her, words she wanted to shout to infinity. The reality was she had no words to say to Tangier. He was right. POVs collected it all. Big Data and the world knew about her. "They don't have my study. That's what they want."

"You really don't get it?" asked Tangier.

"Get what? They are mad that I wrote what I wrote. And only I have the latest draft." Skyla smoothed her coat pocket and felt the data stick.

"Don't tell me you think you are cleverer than Big Data's CSA or POVs or any of the other data mining outfits that overload cyberspace. You don't think you can hide your work from them, do you?"

"Yes, I do. I know how to hide from them. You probably think my data stick is a joke," Skyla said. "It's no joke. The version I saved is different from what exists in cyberspace."

"I don't believe what you say is possible. But if it is, what's the difference? What have you held back?" Tangier narrowed his gaze on her face. He craved a cigarette but had none.

"My notes on how to make the world a better place. Without Big Data."

"You're joking, right?"

"No. There's nothing sacred about this hateful world of ours." Skyla paused then added, "I downloaded files on alternate societies only a few days ago but thanks to this shit-storm I haven't read them yet." Skyla touched the rifle on her lap and wondered if she'd ever have to fire it or any other gun.

"And you think your new design could make the world change?" Tangier shouted. "Make this sucky world a better place?"

"Don't shout at me. What are you talking about? Change? Make what happen? I was just writing a study to get my degree to get a better job."

"So, you aren't planning to lead a revolution?"

"Are you kidding me? Do I look like a revolutionary? I live alone, slave away at a boring job, go to grad school, have a boyfriend, and a cat that I adore who is missing because I am such a fool. That is what I am sad about. That is the dark hole in my heart, the thought that Jaguar has been hurt. My life was a speck in a mass of monotony until Mae Carrington called me. The biggest crime I committed was using a Celebration Wholesale computer on my break." She rolled her eyes and wound a lock of her hair into a knot.

"I don't know who you are," said Tangier stopping the van. He sighed with his whole body. "You wrote all that because you like the topic? Not to avenge our parents' death and take out the people who dumped us in an orphanage?"

"Just the studious little kid you always knew. The kid who always liked school," said Skyla. "That's me. If you were looking for a conspiracy, you were looking in the wrong place."

"I'm not looking out for anything but your safety."

"Maybe someone is playing you. You sure CSA is cool with you? They know everything about us if they bother to look. Me? I follow the rules, even the fake traffic rules, just to avoid attention. I want to avoid POVs."

"You try to avoid POVS? That's impossible, you know," said Tangier.

"I hate POVs and all its sneaky forms. It's nothing but digital dumpster diving. It could live your life for you, it knows so much. Sometimes I think there must be actual, pure data beings that live somewhere, laughing at us pathetic humans, so easy to control. Fear, shopping, and money power. That's all it takes."

"Hyper down, Skyla. You have to deal with the cards you are dealt, and this is the world, our world. You can't recreate the past no matter how much you want. Our parents' world crumbled around them. It cost them their lives. Make the best of our world or you'll get deleted," said Tangier. He stared out the window at something far away, only he could see. "I did my best to prepare you to survive this insane world. I tried."

"You did. I know that. I am grateful." Skyla leaned toward Tangier. "It doesn't change our reality, our here and now. Look out there at this nightmare. Do you know there was a time when people could walk on the street and no one recorded it? That you could travel in a car, drive it yourself, and get lost? Actually lost? No one would know where you were. People actually died because they got lost. That must be what it is like to be free."

"You couldn't call for help. You could die. Free to die."
Tangier shrugged and began to move the van.

"Yes, there would be risk. But you would have the
choice to take the risk or not. Plus, you wouldn't have to be
stupid about it. Take a map. Imagine. A paper map." Skyla
sat back and smiled. "What would it be like to turn off
POVs? What do you think people would do?"

"Nothing and chaos. Two sides of the same coin."

"Good point. Right now, out here, they don't worry if
POVs catch every horrible act they commit. That guy who
snatched me didn't care. But then, he was one of yours,
wasn't he?" Skyla felt a bit disloyal. Although Tangier had
rescued her from a certain and ugly death, the fear of CSA
haunted her. "You really believe in CSA, don't you?"

"It's been my life since the Institute. It's all I have. You
can't leave it, only survive in it."

"Survive. Guess that's all any of us do," said Skyla.
"Where are we going?"

"To the Core. I told you that the Rules of Words
Committee demands to interview you. I've made it step one
of your escape route." Tangier aimed toward the edge of the
Outlier town to the wider roads that led to the Periphery.

"Now I'll never find Jaguar. And Jaffa will never look
for me in the Core. Why are you doing this to me? Skyla
wiped her eyes before tears could show. "I trusted you."

"And you must still trust me, now." The van swerved
onto a connector road. Tangier lowered the window and let
the lighter air fill the van, erasing away the musty stink from
the camp towns.

Skyla felt the data stick in her coat pocket, sure she never told Tangier she had it with her. She drew strength from knowing the possession of knowledge cuts both ways. Tangier didn't know everything and trust goes both ways.

Jaffa had given her the sticks. He told her they could hide data from POVs telematics, and the caché. The trick was to save files as music. He had given her the gift of privacy. The data stick in her pocket was all she had of him, their private life, their private dreams. It kept him close, but she could not afford to let herself dwell on this now.

She summoned what reserve she had to brace for the next onslaught. The van again lurched again away from a pothole. Skyla looked at Tangier but said nothing. She patted him on the shoulder. He winked back at her. She loved her big brother. A few tears began to collect and she wiped them away with her sleeve.

CHAPTER TWENTY

POPPY

Jaffa listened to the thud of drops of water rolling off roofs and hitting objects below. A rookie CSA agent stood on the corner of the alley, nodding her head to count the passersby. She'd file the number of nameless bodies to her command where her count would be compared to POVs records. The young agents resented the task of counting as busywork because there was no escape. Everything is known.

The agents ignored the unstable tunnels dug shovel by shovel over years by drifters with nothing to do. They snaked back and forth like a subway but fell into disuse. People were afraid of being lost among the ghosts of the insane, who lived there in disarray and died alone in the dark. Jaffa knew the about the tunnels from Zeinab. He could use them to get around, unobserved, as a last resort. He could see the roofline of her little shack, next to a turret of a very old building, once used, at least a hundred years ago, as a prison. As the CSA agent moved on, Jaffa pulled his hood up against the increasing strength of the drizzle and set out on the trek toward his grandmother's house.

He felt for his phone in the Faraday case, locked in his pants pocket. His pack of supplies had no doubt been long discovered by scavengers. CSA would soon note that he hadn't signed out of his shift. It would notice he didn't return to his apartment in the Periphery. It would notice that he doesn't show up anywhere he is expected to be. He worried a visit to Zeinab might put her in needless danger. But he had to find Skyla.

The brown clouds thinned and the drizzle eased into a mist, carried on the gusts of wind. It rained with a constancy by which one could set time. Jaffa peered around a corner. He watched a white unmarked van rock back and forth, groaning its way along the alley. CSA on the move, he thought. Where was Tangier?

He avoided a gang of kids engrossed in an old super-hero video playing on a modified scrap vintage tablet. Blaring noise from a screen balanced on a windowsill filled his ears. An Affiliation Red recruiting announcement for EME flashed on the rickety screen for a few seconds.

Jaffa stepped onto the corner where the CSA van had turned. He watched the distance grow as the van lumbered away. The rain stopped as the clouds regrouped. He kept his hood up and slurked along like Jaguar. The thought of Skyla's familiar made him smile. Until he met Skyla, which he did thanks to Tangier's match making on the sly, he had known nothing about cats or familiars or openness or invitations. His heart began to pound at the thought of her lost and in danger. Up ahead, a skinny shape leaned against the wall of a shack.

"Poppy." He took gentle steps toward her.

"My little lovesick puppy." She lifted her arm in an arch like a ballet dancer and slipped a lit cigarette into her lips. She sucked in the tobacco air and blew white smoke from nostrils that flared just so.

"What are you doing here? Are you ok? Have you seen Tangier?" Jaffa fired off questions as if he was doing a cardiac resuscitation.

"Easy, little puppy. Easy. I saw your girl. She's with Tangier. He rescued her."

"Rescued? From who? What?"

"I guess you don't watch Swillian's show." She raised her cigarette, holding it beside her face, elbow on her hip.

"Swillian? I don't watch that pervert. What are you talking about?"

"She was about to be the next star. One of his minions kidnapped her from the street. That's how her cat got away. Luck he found you or he would have been in someone's stew."

"Are you serious about Swillian?"

"Would I make this up? Little puppy, Skyla's big brother got her out of there in the nick of time, before she was assaulted and murdered. Then he blew the studio up. Nice and tidy, that Tangier. He is CSA through and through even though he thinks he can escape it. But he never can. He never will." Poppy gave Jaffa a soft smile. "It's tricky."

"What do you mean? You know something, don't you, Poppy?" Jaffa paced in a circle. "We are old pals. Tell me what you know. I must get to Skyla. I can help her."

"You think you can help her now? After she has been seen by the world on Swillian's show? CSA will get her. I don't know if Tangier can do anything. He has to save himself too. Will he sacrifice everything for her? His life? Because that's what's at stake. CSA has grown bigger than any Affiliation. They know everything all the time, everywhere even about them. CSA is money power's strongest most faithful servant. Big Data is CSA." A long white stream of smoke blew out from Poppy's pursed lips.

"Where was Tangier taking her?"

"To the Core. To whom, I don't know. She appeared calm but was staring straight ahead. She held a rifle across her lap. I think she was chilled because she had her coat buttoned and belted tight. Poor thing. She must be shattered thinking her cat is lost. That cat is something special to her."

"Didn't you tell her I was coming for her?"

"I never talked to her. She was in the front of the van to cover Tangier and me as we grabbed some kids that were being held by that Swillian. I looked after the kids. Like I said, Tangier blew up that cesspool of Swillian's, and he drove us away. He dropped us around the corner over there, to a shelter where I left the kids."

"So you never told her I was coming for her? She doesn't know I have Jaguar?" Jaffa kept his voice even.

"Sorry. Never had the chance." Poppy put a bony hand on Jaffa's shoulder. "It was pure chaos. Just be glad Tangier got her out. She would be dead this very minute if he didn't act like he did. He will do right by her. He always has."

"I get it. I get it. It doesn't help much. I still don't know where they are." Jaffa turned toward the alley where the white van had been. "Tangier could go anywhere in the Core."

"Hey, are you safe? Have you checked in or whatever you have to do," asked Poppy?

"No. I'm AWOL. Never good. I'll think of some excuse."

"Can't say you followed a raven with a cat, can you?" she laughed.

"You know about Poe?"

"Some of us, Genesee and Grenadine, Zeinab, even Mae, we all go way back."

Jaffa nodded. "Now what?"

"You go to your grandmother, Zeinab. Things are aligning, things that must happen if we are to ever break away from Big Data," said Poppy, inhaling the last bit from her cigarette. She looked around at the slum surrounding them. "I will never get away. I am too old. You and Skyla have to get out. I got to go now. Scat, you little puppy." She gave him a tender shove.

Jaffa leaned over and kissed her cheek. "Thanks Poppy." He slipped a box of cigarettes into her hand and closed her fingers over it. He looked up to find his direction, the turret of the old prison near Zeinab's house. Dark clouds resting on the horizon were heading his way. He put up the hood of his jacket and thought about what Poppy had told him. Skyla was with Tangier but that did not mean she was safe because Tangier was always CSA. Skyla had her coat, which meant she had the data stick with her final draft, hidden in the pocket.

He could only trust that the encrypted hack proof digital vault he had built would protect her work and keep her safe. Everyone knew CSA hackers could break into encrypted temporal or audio files. So, he reconfigured the actual audio file itself. Skyla's data lay hidden in plain sight, in a long forgotten, centuries old song on her playlist of vintage songs. It could never be detected by CSA. Tangier once told him that song playlists held no security significance. He had hedged his bet on this.

Jaffa picked up his pace, anxious to reach Zeinab. He kicked through a puddle of black water as the heavy mist pushed against him.

CHAPTER TWENTY-ONE

EXPOSED

Riff followed Stilton to a pub where the drinks were free for any CSA agent. He squeezed his butt cheeks with every step he took to keep up with his boss. Stilton stepped up to the bar and ordered two beers. He pointed to Riff. "He'll pay for them. I never accept freebies."

Riff tapped his wristband twice and waved it across a recessed screen in the countertop. It lit up green. "Done, sir."

"Good. Take a seat over there." Stilton followed Riff to the table. "Now. Where is the video you recorded in the garage?"

"What makes you think I have any video?" Based on his training Riff knew to answer with a question. He also braced himself for being slapped across the face, the typical next move by the interrogator.

"I am not going to hit you here. I am giving you a chance to man up," said Stilton. "Are you a man?" He took a big swig of beer.

"There is no video. I swear. You can look at my wrist phone." Riff yanked off his wrist phone and tossed it on the tabletop in front of Stilton.

"Why did you sneak out like a weasel? Why not just leave by the door? Why didn't you want me to see you? That was not very smart because I did see you." Stilton spun the phone like a top.

"I figured you had man to man business. I did not want to interfere."

"Well, aren't you the little gentleman." Stilton studied Riff's face, colorless and framed with beads of sweat. "There is no record of any event taking place in the garage?"

"No, sir." Riff looked at his beer but did not dare take a sip, his gut knotted and about to explode.

"I am not going to bother looking at your phone. I know you are a tech weirdo." Stilton leaned in closer across the table. "If a video ever sees the light of day, you are a dead man."

"Yes, sir," said Riff. "There is no video."

Stilton took a final gulp of beer and slammed the glass down on the table. Riff watched him survey the crowd in the room. The CSA senior agent turned without a word and walked out. Riff counted to ten then grabbed his phone and ran to the hallway toward the men's room door.

CHAPTER TWENTY-TWO

GRANDMOTHER

Zeinab folded a soft cloth and wiped the top edge of a wooden picture frame propped up on top of a bookshelf. She treasured this picture of her husband, Terry Fitzpatrick, and her on a holiday to a white sand beach with turquoise water. Terry's mop of red hair had caught the sunlight and glowed like a halo around his sunburned face. Mae, her best friend, had taken the picture.

She remembered when Bill Carrington asked Mae to marry him. Who'd have thought Mae, a girl from Casablanca, and Zeinab, a girl from Jaffa, would marry white guys and live happily ever after until death do us part.

Zeinab picked up another framed photo of her daughter, Amira, their princess, on her wedding day to William Seneca. She noticed the white clouds in the blue sky. But, with fires, radiation, and pollution everywhere during the Collapse, she couldn't save them from the massacre that engulfed them. They were killed outright by old fashioned machine gun fire sprayed at any moving vehicle.

Their slow-going SUV was hit as they returned back from the grocery with food for Jaffa, their little baby boy. Terry died from a sniper shot as he attempted to bring their bodies home. That day, the world lost Amira, a pediatrician, William, a math teacher, and her beloved Terry. That sad day she cradled them all, one by one, when Bill Carrington brought them home under cover of night. Zeinab stepped up like all grandmothers do and raised Jaffa, her grandson. She refolded her dust cloth and wiped the top of a picture of Jaffa at his graduation from medical studies.

Zeinab listened to the wind and adjusted the bucket on the floor as it caught drips from the leaking roof. She ignored the noisy people next door who never shut up. She slid onto the piano bench and played a few notes of Terry's favorite song. She felt a case of the blues come on even after these many years. "I still love you. Always," she whispered to herself and played a few more bars before she stopped with a jolt.

The stairs outside her door creaked with each step approaching closer and closer. A key turned in the door lock. The door swung open. "Grandma."

"Jaffa. What are you doing here?" She stood up and dabbed her eyes with her dust cloth.

"Were you crying?" Jaffa put his arms around her and patted her head. "What's wrong?"

"Nothing. Memories can pain us, even old ones." She pushed him to sit down on a chair. "Shouldn't you be at one of your clinics?"

"I should, but something's happened."

"What? Tell me." Zeinab plopped back down on the piano bench. "Are you in trouble?"

"It's Skyla. She's in trouble. She was kidnapped by some Outlier ring that traffics in porn and organ harvesting."

"Oh no! How can we get her back?"

"She's safe. Tangier rescued her. He has her. I have no idea where they are or where they're headed. Tangier would never hurt her. As long as they're together, she is safe. In the meantime, Jaguar is staying with Genesee and Grenadine." Jaffa sat back in the chair. "You know them, don't you?"

"Yes, of course. They're old friends."

"How close of friends? I didn't know them. Jaguar followed their raven, Poe, to their house." Jaffa remained still. "Grandma, why don't I know them, if you are such good friends?"

"You don't know everything," she said. "But it is time you do. Are you sure, Skyla is safe?"

"She is safe, I am sure. Now, Grandma, I need to know everything." Jaffa spun around toward the framed photos. "Everything."

"Then make some coffee," said Zeinab. "I will keep nothing from you."

Jaffa poured hot water from the dented kettle through coarse grounds in a sieve into a metal pot. After letting it steep for a couple minutes, he filled two mugs with a steaming black brew. He set them on a small table by the worn sapphire blue chintz chair. Zeinab moved to her once chic chair and he took the piano bench.

"The truth is, I tried to protect you from all the craziness during the Collapse. Mae could not keep Tangier and Skyla since the new CSA surveillance was fixated on her and would have exposed those kids to danger. Some CSA agents even wanted to kill the kids of the traitors. She thought they'd be safer in an orphanage with the both of us keeping tabs from afar. I set up the money accounts. Mae worked all the time and put every bit she earned into them. I could not be that selfless. I kept you with me."

"Were you in danger all those years, too?"

"It was not the same for me. Your parents' death was ruled collateral damage. In time, they might have been a threat to the new Affiliations but they died before they were labeled traitors. You and I were not considered threats." Zeinab wrapped both pale hands around the warm mug.

She took a sip of coffee. "Did you ever notice we never saw your other grandparents?"

"I guess so. You never spoke of them and kept me very busy if you recall." Jaffa paused in silence. "Many kids I knew did not have parents or grandparents. So many were killed in the fighting like Skyla's."

"That's true, but William Seneca, your father grew up with his mother. He was an only child of a single mom."

"Is she still alive?" Jaffa leaned back in his chair.

"Yes." Zeinab gazed past him. "You spoke with her today. She has a familiar, a raven."

"Genesee? Are you telling me that Clan Mother Genesee is my grandmother?" Jaffa stood up and walked toward the window. He peeked out behind the shade at the dark sky. "And Grenadine is my auntie? Where is my grandfather?"

"Genesee was raped when she left the reservation for college in the city. She never knew her attacker," said Zeinab. "She kept the baby and named him William."

"You knew all this and never told me? You let me believe some vague fairy tale about them living so far away we that lost touch? What else did you leave out?"

"Don't be angry. I wanted to protect you." Zeinab tried to stand but couldn't move.

"Protect me from what?"

"From CSA," she whispered. "From what Skyla calls Big Data. Within months after the Collapse, CSA began to penetrate everything with their surveillance. Why the details of daily life were so important is beyond me but I think they combined two beliefs about surveillance into one."

"What do you mean?" Jaffa asked.

"Well, there is the total surveillance that is real, that keeps people in line. But, there is also the type that as long as the people think you are watching them, they will adjust their behavior and act in a way that will not bring them trouble from the authorities. You put up lots of cameras, like POVs and talk a lot about surveillance, but who knows; all those cameras could be fakes. It's just for the look of it.

Either way, you never know, so people assume they are being watched. For months, no one would talk out loud, no one would go outside. They only left their houses to go to work and back. It took months for people to start going outside to garden or take their kids to a park if they could afford it. Surveillance was cheap, easy and total. That's CSA. And it works. No one really knows how much he or she is being documented and why? In the end, crime is gone in the Core, rare in the Periphery, and no one bothers about Outlier towns."

"That may be the story, but I can assure you that CSA is actively watching the Outlier towns. There are more mosquitoes and bees flying around than nature could do on its own. Real insects don't survive for long in the radioactive cesspools of the Outlier towns. Only the bugs with tiny glass eyes exist." Jaffa stopped. "But let's get back to Genesee?"

"Genesee and I agreed you would be unnoticed living with me. She could watch over you like a guardian spirit throughout your life."

"But, why?" Jaffa flattened his voice. "Why didn't she want to see me?"

"Genesee and Grenadine had founded Longhouse by then. They launched the resistance." Zeinab let out a sigh. "We loved you. We wanted to keep you."

"So the old reservation is the Keep?" Jaffa spun around. "This is where you all want Skyla and me to go?"

"Yes. The Keep is your people's land. Genesee appears to be a doddering old lady living in a dump with her sister, but she along with other Clan Mothers, saved the land, your people, and many other people. She saw the future in a vision. Look around, Jaffa. None of this can last.

"Looks pretty stable to me. You have not been out on the frontline like me. CSA is strong as ever, POVs is almost sentient like artificial intelligence."

"I have seen more than you know. I know more than you know. Even now." Zeinab pushed herself out of the chair. "Come, sit next to me, sweetie." She put a finger to her lips for Jaffa to be quiet. She grabbed a chair next to the table and sat next to him. She pulled a bag of yarn and knitting needles up to the table, along with a small pad of paper.

"Why the silence? Why the drama?" Jaffa made room for her bag of yarn.

Zeinab ignored him and began to write in cursive on the paper. "Terry F." Jaffa nodded. She then wrote "NOC."

Jaffa's eyes widened. The Network Operations Center controlled satellites in space, their trajectories, their angles, and their motion. He wrote, "tech?"

"Director," she wrote. "Big one."

Jaffa put down the pen and took the paper from her. He lit a match and burned it in a small dish. A sort of reverence swept over him as he grasped the revelation that his dear, sweet Zeinab was also not a doddering old lady and never had been "just a sweet, old grandma." He took her hand and gave it a little squeeze. He whispered, "I get it. Extreme top secret."

Zeinab breathed a deep sigh and put her head on his shoulder. "Do you want something to eat? I can fix you a little something," she asked.

"Grandma, I need to go. I need to check in with the hospital. I want you to stay here. Don't change your routine." Jaffa stood up and zipped his coat. He drained the remaining coffee in his cup. "I have to check in with some story to stay out of CSA's way. I won't be away long."

"You still need to know more. There's much more you must know, now. I should not have waited so long." She stood up to hug him tight, the little boy, now a grown man, whom she had cared for all these years.

"You'll tell me tonight. I'll be back soon, but pack a few things in case we have to stay at my house for a bit." He put his finger to his lips to quiet her. "We'll talk more tonight. Promise." He kissed her cheek and then slipped out without a sound.

Zeinab waited a moment. She fell back into the chintz chair, her head in her hands.

CHAPTER TWENTY-THREE

TRAITOR

Stilton swung open the door of his office. He stood apart from the agents monitoring the screens. He had missed something. Without a sound, he sat down at his desk and tapped the computer keyboard. He was tempted to start digging into CSA files, but he held back. The telematics would alert the deep history registry to an unauthorized search. His senior agent status did not give him total security clearance. Only heads of rules committees had total security clearance. He would have that one day, he knew with certainty, but that day was yet ahead. He closed his eyes and took a deep breath, to begin again.

It was all about the girl. Who tipped her off at Celebration Wholesale? What made her run?

Skyla could be a pawn in someone else's game. He wondered about Tangier's elaborate scheme to soften her up before she was arrested. She would have been in custody

223

days ago, but for Grub's insatiable greed. Tangier's plan for her was sound, but his flair for jazzing up any operation struck Stilton as too laid back. Why the fuss, he would ask Tangier. Why not the fuss, Tangier would challenge him. What else do we have to do? Constant surveilling dulls our skills and bores us to death, Tangier would argue. Stilton agreed.

"Sir," said an agent now standing at Stilton's desk.

"What is it?"

"I review the data for Affiliation Yellow."

"Your point is?" Stilton replied.

"One of the doctors has not reported in from the Outlier clinic where he goes for his weekly clinic duty," she said.

"Why is this important to me?"

"His name is Jaffa Seneca. He was last seen leaving the clinic with a black cat."

"Round him up. Bring him to me. Priority Red." Stilton stood up. "Pets are always the weak link."

"Sir, he is off the grid," she replied standing at attention.

"Then use the old methods. Do you remember them?" Stilton rolled his eyes at her. "Do you need a short review?"

"No sir, I know what to do. Contact our embedded agents in Outlier towns and program POVs to scan for the last visual."

"You should alert agents in the Periphery and Core as well. And look for a god damned black cat."

"Yes, sir."

"Now get out of my sight and don't come back until you have this Jaffa Seneca." Stilton sat down at his desk. He began to search the database for Jaffa Seneca. The screen read, No record of this name. He lowered his head as sudden insight burned in his temples: the enemy within. CSA had a traitor.

CHAPTER TWENTY-FOUR

SUSPECTS

Skyla thought she knew a lot about CSA spying in the Outlier Camp towns until now. She watched Tangier's simple nod of his head to random undercover CSA agents along the twisty way out. He had proved her wrong. Once they entered the Periphery, she realized the alleys were not random at all. CSA's agents had seeped into daily life beyond the obvious POVs lenses. Whether he intended to or not, Tangier had shown her how CSA was the building block of the world as organized by the Affiliations.

Skyla saw its terrifying power as the out and out best tool to keep order, the soul of Big Data. All it took was a network of spies sent everywhere and the technology of POVs lenses for CSA to control it all. Skyla sifted through words rising up in her head that could explain it all. She let go of any thought of revisiting her beloved study, which would stay just an unfinished draft in her data stick. But in the shadow of its forgotten and forbidden words, the outline of a manifesto had formed, which she felt fated to write. She repositioned the rifle on her lap and felt her data stick. "Are we there yet?" she asked.

"Cute." Tangier turned to look at her. "Almost there."

"Where are we going exactly? You owe me that." Skyla sniffed at her arms. "I stink."

"You have smelled better, but in Outlier towns, you don't really notice any one person," he said laughing. "You can wash up at my place."

"Your place? I thought we were going to some secret place to meet with dangerous people," she said.

"After my place," he said. "And they are dangerous to anyone who dares to use words that are not official words. For you, they are very dangerous, but I will be there."

"Isn't this a trial? My trial? How dare I write against Big Data and all that?"

"It is not a trial," replied Tangier. "You know as well as I there are no such things as trials anymore. There are only interrogations to locate the weak spots where the rules of words failed. Follow the rules, no problems. Break the rules, well, you know."

"Yes, I know. Smells like a trial to me." Skyla sniffed her other arm. "Do you have any clothes at your place?"

"Yep. You get new ones."

"Oh, I see. Prison garb."

"Something like that." Tangier nodded to a traffic officer. "We have to play along if I am going to get you out.

You have to believe me that I won't turn in my own sister, even though that is what they want."

"So they know you're my brother?" She patted the rifle with her fingertips.

"Only the head of the Rules of Words Committee, who is also head of Affiliation Red, and CSA knows. He is the chief disciple of the knowledge is power school of thought. The bigger the secret, the bigger the power. He is the one who set up the network of orphanages way back when."

"Wow. The guy who heads up CSA?"

"Yes, it was his idea. He ordered them to be set up. He wasn't the head of Affiliation Red yet. That came years later."

"But, how could he know you and me? Did he see us?" Skyla thought back to her childhood but came up with no memory of any visitors.

"Actually, yes. Soon after we arrived. There was some official meeting there. Men dressed in fancy uniforms inspected all the kids. I was standing next to you, a scared toddler, with my arm around your shoulders when he came and stood in front of us. I was afraid that he was going to take you away. I told him not to touch you, that I can take care of my sister."

"What did he say?"

"Nothing. He nodded his head," said Tangier. "He might have been the same guy who let me keep you when the police took our parents away. But there is no way to know. This guy, the head of CSA, I think he is the reason we were not split up along the way. He keeps many secrets from those early days post Collapse."

"Even from CSA?"

"Sure. It gives him an edge over any Senior Agent like Stilton, my boss, who has not yet put us together."

"Why would the head of the Committee consider us a valuable secret?"

"We held no strategic value at all until you wrote your dissertation. That put us back into new intel, possible threat mode. My loyalty to CSA is as of yet unquestioned and the head knows this. After all I am bringing you, my sister, to the Committee myself."

"Ah, yes. I can see that," said Skyla. "Proof CSA is stronger than family."

"That is exactly the message we need to give, in order for me to get you to safety. The head may know many secrets, but he doesn't know everything."

"But Senior Agents are usually cunning and smart. Couldn't Stilton look us up himself?" Skyla began to twist a lock of hair into a knot.

"I suspect he is doing so right now. Years ago, I blocked any records related to us." Tangier sighed. "But he will not know that and think some other agent is sabotaging him. He will be pissed and start to suspect a traitor in CSA."

"You?"

"Me, and a few other agents with excellent computer skills will be suspect. Anyone that can hide data, lose it, or cover it, will be on his list. He will come after one of us like a cobra, laying low, in the shadows, striking with lethal force."

"I knew a guy at Celebration Wholesale who could muck around in deep files and find anything. He bragged to me about it once, thinking it would soften me up for a date with him."

"What was his name?" Tangier leaned forward to look up toward the sky.

"Riff." Skyla winced at the sound of his name.

"He's one of ours. He'd be on Stilton's list."

"Riff is CSA? You can't be serious. That disgusting lard ass?"

"The very same. Stilton hates him but knows he's smart with data. He's valuable, "said Tangier, "but he'll be a suspect."

The van turned onto a broad boulevard that separated the Periphery from the edge of Cap City Core. Tangier swung onto a frontage road and approached a plain, electrified, iron gate with guards in a gatehouse.

Tangier stopped the van in front of the gate. A guard from the gatehouse stepped toward him. He nodded toward Tangier and activated the doors, which opened inward without a sound.

Tangier drove the van through without delay.

"Did that guard know you?" Skyla asked.

"He knew me."

"Will he report he saw you with me?" Skyla squirmed in her seat as she pulled back from the windows.

"He will not. He will say nothing." Tangier turned to a tree lined avenue. The steel and glass homes shined in the bit of light breaking through the clouds. "Not all CSA agents love Big Data."

"Are you saying CSA is infiltrated by the resistance, by Longhouse?" Skyla shook her head. "Or are there other groups?"

"We call them crews. I lead one crew. Stilton has his crew. Sometimes we work together." Tangier pointed toward a traffic cop on a motorbike. "He is part of my crew."

"I thought you all worked in sync for Big Data like a spider web, spread out everywhere."

"Big Data wants you to think that. But, face it, there will always be internal competition for promotion, for power. Stilton wants it the most. He is the most ruthless."

"What does he want?" Skyla shivered as she remembered the cell at Swillian's.

"He wants CSA to become an Affiliation in its own right and to rule the other ones."

"That is scary. Is it possible?"

"He is working on it. That's why you have to get out. And Jaffa. He not only wants to kill what you wrote, but to kill you. A crack in the propaganda wall can ruin everything." Tangier turned into a driveway in front of a posh, white stucco building, containing half a dozen small condos. "Home." He opened a garage door by remote and pulled into the clean empty space. "We are safe from view now. The lens can see only the top rear of the vehicle."

She closed her eyes and jumped down to the floor. She pulled the data stick from the coat pocket and slid it into her hair behind her ear. Skyla had never been more alive than when she wrote her introduction a few days ago and saved it to the music files. As Tangier waved for her to come to the door, she promised herself, that whatever it took, she would see Jaffa and Jaguar again. For now, she smiled at her big brother and walked to the door, the rifle swinging by her side.

Once inside, Skyla searched for the bathroom door. "I am filthy. I must clean up."

"First, give me your coat and shoes. I need to get rid of them right away." He opened a plastic bag and held it open for her. "Here, take this one with you for the rest of your clothes. I have to burn them all."

She took the other bag and pointed to a door.

"Yes, that's it. Take your time. We are not going anywhere for a while. I have a few things to do." Tangier sat at his desk in front of the computer. When he finished filing a routine report, he set the computer to alert mode on the slim chance Jaffa might try to contact him over his rogue secure site.

He noted the time and grabbed a small box from the drawer. He lifted it out a small metal battery operated tapping machine and old headphones. Using low frequency radio waves, he tapped the lever to send a message. He closed his eyes and listened. Members of his crew and people with no names, but only allegiance to him and Longhouse, tapped back messages in return. Tangier took no notes, committing all communication to memory. After a few minutes, he tapped a few bits and switched off the machine. He placed the set back in the box and slid it into the false bottom of the drawer.

He rested back in the chair and put his hands behind his head. "Tomorrow is a go," he said to himself. "Jaffa, where the hell are you?"

Sometime later, Skyla emerged from a steamy mist and wrapped herself in fluffy white towels. She stared at the thin data stick propped up alongside a toothbrush in the holder. It reassured her to see it there.

She enjoyed the peaceful moment that would not last long. The heat and soap cleaned away the dirt of the last few days, but the memory of Grub and Cheddar resisted scrubbing away. Even Ruby, a traitor to all womankind, the faithless lackey who could have cared less about her own or any other poor child, stained her memory. She looked into the mirror and wondered if someone was on the other side looking at her.

Tangier was right about the prison clothes. She pulled on the grey tank top and tucked it into the dark grey cargo pants. She put on the light grey shirt with an interior pocket along the shirttail and rolled the sleeves to three-quarters length. Skyla took a deep breath and stepped back in front of the mirror. Yep. Prison garb.

She picked up the data stick from the toothbrush holder and shoved it into the shirt's pocket along the hem. She rolled the back shirt tail up above her hips and gathered the sides into two long ties in the front. She entwined them into a knot just slightly below her waist and buttoned the shirt up to the third button. The data stick, undetectable in the fabric of the knot, was secure, and she did not look like a jailbird. Satisfied with her look, she tugged new smooth leather boots on over thick white socks.

"How do I look?" Skyla stepped out to the kitchen where Tangier sat on a barstool.

"Clean, the shiny black hair like I remember when you were a kid," he said.

"That was a long time ago." Skyla sat on a stool next to him. "The boots fit great."

"They are tracker free. You are undetectable in them." Tangier studied his sister's face. "The world was screwed up when we were kids. It is worse now."

"So what happens? How can you stop the Rules of Words Committee?" Skyla studied his downcast eyes. "Is this the end of me? I don't blame you, for anything."

"You have always been a smart girl. Looking after you, even when you didn't know it, made my life special. I had a relationship that had nothing to do with profitmaking and money power. We mattered to each other." Tangier patted her shoulder.

"But I have put you at risk. This is all my fault." Skyla stood up and walked toward the futon where she stopped and turned. "Why don't you come with me to this place, the Keep. You, Jaffa, Jaguar, and me. Why can't you go with us? You have nothing here. I don't know what the future would be, but it would be better than the rotting Custodian Service Agency."

Tangier looked up at her and smiled. "Skyla, if you are to get out, with Jaffa and Jaguar, I have to stay here to make it work."

"Why?"

"I have to take someone down to do it. It will be messy. For me to do this, the price is staying here. I am willing to pay that price."

"You can't imagine life outside CSA, can you?" She spoke with as much gentleness as she could. "You do have power and could be more powerful with Big Data."

"I hate Big Data as much as you do, but I cannot run from a life I have led for so many years. Remember, I am older than you. But I can promise you that when I can get you out, you will have a valuable asset, an ally here within Big Data that someday will be of service to you, to Jaffa, to all. We will be together in the end."

"Will it hurt?" Skyla wrinkled her face.

"Will what hurt?"

"I know you are going to take me for interrogation first, before any escape attempt. Will it hurt?"

"It is a verbal interrogation, not physical torture. Think of it like a meeting of professors gathered to discuss your ideas. They will push you, they will insult you, they will challenge you. You must fight back as much as you can. You must not let them win with words or theories. You must not let them ever think you doubt your own work. If you believe in what you wrote, let your words be knives. Let them impale themselves on your words, so razor sharp, that they begin to bleed to death. Then I can take action, as

CSA, and stop the proceedings. You'll be whisked away to safety. I will remain to tidy up the mess."

"So, you have help?"

"Even now, as you and I sit here, Longhouse is at work. I have certain CSA agents at work although they don't know it." Tangier reached for a bottle of whiskey from the cupboard. "You and I shall take a drink together. Mae told me once that Mom and Dad used to drink a smoky Scotch to celebrate special events. This is not so smoky, but it is the only Scotch made since the Collapse." He poured two shots of the amber drink and pushed one toward Skyla. "To the future."

Skyla raised her glass, "To my big brother."

They drank the shots and sat still, without a sound. Skyla broke the silence with the question she had waited to ask. "Mae's gone, right?"

Tangier nodded. "Free at last. I'm glad you saw her."

"Me too," said Skyla.

"We should get as much rest as we can," said Tangier. "You stretch out on the futon. I'll take the lounge chair. Don't worry, I'll wake you." Tangier switched off the light. Bits of soft light from outside the windows coated the tiny apartment in eerie shadows.

"My one and only night in the Core." Skyla took off her new boots and set them by the futon. She unwound on the thin mattress and said, "It's good to be with you."

"Go to sleep."

CHAPTER TWENTY-FIVE

ROSARIO

Jaffa slurked back into an alleyway scoping out the shabby groups of people. He saw some rough teenage kids sitting near a screen playing an old computer game and began to dig in his pocket for his wrist phone. He eased it out of the Faraday case, which made it trackable to POVs. With that, he'd be back on the grid soon. He knelt down and dragged the phone back and forth in the water of the puddles at his feet to drowning it. He knew the damage would match his new cover story. He tossed the phone near the kids who were too busy game playing to notice and hid down the street with them in view.

Within a few minutes, a CSA Agent disguised as a shuffling tramp approached from another alley. She walked up to the gang, her shiny metal tipped boots almost hidden by the long scruffy pants. She dug around near the scrappy kids, kicking away rubbish. The phone slid out from a carton to the ground. She barked orders to them to stand up and explain where the phone came from. They denied knowing about it and cursed her to hell and beyond. The agent realized they had nothing for her and turned away. She had the phone, the prize.

Jaffa watched the CSA agent retreat back to her post, so he made his way in a different direction towards a clinic close by. He had to get back onto the grid but with his new story as someone who was mugged and beaten when he was at the clinic. This way he could explain his missing backpack and being passed out for hours in some alley. Tangier had always told him to keep the story simple, possible, and probable.

The clinic came into view and Jaffa sped up. He stopped to mess up his hair. He smeared some dirt along one side of his face, the side that had fallen into the muck of the alley, or so the story would go. He tossed his knit cap into a barrel he passed on the way. He developed a limp to show he had been beaten up.

"Eh, Jaffa! Where have you been?" asked Rosario, the receiving doctor, standing by the door of the clinic entrance. "Let me look at you. Who mugged you?"

"Some little shits. I left early because I had a headache and didn't feel well at all. There were only a few patients anyway." Jaffa followed his petite brown haired colleague to a small room with a desk and chair. "They got me right away."

"How did you get here all the way from the clinic in the south?" Rosario took a piece of gauze and wiped at the dirt on his head.

"I must have stumbled my way toward home nearby. I woke up in a corner a few alleys from here. So, I headed this way and hoped you'd be on duty." Jaffa looked away and shrugged like a child hiding something.

"Wow. For the record, you're a crummy actor." Rosario stuffed her hands into her lab coat pockets. "So, you want me to legalize your story with a write up, a record that matches what you say? How much trouble are you in?"

"Probably a lot," he said. "I don't want to say more than this. You can deny any knowledge other than you treated me."

"Fair enough." Rosario sat down at the desk and turned the screen toward her. "I'll enter an airtight cover story for you."

"I swear I have done nothing wrong. I am indebted to you." Jaffa placed his right hand over his heart and leaned toward her.

"On one condition," she said, looking at Jaffa straight in the eyes.

"Name it."

"You and that girlfriend of yours—get the hell out of here. I mean really out. You don't have to tell me what's going on because I know. All of Longhouse knows the two of you need to get out or be killed." Rosario put her pink, nail polished fingers together and tapped them against each other.

"You make it sound like we are important. We are just two people trying to exist together." Jaffa squinted his eyes at her. "There is something more?"

"You don't realize that CSA is chomping at the bit to launch a takeover of the Affiliations. You must be out before that happens. You and Skyla can survive only if you get to the Keep. Someday, from there, you will fight CSA and the Affiliations."

"Skyla and I are no heroes, nothing special. You sound like Zeinab, "said Jaffa. "I must get back to her. She wanted to tell me something."

"You are the children of heroes. You inherit their legacy. Zeinab knows everything. She'll explain it to you. I have known her for years working with Longhouse. She should have told you long ago, in my humble opinion." Rosario studied the young man in front of her. "First you take this. A temporary phone. The clinic provides these simple types to keep in good graces with CSA. Let the tracker show them you are resuming normal activities. Go home. Take a shower. Take a nap. Report to your usual office and resume your usual duties. Then tomorrow after your shift, come here. I will write that I want to see you again as a follow up."

Rosario's calm, but bossy voice stopped him from questioning her orders. "Ok, I'll do it.

Rosario continued. "I'm scared about Skyla But, she's in Tangier's hands now, deep within the hold of CSA. We can only hope he knows what he is doing." Rosario shrugged. "Now go. Do as I say."

"Yes, ma'am." Jaffa stood up.

"Now. Go. Get out of here!"

Jaffa put the temporary phone in his Faraday case and wove his way through the trash alleys to the Periphery where he lived, unaware that the CSA agent who found his real phone had followed him to the clinic. There, the nameless agent confronted Rosario in the back hall.

"Where is that guy with the limp?"

"Gone." Rosario shrugged. She put her hands in her lab coat pockets.

"I said, where is he?" The agent stepped closer. She bent over to scan the main hall and opened the door of an exam room.

"Gone." Rosario turned away from the CSA watcher and dug into her pocket. She swung back around. "I told you he is not here and neither are you." Rosario took aim and shot her dead with a Frankenstein gun and silencer. As the CSA agent lay in a pool of her own blood, Rosario called into the CSA alert line. "One of your agents stumbled into my clinic, hemorrhaging from a gunshot to the chest, keeled over and died on my floor. Come get her." A skinny white van arrived within minutes with two husky agents, who scooped up the body and shoved it into the cargo hold in back. Rosario watched them with calm. She knew the hall was a surveillance desert where nothing could be seen or heard. Tangier had rigged it for her years ago when he was a young agent.

She felt for the gun back in her pocket but it gave her no pleasure. One life extinguished by her hand, to save many more. She took a deep breath and returned to seeing her usual patients in the line that had grown very long by then.

CHAPTER TWENTY-SIX

LOST

"Jaffa Seneca is back, and one of ours is dead." His voice rose in volume until it cracked. Stilton stared at the screen on his desk. "This is no innocent coincidence. I want that little punk. I want the whole criminal Longhouse brought down." He pounded his desk and stood up.

The agents viewing the other screens turned to look at him. They had never seen Senior Agent Stilton lose his cool. "Get back to work," he commanded with the slow, growl of a wolf. He recognized right away he had violated his own mantra, the one he drilled into his agents: "keep your composure, win your battle, win your war." Barely seconds passed before he recovered. He took a deep breath and walked out of the office without hurry. He had found his lost composure.

The door to the stairwell leading to the rooftop was at the end of the hall. Stilton pushed it open, smacking it into the wall. He let it close by itself as he climbed the cement stairs to another landing and door. This one he opened with hesitation, knowing that he would be visible on the rooftop to POVs and any drones be they birds or insects. Although he spent his life observing every other living being, he avoided the spotlight at all times. He created a face of strength and power by being cagey about his own personal life. He varied a portrayal of the tough guy or the silent guy or the smart guy, but never the showy guy. Cool damp air covered him within an instant after he opened the door with a shove.

What sun had been visible behind dark brown clouds sank below the horizon. He didn't care about soft things like sunrises or sunsets. He only believed in the mission of CSA to keep the security of the Affiliations. Stilton stepped along the wall of the elevator shaft and other maintenance machinery. He balanced against the wall with one knee bent, ready to push off if needed. An insect drone circled nearby, scoping out something in another direction, so he held still while it flew away from him. The smack of sporadic raindrops on the metallic grates in the rooftop grew louder and drew his attention. Evening thunderstorms came and went on a daily basis. Tonight, Stilton welcomed the claps of thunder and bolts of lightning cutting across the sky, for they expressed the very storm raging in him.

When the rain had soaked his uniform and enough time cooled his temper, Stilton re-entered the building, but he did not return to his office. Instead he headed to the garage. Once there he made his way toward the Phantom and powered her up. Of all his many secret abodes, tonight, his condo in the Core appealed to him the most. He craved the feel of luxury. He wanted to surround himself with the finest things money power could buy. That was the point of it all. He could serve the Affiliations, but he wanted more. He wanted to taste obscure cognac and feast on hormone free meats and fish. He craved authentic green vegetables, free from radioactivity that only extreme wealth could buy. With loads of money units stored in secure accounts, he was already a rich man, but that was not his endpoint. Revenge powered his ambition. His target lay in front of him, close to him, all around him. The Affiliations hovered in the crosshairs of his aim, a retribution so ferocious he would take them all down. He had sworn an oath to rise up and rule them.

The Affiliations had put him in that cold orphanage, never to know parents or family, cut off from the pre-Collapse world. Even his name, Stilton, a typical second name, came from a computer-generated list. His first name, Perdu, meant "lost". He was not so much named as la-beled, Perdu Stilton, a description of who he was, a lost baby, belonging to no one, no family, no people. CSA surrounded him with agents, but no friends. Big Data had provided for him but he did not love him back. The only healing cream that could close his perpetual wound of lifelong abandonment would be to control Big Data himself. When CSA took over the Affiliations with Stilton in charge, the world would belong to him.

Stilton peered into the rearview mirror. His sharp eyes searched the shadows for movement or stray light. Satisfied that nothing appeared out of order, he maneuvered the Phantom out of the garage and into the steady rhythm of traffic, using it to blend into the scene. He nodded to a traffic control officer as he passed and saw a red light flash on the dashboard touchscreen of the Phantom. He tapped the touch screen and stated in a deep CSA business voice, "Stilton here."

"Tangier just reported in. He has the girl," said a voice of one of his agents.

"Excellent. Tomorrow belongs to me."

CHAPTER TWENTY-SEVEN

KISS THE ELDERS

Jaffa opened the door to his apartment but did not turn on the light. He sniffed the stale air and listened. Silence. He approached the short hall to the bedroom. When he had checked every bit of space, confident he was alone, only then, did he place his computer on a table and hook up to a secure, encrypted, rogue network. He and Tangier had agreed on which one to use for emergencies.

He kept the screen within eyesight as he grabbed a bottle of whiskey. He chugged a shot from the bottle. The fiery whiskey scalded his throat as he swallowed. He sat down and opened another pathway to check in and confirm for tomorrow, he would be in his usual office seeing patients. No alerts popped up. He left the phone in the Faraday case. No need to activate it yet. He took another swig of whiskey and began.

He opened another self-designed secure route to a search engine used by rogue groups who dig radical music.

He typed the words "NOC directors" but did not hit enter. He paused to consider the risk of discovery while searching in databases marked classified. Sooner or later CSA would know he rummaged around in classified files and would track the route he took to get there. That would connect to Tangier, which could also hurt Skyla. He closed all digital paths but the one he needed to contact Tangier.

After one more chug of whiskey, Jaffa mustered the nerve to poke Tangier using the encrypted access code that led only to his secure cyber site. Only seconds after he hit send, the prompt lit up the letter J and question mark.

"U with S?" replied Jaffa.

"Yes."

"Where? She ok?"

"Yes. Safe place."

"Nowhere safe," typed Jaffa.

"Yes."

"Will see C. M. G. tomorrow," typed Jaffa.

"Go tonight. Not safe, U." replied Tangier

"Ok."

"Will find U. Jag?" typed Tangier.

"Jag ok. C.M.G."

"Kiss the elders."

"Ok."

Jaffa closed his eyes to absorb the meaning of the chat he had with Tangier. This mess was not just about Skyla's abduction by a porno film crew only to be rescued by Tangier. A simple rescue would not involve security risks or secrecy about locations. The order to go see Genesee tonight only made sense if another risky plot was in play.

Then it hit him. Genesee held all the answers to his questions. Forget kisses, he couldn't wait to demand to know what the hell was going on.

Within an hour, Jaffa put on fresh clothes, heavy socks, and boots. He filled the pockets of his cargo pants and vest with suture and gauze, anesthetic cream, glue, scissors, clamps, and a few syringes. He placed a few Ace wrap rolls and bandages in the pockets on his jacket sleeves. Genuine aspirin was still his favorite "works for everything" pill. He stuck a bottle into his interior coat pocket. If he were to be prepared, he would be armed with the tools he knew best. He stuffed his stethoscope into a remaining pocket. His spare backpack hid his computer and a blanket.

He left his apartment in the Periphery and made his way toward Genesee's shack in the Outlier town. He pulled his hood up against the night air and slight drizzle. For the moment, he was untraceable. For the moment, he felt free.

The dark alley's residents slept in the steady rain, and Jaffa slurked closer and closer to Genesee's shack. He located the slits of light almost invisible around her window. He tapped on her door. A tap returned to which he tapped again. The door opened without a sound and a sturdy hand reached out and pulled him in. The door closed behind in silence.

Zeinab sat next to Grenadine on an old couch in the parlor, a little alcove next to the front room. Genesee sat erect on a straight chair. She wore an antique set of wide padded earphones and listened to someone. She nodded to Jaffa without saying word. He went to his grandmother Zeinab and kissed her on the cheek. He turned to Grenadine and did the same.

"Back so soon?" asked Grenadine.

Jaffa slid onto a chair next to her. He turned to the other woman in the room. "Rosario, why am I not surprised to see you here?"

"I told you, Grenadine, he's cute and smart." Rosario crossed her arms and smiled.

"You did and now we can get all our little duckies in a row tonight." Grenadine reached for a teapot and drew it closer. "Tea, Jaffa?"

"Yes, thanks." Jaffa smiled at Zeinab who put her finger to her lips while rolling her eyes over to Genesee.

Genesee switched off a lever and pulled the earphones from her head. "Jaffa. We have much to discuss."

"Shall I call you grandmother?" He stole a glance at Zeinab who shrugged and smiled.

"I think you should call me Genesee," she said, "and I ask your forgiveness for not making myself known to you before now. Zeinab did the heavy lifting of raising you and to her I am forever grateful."

"Genesee." Jaffa tried to summon a feeling of kinship.

"As we know, Tangier sent you here tonight. Let me catch you up on the predicament we are all in, the danger that hovers close to us." Genesee stopped and took Jaffa's hand. "I owe you some family history and I will make good on that debt, but for now, let's solve the immediate crisis."

Genesee began with the account of how a CSA agent, with a cover as a student, seduced a professor at the Institute where Skyla studied. The agent discovered the professor had skimmed money units from extra tutoring sessions and had not reported it as earned income for toll collection purposes."

"So what? People try to avoid paying tolls all the time," said Jaffa.

"True." Genesee shrugged. "People know that they are being extorted for the cost of their own surveillance. It's a forced toll for a privatized service you despise but can't reject."

"Skyla always complained that a toll was the soft word for taxes." said Jaffa. "The jailed pay for the jailers."

"She's right. The Affiliations sell the idea that there are no taxes since there is no state. It's just the old con, free speech but not any speech. It's a game they play. However, back to the story: The cheating professor could not bear being cast out to an Outlier town. She gave the CSA agent a prize, something of value in trade for immunity from punishment for theft."

"Skyla's study?" Jaffa said. "There must be something else. CSA infiltrates all the Institutes. All the academic work is known. CSA can always make up charges against a professor for failing to report a student using unapproved language. The Behavior Studies students write about the Affiliations all the time."

"True. On balance, they do write about the Affiliations so that in of itself is no consequence," said Genesee. "Skyla had mentioned to them her intention to use the name 'Big Data' and that fed the flame of fear in them."

"Why? It's just a catchy turn of phrase against the power of the Affiliations. It's just some words." Jaffa looked to Zeinab who looked back to Genesee.

"Words. That's the point. Words hold power, and the group that gets to define them and regulate how they're used control that power. She coined the term 'Big Data' to call into question the whole structure and power of the money economy. Skyla's words removed the cover, opened the drapes, whatever metaphor you choose to use. It exposed the Affiliations for the money grubbing machines that they are and saying they're persons like us. Every human interaction is a for-profit deal in the world of Big Data." Genesee took a weary deep breath. "Skyla shouted unapproved words to the whole world."

"That may all be true, but Skyla wrote her study to get her degree so she could teach, maybe even in the Core. She had no intention of doing anything else." Jaffa stood up and paced back and forth. "When did this turn into something political?"

"When CSA got hold of it," answered Genesee. "When the Rules of Words Committee got hold of it."

"Tangier must have seen that she was in trouble."

"That's it. He was briefed on the dissertation of a Behavior Studies student, a girl named Skyla, and was told to pick her up." Genesee shifted her gaze to the women on the couch. "He called Mae knowing she was unmutual. Mae demanded the right and responsibility as grandmother to communicate with Skyla, to warn her. She escaped from Celebration Wholesale and Tangier picked her up in a trash alley. He brought her to Mae, although Skyla had no memory of her. Before they all could truly reacquaint themselves, Tangier and Skyla were forced to flee. CSA was following Mae and Tangier knew it. He had to choose, save Mae or save Skyla."

"Skyla. He chose Skyla." Jaffa reached out to Zeinab and patted her knee acknowledging her lifelong friendship with Mae. "But how did Skyla get abducted by the porn guys?"

"Tangier left her in an Outlier town, planning to go back for her after he checked in, giving them some cock and bull story to delay the whole thing. Out of nowhere came this other situation."

"That must be how Jaguar came to be lost. Somehow he got away and found me." He looked at Poe sitting still on a perch near the window. Jaguar, curled into a ball, slept next to Grenadine on the couch.

"And Poe brought you to me." Genesee smiled at the raven. "You know the rest. Tangier rescued her, but now he must still bring her to the Rules of Words Committee. They will talk to her then kill her. They fear long forgotten words used to speak truth to power. They fear if her work gets to the underground it will bubble up here and there beyond their control. In time, it will expand and strengthen the resistance. The Affiliations intend to survive at any cost, even the cost of human life."

"That is why we want you to go to the Keep," said Grenadine, stroking the cat. "With Jaguar, of course."

"What about all of you? Why don't you go to the Keep?" Jaffa retook his seat in the chair with his arms crossed and his fingers clenched together. "You are not safe here either. CSA will launch a takeover. They will kill anyone connected to Longhouse. That means you." He paused, "I hear plenty out there, too. I am no innocent."

"No one said you were." Genesee reached for Jaffa's hands and held them in her own. "Dear boy, you are young. Skyla is young. We are committed to seeing you both to safety. We will follow, I promise. But, you first. You are the future."

"Tangier? What happens to him?" Jaffa frowned and looked to Zeinab.

"He is CSA. He cannot leave if you are to go. Someone must stay back," said Genesee. "He made his choice long ago. He will always provide the Keep with protection as long as he is with CSA whatever shape it takes."

"Do you have a plan? There is total surveillance even beyond Outlier towns. POVs and CSA penetrate into the most abandoned territories, even to the radioactive badlands and beyond."

"Of course, she has a plan," said Grenadine. "She's the Clan Mother!"

"Yes. I know how you will escape once we get hold of Skyla. Timing will need to be perfect," said Genesee. "Grenadine, make some more tea, please. The telling of this plan requires hot, strong tea."

CHAPTER TWENTY-EIGHT

ALLEGIANCE

Riff, home alone, deep in a dig of a new Celebration Wholesale worker, shoved back his chair with a jump, then ran toward the bathroom. His gut churned from the CSA special alert that showed up on his screen. He had never been to any of Stilton's shadowy hideouts, but just now he had been ordered to the one in the Core. There can be no good end to this, he thought. He would make Stilton happy or not. If not, he'd be demoted or fired from CSA.

He dressed in a fresh regular duty uniform and buffed the tips of his boots with a clean sock. Stilton would want help with accessing files, the one skill Riff had that his boss did not. It made him handy to Stilton, but there were others just as skilled. Riff radiated the scent of weak prey, of being an easy target for a guy like Stilton, and this insight shamed him. His bowels always betrayed him, making him not a gutless man but rather a gut filled man, always slow out of the blocks. He grabbed his computer and put on some speed. He stepped lively down the stairs to the street where he met a CSA hover vehicle Stilton had sent to fetch him.

The unmanned grey hover vehicle sped through the traffic, its blue rooftop lamp flashing the light of dread, for no resident of the Cap City welcomed it. Riff watched the bland skyline of the Periphery fade away as the vehicle crossed the boulevard into the Core. At the gate to Stilton's neighborhood, a guard waved him through without a pause. No guard dared stop a CSA vehicle with its active, flashing light of dread. The vehicle slowed its speed before coming to a standstill in front of a three story building, not quite visible behind a tall hedge of prickly bushes. Riff swallowed an antacid pill before lurching out of the cramped sedan.

He could see a dull light, the shadow of his unpleasant boss, in a window on the third floor. The steps to the door were made of something artificial, making each boot step sound like a tap dancer on a stage. There would be no sneaking up on Senior Agent Stilton. If POVs failed him, his own ears would detect any unaccounted steps. Riff pushed a rush of jealousy way down into his gut. Jealousy was a distraction he could not afford. If he ever had a chance of reaching the Core it could well be from today's performance with Stilton. He looked up at the POVs lens and gave a brief nod, rather than a salute. Confidence rather than nerves, he hoped that was what Stilton saw on his monitor. The door lock clicked open. Riff pushed the door and trekked up the cascade of marble steps toward the third floor.

A single recessed light above a single door on the third floor lit the landing, casting stretched shadows against the wall. Riff noticed his shadow as he reached the last few steps. He smiled at the clever way Stilton could view any movement at all from inside his apartment through a glass marble in the door. It was a throwback, a retro tactic of surveillance, one that did not require a power source. The tiny skylight in the ceiling would always provide a bit of light so there would be no hiding on the third floor. Shadows and light, Riff thought, that was the life of CSA agents, and mostly shadows.

Before he raised his hand to knock, the door opened.

"Come in. I detest knocking. No one comes here unless I ask them to come. If I ask them to come, as you have no doubt figured out, no one else is to know." Stilton closed the door behind Riff without a sound. "No one knows you are here?"

"No one knows." Riff stood still, waiting for Stilton's next move.

"Riff. Reliable Riff. You sit at the table." Stilton pointed to a teak table with a zebra wood inlaid border.

"Yes, sir." Riff pulled the solitary, antique ladder back chair from the table and sat down. He set up his computer while vowing to himself that one day he would own a table and chair like these.

"We have a problem. CSA has a problem. As of right now, I am raising your security clearance. What we, that is you, have to do is find a traitor." Stilton walked toward his shelf of rare whiskies. "Want a drink?"

"Vodka, sir," said Riff. "What sort of traitor? Where are you looking for him?"

"Hell, if I know. That is why you are here. I know you are the best hacker around." He slammed the glass down next to the computer. "When I typed in the name Jaffa Seneca, I got a screen telling me there is no file on him. Now, I know with certainty this scum doctor exists. I want to know who hid the files and why."

"Yes, sir."

"No one messes with me and CSA. You understand?" Stilton gritted every word.

"Yes, sir." Riff stared at the shot glass of vodka. "Jaffa Seneca. I'll find him." He picked up the glass and drank the shot. It tasted like lemons. Stilton had given him flavored vodka available only in the Core.

"I'll just sit over here. You let me know when you find the file and who the hell hid it." Stilton eased into a couch. He opened a black walnut box and picked up a cigar. He cut the tip and balanced the robusto in his lips. With a silver lighter, he lit the end and dragged in the flame, puffing out clouds of smoke that swirled around his head. "Now this is a nice cigar."

Riff smelled the cigar and added unlimited cigars to his list of musts have items he would get once he made the Core. With a couple of keystrokes, he began to search, to dig, to excavate for Jaffa Seneca. Although confident in his own skills, it was much more difficult to extract a trail camouflaged with purpose than muck around existing files. "Sir, this could take some time."

"Take all the time you need. You are not going anywhere until you find the files. Take all day; take all night.
Find the files." Stilton tapped the ashes from the end of the
cigar into a red ceramic bowl shaped like an angelfish.

"Yes, sir." Riff took a deep breath and clicked away. If
he found the missing files with too much speed, he risked
making Stilton look incompetent with the Custodian Service
Agency file system. It would be better to take time, make
Stilton think he needed a guy like him. All this played back
and forth in his head as he dug into databases that cross-
referenced or intersected with other layers of encryption.

To his surprise, the word "lynx" reappeared as a marker.
Lynx as the cat, lynx as a name, lynx as the veil rendering
the Jaffa Seneca files invisible. Removing a veil took time.
Riff glanced toward Stilton who had relaxed into the couch,
his head resting back on a pillow. The cigar still burned but
not for much longer. Riff turned back to the computer and
pushed on. He used "lynx" to access various databases and
categories of people. He added "historic" to the search and
references to great cats appeared on the screen. He
recognized the Sphinx in Egypt, drew a blank on Shere
Kahn from a kid's story, but noted an old logo of a cat on a
car bearing the name Jaguar. Riff recognized at once that he
was faced with a question of allegiance.

Stilton had closed his eyes, the tan cigar tamped out a
while back. Riff did not think he was asleep. With a few
more keystrokes, Riff cracked the encrypted veil and knew
who constructed it in the first place. He knew who belonged
to a cat named Jaguar. The cat logo he had seen once on a

ball cap that Tangier would wear now and then while undercover in Outlier towns. So, Skyla and Tangier are brother and sister, he thought, a shock to be sure, but meaningless to him.

He dug a little more and found that the lynx cyber clue that connected to the Jaffa Seneca file added yet other layers to the complicated crosshatch of code. Riff could decipher the presence of another file linked to a lynx but his attempt to decrypt it failed because an even denser veil covered this additional file. He made a mental note to excavate here on his own, not because he cared about the identity but he was intrigued by the brilliant technique used to create an impenetrable cyber veil. Whoever built it had to have CSA access and possess skills beyond his own. Riff did not think the identity of this other person would be of interest to Stilton as all he wanted was the Jaffa Seneca file, which he had found. He had learned in CSA never to volunteer information, rather, answer only what was asked, do only what was ordered.

This Jaffa Seneca, he discovered, was an everyday guy, a doctor who served time at the EME front, who occasionally worked in Outlier clinics, who at this time was engaged to Skyla Roseau. No wonder she snubbed him, Riff thought. She wasn't available, so of course she would not be interested. He thought further, that Tangier had always treated him well, with respect unlike Stilton whose arrogance nicked him over and over again like a cheap, rusty blade. He looked at the empty shot glass and wondered if the fine vodka was a bribe. The choice before him evoked cramps in his stomach, and he struggled to ignore them. Today, he had to choose a future, pick a champion, be on the side of the winning ticket. He could see the war brewing between Tangier and Stilton laid out before him like a map on a wall.

"You stopped. Find the file?" Stilton barked like a dog startled out of sleep.

"I found the problem. The file is corrupted."

"What do you mean corrupted? By whom?" Stilton sat up straight and took a swig from his glass of whiskey.

"It was not corrupted by anyone. When there are electrical storms, there can be overloads that fry certain segments of various mainframes. His file is in a section that was hit by a storm a week or two ago. The self-repair of the files is in process. It will all be back within a week." Riff kept his voice even.

"You can tell this? Are you playing with me?"

"I can tell by collateral files. No, sir, I am not playing here. The files are all in regeneration mode. It was not a deliberate act." Riff turned around to face him.

"Son of a bitch." Stilton stood up and walked toward Riff. "If you are lying to me, you are a dead man."

"I have no wish to die. I'd be glad to monitor this and tell you when it's back online," said Riff.

"You do that." Stilton walked toward the door. "Get your stuff and get out of here. Not a word to anyone."

"Yes, sir." Riff rammed his computer into his pack and pushed the chair toward the table.

"I still think there is a traitor," said Stilton. "I can smell it. I am CSA; I don't need proof. I want you to take him out."

"Sir?" Riff stopped in front of him and could feel his hot cigar breath on his face.

"Tangier. That son of a bitch is playing me. I know it. I hated him since we were kids."

Riff stood still, unsure of what to say. "I should go."

"Yes, you should go now." Stilton opened the door. "You will kill Tangier by the end of this week. I will set it up. Then you'll be my new senior field agent. I know you'd like that. You can taste it."

"Yes, sir." Riff walked down the steps, unhurried until he heard the door slam shut. He waited a few seconds then revved up to run down the rest of the stairs and out to the CSA vehicle. He jumped in, shouted the return instructions and sat back for the ride.

The coveted job of senior field agent was in his grasp, if he trusted Stilton. All he had to do was kill a respected agent who had always treated him well. He counted the minutes before he was back in the Periphery and outside his own place. He raced up the stairs to his apartment and flung open the door. There in front of him sat Grub, propped up on a chair, blood pooling on the floor from the deep slit in his throat, his eyes still open, his head dangling to the left. Only the back of the chair prevented it from ripping off. So Grub had met the CSA traitor's fate with a silent, speedy kill. Riff understood this bloody execution done in his own home as the coldblooded reminder of what he was expected to do by week's end. In his heart, Riff knew the greed and shiftiness so typical of Grub had nothing to do with loyalty to CSA. Didn't everyone claw their way to more and more. Wasn't that the point of life, to get more and more?

Grub was no traitor. This unfair mess was a warning from Stilton to Riff. There was no justice in the CSA, only rules, Stilton's rules. Before he could think another thought, he ran to the bathroom and exploded.

CHAPTER TWENTY-NINE

TIME

Genesee inhaled the steam from the hot tea Grenadine placed in front of her. Jaffa cleared a place on a side table for the cup he brought to Zeinab. Poe fluffed his feathers then paced on top of a bookcase above a bowl of water. "Thank you, dear." Poe tilted his head and turned his beak toward Genesee. "Thank you, dear."

"Thank you, Poe," Genesee called back to him.

Jaffa squeezed into the space beside Zeinab on the couch. "I didn't know a raven could talk."

"Ravens are clever, smart birds. Poe can be quite a chatterbox at times but I am always grateful to him for choosing me," she explained. "You saw for yourself. He saved Jaguar and brought you both to me."

"That he did." Jaffa reached over Zeinab to massage Jaguar behind the ears. "So, what is the big secret? There have been many secrets these days."

"I'll start with tomorrow. Then I'll conclude with yesterday." Genesee sipped her tea. "Grenadine, you make the best cup of tea!"

"That, I do. Every time," she answered, "Let's get this thing done. There is a lot of work to do. It is a frightening time."

"Let us begin. Jaffa, son of Amira and my son, William, once I reveal what I am about to reveal, there is only forward motion. To hear this truth is to accept the decisions of your grandmothers, taken with great deliberation, with the best interests of you and seven generations ahead. If you are unwilling to accept this condition, I will stop here."

"It is pretty hard to agree to something when it is shrouded in mystery," said Jaffa. "Grandma Zeinab, are you in on this?"

Zeinab nodded. "Genesee, just cut to the chase. You are scaring the poor boy."

Genesee took a deep breath, letting it out in little puffs. "Tomorrow is the only day possible to get Skyla and you to the Keep. We cannot fail. The alternative is too awful to imagine."

"The Keep? Tomorrow? That is the secret? We don't even know Skyla and Tangier's whereabouts." Jaffa held his forehead with the palm of his hand. Deep furrows appeared along brow of his face. His eyes darkened.

"We do know where they are and where they will go. The timing is fluid but you all meet tomorrow at day's end. You will meet up with Tangier and Skyla at a point we have already arranged. Then you and Skyla will set out for the

Keep together. Longhouse will assist you along the way and us from here. There is only one chance, one hour of opportunity at the end of your trek to cross into your future." Genesee nodded to Rosario who until now sat motionless with her hands folded on her lap.

"Jaffa, you will have tools, drugs, to assist you on your journey should you need them. I will prepare it all for you. You must use the tools with care as they are powerful but few in number." Rosario spread her hands out on her lap, the pink nail polish glowed in the soft lamp light, the only one illuminated in the room. "Think poison darts."

"With respect, I do not know what any of you are talking about. What trek? Poison darts? Where in the world is the Keep? And what is an hour of opportunity?" Jaffa softened his expression in an attempt to keep calm. He scanned the roomful of women who together formed a council with authority over him. "I'm listening."

"Let's start with your grandfather, Terry Fitzpatrick, who directed the Network Operations Center for Global Satellite Inc. This corporation over time amassed complete control of all the communication and surveillance satellites that existed at the time of the Collapse. What else do satellites do but transmit or record in endless arcs surveilling everything. Global Satellite thrived as a stand-alone, independent contractor, a monopoly. Every state and every other corporation the world over paid them well to provide the satellite service they each needed. And Terry ran the whole thing." Genesee turned to Zeinab and added, "He saw the future and created an escape route for us. He was a brother of the heart to me and my people."

"Terry cherished you all," said Zeinab, "And Jaffa, you, and Skyla will take this escape route he formed out of digital code. This is not negotiable."

Jaffa did not move but for an occasional stroke of Jaguar's tail. He betrayed nothing from his face, not a flinch. He had never heard his grandmother speak with command authority like a general, much less talk about sculpting digital code.

"Tomorrow is the one day each year that the escape route is open. It is the one hour each year that all POVs lenses are blind. It is the one hour each year that CSA knows nothing about anything. In our capital time zone, from ten o'clock in the evening until eleven o'clock in the evening, all, that is, one hundred percent of all satellite activity, is reset. Global systems go down. They reboot by the end of the hour." Zeinab took Jaffa's hand keeping a tight grip. "Your grandfather, like all of us during the Collapse, watched governments fall like dominoes only for rich, powerful men to regroup everything into Affiliations."

"Jaffa," said Genesee, "I told your grandparents we could all go to my people's land. We could be safe there. But it was not to be. Like a wind storm, the new Affiliation Red sucked up all the police, spies, and military forces cut loose from the old system to form the Custodian Service Agency. So the new CSA forces stopped all air travel and blew up roads and railways. They broke apart families, friends, and communities to redistrict the world into the countless Cores, Peripheries, and Outlier camp towns. The capital city became Cap City and numbers replaced the names of all the rest. We were sorted into Core, Periphery, or Outlier towns, the new social prisons. Which brings us to tomorrow."

"Tomorrow is the one day and time in a three hundred sixty-five-day cycle that the prison gates are unlocked. And the prison guards don't even know it," said Zeinab.

"How do you know this? How do you know this time and date, when the fine-tuned CSA security machine, is guarded by every known weapon, digital or physical, in the universe?" Jaffa resisted taking his hand from his grandmother's tight grip.

"Laylat al-Qadr. The Night of Power." Zeinab's eyes grew still as if she had traveled to another time and place. "This was your grandfather's gift to us."

Genesee patted the armrest of her chair. Poe hopped from the bookcase to her. He nudged his beak against her cheek and quieted himself. "Before Global Satellite fell under the rule of CSA, Terry put in the fix."

"You mean he rigged the satellite command protocol?" Jaffa slipped his hand away from his grandmother and crossed his arms. "In what way?"

"In a clever way, replied Genesee. He knew about Laylat al-Qadr from Zeinab. As her grandson, you no doubt know, it is the most holy night of the year in which Muslims believe the first revelation of the Quran was sent down to the Prophet Muhammad. It is stated that this night was "better than one thousand months [of proper worship], as stated in Chapter 97:3 of the Qur'an. It more or less, over time, occurs on the twenty-seventh night of Ramadan." Genesee stroked Poe with her fingertips.

"Yes, Ramadan. What exactly did Terry do?" Jaffa began to rub Jaguar's shoulders with such deliberate strokes that he raised his head and his motor started to run.

"Think." Zeinab barked at her grandson as if he were a new recruit. "Ramadan is special, why?"

"Why? I don't know. Fasting? It comes once a year." Jaffa turned to Zeinab. "Time. Time is the key."

"Bravo! You are going to be just fine in the Keep," said Genesee. "Ramadan is the ninth month of the lunar year, approximately 354 days long. Terry knew the months rotate backward through the seasons and are not fixed to the secular calendar the Affiliations use."

"So," Jaffa said, "Terry rigged the whole CSA satellite system to go offline for an hour on the 27th night of Ramadan because it rotates with the lunar calendar? And, no one at CSA ever thinks of a lunar calendar? So, it is undetectable?" Jaffa gazed around the room at their grave faces. "You really believe we, the people in this room, are the only ones who know about this? That is impossible. CSA is filled with cyber, satellite, and data wizards."

"Tangier knows. Those of us here know. That is all," replied Genesee. "Those Longhouse operatives working with Tangier only know a day was chosen for the escape without the rationale. They are used to 'need to know' orders and ask no questions."

"Jaffa, your grandfather fixed the system using a plain, low level program. Think of it as a little movie that loops over and over again, so a network operator or CSA agent never sees anything out of place." Zeinab let her head relax onto the back of the couch. "He had it in place before he was killed. He thought he could get us out, get us to the Keep, but it wasn't to be. That's why you and Skyla must go." Rosario leaned over and patted her arm.

"So, Jaffa, you see, tomorrow is possible because the story began in the yesterdays," said Genesee.

"Now, Jaffa, my dear boy," said Grenadine, "you don't mind me calling you 'dear boy,' do you? No matter, my dear boy. You're going to play catch up with your Haudenosaunee family, too."

"Family? How about the whole damn culture? I was told my father came from somewhere west and he was an only child whose parents were gone. Yet, all this time another mysterious grandmother was right here in the same town." Jaffa glanced back at Zeinab.

"Young man, we did a lot of shady things to protect you," said Zeinab who pushed off of the couch and stood up in his face. "We lost everything in the Collapse. What would you have us do? Surrender? No. Once we got past the grief and loss that paralyzed us, we fought back. To build a resistance, sacrifices had to be made. Don't you think for a minute it was easy for either of us to shield you from Genesee. There are costs all around suffered by many to keep you, Skyla, and Tangier, for that matter, safe from the clutches of CSA."

"Enough. Zeinab, you'll start to cry or cough." Genesee pointed to the couch. "Sit down." She turned to her grandson. "Jaffa. Your anger is justifiable. Skyla was angry when she met Mae and Zeinab."

"As she should be. When were you going to let us all in on the family secrets? Jaffa scowled at the group then settled on Genesee. "When did Tangier learn about all this?"

"Only a few months ago when Skyla began to sharpen the focus of her thesis. Tangier fed us her chapters and together we saw the threat to the Affiliations." Genesee started to chuckle. "She really came up with a good one, lumping CSA and the Affiliations together as Big Data."

"Yeah, it's a game changer. She has guts. She calls it like she sees it," said Jaffa, putting his hands in his pockets. "I'm sure she has shared a few choice words with Tangier by now. Whatever your intentions, you waited too long to tell us the truth." He shot a glance at Jaguar who had raised his head. "You even put Jaguar in danger and that's unforgivable."

"We did wait too long. Neither you, Skyla, nor Tangier are kids anymore." Genesee looked to Zeinab who nodded. "Jaffa, you will soon meet your family that lives in the Keep. Skyla's too."

"Oh, that's right. Skyla, the Joan of Arc?" said Jaffa.

"Just listen for a moment and don't get mad." Zeinab, scooted to the edge of her seat. "Mae trusted me to keep secrets, to look after Skyla. We lived through hell to keep Tangier and her alive. I am not sorry."

"Zeinab, calm down," said Genesee.

"How much does Skyla know of this yet?" Jaffa sat down on a chair near Jaguar, who had stretched out with a better view to Poe.

"I don't know," said Genesee. "Tangier was going to tell her. Remember, this is not how I intended this discussion to take place." Genesee checked the time. "I must check in with my scouts. Tangier and Skyla will be traveling early tomorrow to be with the Rules of Words Committee."

"Then what?" asked Jaffa. He inhaled slowly and held his breath. The exhale was silent.

"Tangier and Skyla must survive the committee and escape to our meeting point, and you'll be there waiting for her. Then Tangier will escort you as far as he can go, and you'll be off. Genesee turned to the console. "Now for the scouts, then I must sleep a bit. Morning will greet us early." She picked up her padded earphones. "As for all of you, it is much too late for anyone to leave. You must all stay here tonight."

The room fell silent, only Poe and Jaguar moved. Poe climbed up Genesee to perch on her shoulder while Jaguar stood up and arched his back, then turned around in a circle and plopped back down in his place. Jaffa sat still as stone.

"This may be our last night together ever, the little bit of family that we are," said Zeinab. She turned to Rosario, again, and buried her head in the doctor's shoulder. She could not stop the tears and muffled the words, "I will never see Jaffa again, after tomorrow."

Grenadine snapped her fingers at Jaffa and waved for him to follow her to a closet full of blankets and sleeping pads. He made up beds for himself and Rosario on the wooden plank floor. He arranged pillows and blankets on the couch for Zeinab. He sat down next to her and held her hand in his. His grandmother always told the truth and tonight, their last night together, he hated the truth.

CHAPTER THIRTY

DELIVERY

"We need to go," said Tangier. He tapped his wrist phone to stop the chirp of the alarm.

Skyla opened her eyes and sat up with a start. She pictured Jaguar, a black mound of silky fur curled up on a pillow beside Jaffa, who had stretched out on her couch. She could hear Jaguar's tiny snores as her sweet Jaffa stroked him.

Tangier adjusted the pleat in his black trousers, then smoothed a sleeve of his scarlet collarless shirt, buttoned up at the neck. Only senior field agents and senior agents wore the black narrow band of stiff cloth forming the neck of his shirt. The dress uniform of CSA filled onlookers with fear as it signaled the wrath of CSA about to fall on some poor soul. CSA was well aware the sight of scarlet shirts and black pants, towering over boots with shiny metal tips, served to reinforce that everything is known.

Skyla had never seen Tangier outfitted in his official dress uniform. She wanted to reach up and rip the red shirt away from his face, to replace it with a dull green t-shirt and blue hoodie, the uniform of her big brother when they used to play as kids. Instead, she watched Tangier motion toward the stairs that led to the garage. He opened the door for her. Her hand adjusted the knot of her tied shirt. She felt the data stick, secured deep within the folds. She winced at the clicks of Tangier's steel tipped boots on the concrete floor of the garage but followed him anyway.

Tangier started the van while Skyla climbed in. "I wish we could rewind this week. I am lost, drowning, and float-ing all at the same time. I am cut off from Jaffa and poor Jaguar, my little boy."

"Whatever you think, you don't want to rewind the week. Tomorrow you will be glad this week happened. Tomorrow you will be free with Jaffa and Jaguar, never to return to this hell hole." Tangier pushed the remote to open the garage door. "It's Mae's gift to you. Zeinab's too. She relinquished Jaffa to your love and care."

"Always dropping clues. What are you talking about? How am I to get away? The Rules of the Words Committee will scramble my brains with their dumbass questions. I'll turn into a zombie. Then they will finish me off with a drug that leaves no trace, ordering you to dump me in a morgue to be incinerated by day's end."

"Well, that was dramatic," said Tangier. "Damn, you are a good with words."

"Shut up," said Skyla, "I am serious. Today I will be offed, so what good is it to tease me with thoughts of seeing Jaffa and Jaguar and living happily ever after?" Skyla sat up straight and felt a cold wave of fear fill her chest. "You are teasing me. You are lying about Jaffa and Jaguar. You are driving me to my death. Why? Do you get a promotion? And you never returned the earring you took from me." She touched her ears, feeling one and noting the absence of the other.

Tangier put the van in motion, easing it outside to the street. He pulled over to the side and stopped. He dug into his pants pocket and handed Skyla the earring in an outstretched hand. "Here. Take it."

"Why do you have it in your pocket?" Skyla did not move.

"I was keeping it, a piece of you, just to have." Tangier sat back on the seat and stared out the window. "Silly. Sentimental, I guess." He turned to her and said, "Cut the drama. You're not dying. You must suffer through this with the Committee, but I'll get you out. Then you're going to the Keep with Jaffa and Jaguar. It's not without risk, but our plan will work."

Skyla folded his fingers back over the earring. "You keep it. It'll protect you. I've missed you all these years, Tangier." She could feel tears welling up. "What happens to you? When will I ever see you again?" Chills spread over her like it was wintertime.

"I told you before. I stay. Someone has to run CSA. The biggest threat to us all is Stilton. He wants to set up wars among the Affiliations with CSA to win it all. But, first, let's get you out. Mom drilled it into me that a brother always defends his sister. I have tried to do that for her, for you, all my life. Since Mae first called you at your job, getting you away from the Affiliations has been my only objective."

Skyla fell silent. She vowed to her deepest spirit, that she would not disappoint her big brother, who had never hurt her, never let her down. She knew she could build a defense, plead any case, defend her work against the claws and swipes yet to come from the committee. Words were her stash and she knew many words, old and new. "I won't fail you. I trust you," she said.

Tangier pushed the earring deep into his pants pocket. "We have to hustle now. Can't be late." He revved up the van and pulled out into the traffic. The route took them onto the boulevard where Tangier saw the familiar shape of the skinniest woman he knew.

He slowed the van to a creeping roll. Poppy huffed and puffed as she trotted next to him. "We are good to go whenever you get free from the Committee. Meet me at warehouse row, door number fifty-four. It's on the end. I will be waiting there for you."

"Got it." Tangier waved her a salute.

"POVs are on highest alert," said Poppy, "We are awash with CSA field agent scum sniffing around like rats in the garbage, uploading images from cesspools they never bothered to watch before. Blowing up Swillian's was emotional, but a huge mistake."

"He deserved it." Tangier slowed the van almost to a stop.

"It drew attention to the Outlier towns at a level we never had before. CSA blames Longhouse, so it's rounding up random Outlier people in droves. The agents terrify them into spilling secrets about us. But since we are as visible as air and fly like the raven, there is no catching us. But for you, no doubt CSA is following your every move." Poppy kept her pace with the slowed van. "You must pretend to knock me away. I will fake the fall. Make it look bad. You just keep on going. Good luck. Till soon. Now, shove me away."

Tangier flicked Poppy away from the van. In the van's side mirror, he watched her tuck and roll away from the street, lying still. He could see her prop herself up, leaning against the wall. She rolled up to her feet and began to take tiny steps. Then she put one hand on her forehead.

"She's limping," said Skyla watching from her side mirror.

"It's a fake. All for show." Tangier laughed.

"You sure?"

"I know Poppy. She's fine. You heard, she'll be waiting for us." Tangier sped up, nodding to the traffic control officer who waved his white gloves for him to hurry up.

The white van turn onto an exit route reserved only for CSA. Tangier drove straight on through the open gates, which closed behind him with quiet speed. Two heavily armed CSA agents retook their sentry position in front of the gates. Tangier knew them both. They were his agents, his crew.

Skyla watched the white stucco square building come into view behind lush green trees, a variety she had never seen. The glossy steps, polished like marble, led to a veranda shaded by a roof supported with tall fat pillars. Tangier led her through the thick door to a security checkpoint. A CSA agent, wearing thin, black gloves motioned for them to step through a glass partition to an immense rotunda. He pushed a button and a small buzzer sounded.

"What was the point of that charade?" Skyla whispered.

"Just show," said Tangier. "Follow me."

Skyla thought about her data stick, covered in a Faraday sheath, holding only musical playlists, safe in her shirt as she walked across a black and white mosaic floor. Massive tapestries hung on the walls, each one depicting the industries of their Affiliation. An enormous chandelier hung from the ceiling in the center of the rotunda. It was made of thousands of steel pointed tips representing the Custodian Service Agency who protected all the Affiliations. She stopped beside her big brother in front of an elliptical staircase made of pink and green granite.

"This is it. At the top of the stairs is the Executive Assembly Room. I will bring you in, but remain silent. The head won't reveal that he knows we are brother and sister because that gives him power. I will have proven my loyalty to CSA by bringing you in because they intend to kill you." Tangier put his hand on Skyla's arm. "Of course, that is not what will happen. So trust me. When I tell you to run, we run like the wind, together. It will be ok. I promise."

Skyla could not muster a word, but nodded. The clicks of Tangier's boots sounded like a clock counting down to the zero hour. She blocked that thought with a picture of her cozy apartment where Jaffa and Jaguar would be waiting for her.

She pictured Jaguar. Cats study their prey before they pounce. They consider all the angles of escape or entrapment. I shall be like him, she thought, vowing to reveal nothing by staying as motionless as a black panther, camouflaged by the night. I am not their prey. They are mine. I will eat them and spit out their bones. When Tangier opened the door to the meeting room, the bright light almost blinded her.

She had never seen such cool unfiltered light, pouring in from windows. She followed Tangier to the center of a long table. They stood facing five men seated on the other side. The light from the windows dimmed a fraction, confirming her hunch that it was fake. Natural light had not shined that bright anywhere since the Collapse, when the airborne dirt of endless wars shaded everything.

"The light too much for you, Skyla?" The man wearing a white collarless shirt with a red band around the neck folded his dark hands in front of himself. They all wore the same style shirt Tangier wore, but the fabric was white with the neckband color coded to the Affiliation the men led.

"No, sir." Skyla knew not to volunteer a thing, to answer only what was asked in tight, limited way. Her big brother had rehearsed her, well.

"You see that chair over by the door?" asked the man with red spidery veins that laced across his round, pug nose onto rosy cheeks. He wore a white shirt with a blue neckband. "When you are tired you may sit there, but understand when you do, then this discussion is finished. As long as you stand, we will interact."

"Yes, sir." Skyla scanned the creased faces of the men, dark or light, bald or not, a mixed bunch, but all lounging with the posh, easy air of the invincible. She noted how glib it was for them to toss the final decision to her about her own demise. Talk as long you live, live as long as you talk. When there is nothing more to say, you die.

"Tangier, you may go. You have fulfilled your duty. We, on behalf of the Affiliations, thank you. You are the pride of the CSA," said the man with gentle eyes, in a deep bass voice that echoed in the wide expanse of the room. His white shirt with red neckband shone all the brighter against his black skin.

"Sir." Tangier turned to Skyla and took her hand in a handshake. "Skyla." He tapped into her palm, their old childhood secret code, the number two. Skyla closed and opened her eyes twice, to signal back she understood. It meant they would always be a matched set, neither would leave each other in harm's way. They would always rescue each other. Neither of them had forgotten this in all these years since the orphanage.

Tangier's boots clicked as he walked toward the door by the chair, the upholstered, deep tufted chair with comfy cushions. With a brief glance at Skyla, he opened the door and closed it behind without a sound. In the hallway stood another CSA agent, Zinc, tall and buff, armed and ready. She winked at Tangier as he walked by. He gave her the slightest nod of the head and kept walking toward the interior staircase.

By the time he stepped onto the main floor of the rotunda, his wrist phone had vibrated an alert. He found an extreme alert from Riff who wanted to meet him at the Network Operations Center. He could feel his pulse race. Why the NOC? Why would Riff want him at the NOC? On this day, of all days? Without a change in his pace, Tangier exited the building and jumped in the van. His agents saluted him as they opened the gate for his departure. Once he reached the connecting route to the boulevard, he raced to the NOC at another border area between the Core and Periphery.

He tried not to think of Skyla and the difficult hour ahead of her in that room of jackals. He had not told her about the standing, for fear it would erode her confidence. His plan to return within the hour to create her escape was now in jeopardy. Whatever the hell this was about, Riff had better not be wasting his time. Tangier swung the van onto the side road and the NOC straight ahead. Riff stood by the CSA guards at the gate.

"Get in," Tangier barked, "This better be good."

"It is," said Riff. "It is."

CHAPTER THIRTY-ONE

COMMITTEE

As Skyla looked around the room, for a moment she thought she was in a bird cage. White stone falcons with fabulous wings, spread as if in flight, were scattered around on wood pedestals. Pink marble busts of the men who led the Collapse and formed the Affiliations were lined up like pigeons. Five shimmering silk tapestry panels, one for each Affiliation, covered the walls from floor to ceiling.

Skyla watched as a plain wood panel underneath the Affiliation Orange tapestry swung out like a door. A tall woman wearing a green waitress uniform wheeled out a cart full of pastries and cakes that smelled of honey, almonds and berries. She placed the goodies on the table and set small plates and napkins by each man. From a sterling silver pot, she poured steaming black coffee into china cups and saucers. Then she disappeared behind the door.

"Feel free to walk about." The man with a yellow neckband on his shirt leaned forward to stab a berry-filled crescent roll with his fingers. He wore blue eyeshadow on his heavy lidded eyes. His curvy hooknose, like the beak of a turkey vulture, twitched when he spoke. "I understand you have a cat. I like cats too. They are very clean. They keep the vermin down."

Skyla said nothing, waiting for a question. She did not intend to let them soften her up with friendly questions about pets only to come for the kill later when she was off her guard. Taking note of the space around her, she turned to take a few steps then pivot back to the starting place. She anticipated that a question would come soon and only then would she speak.

The man with a green neckband on his shirt broke the quiet. He had blonde fluffy hair that included his long sideburns. His plump folded hands rested on his potbelly.

"That was quite a blow you dealt that man. Your cunning impressed me. That took strength of will, to cause him permanent disability. Are you always so strong?" He turned his head one side and then the other to view his colleagues. "Tell me, are you always so strong?"

"Yes, sir." Skyla held back the response she wanted to scream: you swine, you watch that porn shit?

"That's it? That's all you have for me?" The man wearing green slapped his hands on the tabletop almost hitting his cup and saucer.

"Yes, sir." Skyla took a slight step to the side.

The Asian man with an orange neckband leaned back in his chair. The long braid of his queue hairstyle grazed his shoulder, visible along his neck. The smooth shaved front and sides of his head gleamed in the vivid light as if he had polished them. He pursed his lips and began to speak.

"It is obvious to me you have a strategy. I believe you intend to answer questions only, not make idle conversation. I believe you take this meeting with the seriousness it deserves. And it is serious. So, let me restart this proceeding." He flashed a half grin and slight nod to the man with the green neckband.

"Now, there is no doubt you are strong and smart. It takes both to write what you did. Let's talk about that, your study. What event first put you on the path of your inquiry in Behavior Studies? Why did you choose your topic and not, for example, the study of children's plays toys or the state of cinema? These would have contributed to our knowledge of the contemporary markets and product consumption. So, what caught your attention to a non-money power course of study?"

"Ads."

"What sort of ads? Ads are the source of life. What aspect of the ad?" The man with the orange neckband brushed his braid off his shoulder.

"Just an ad, an ad on my screen. I saw an ad for a product I had never spoken about to anyone."

He rubbed his neck with his finger, pulling the tight orange collar away from his throat. "What product? What was unusual about this product?"

"Nothing. That is what interested me." Skyla did not want to confess the product was a brush for grooming

Jaguar. All thoughts of him were tucked away for the moment.

"Enough of this game," said the man with the green neckband who ran his hand through his sticky hairdo. "I don't care what ad you saw, the ad itself is not the thing, is it? It could have been any ad." His voice held traces of an accent used by old, rich, white folks who got even richer by supporting the rise of the Affiliations. Skyla knew the accent from her work at Celebration Wholesale. And, this one just kept on speaking. "You see, you are not the only smart person in this room. This is not a question but a command. Explain your study choice."

She took a few steps and took an at ease stance. She tried to read their intent, their level of hostility; their level of defensiveness about the system they knew was under attack from her. "Sir, the image pushed onto my screen was a product I only saw in a store window, where I had paused for no more than a few seconds to read the price tag. POVs must have seen me stop, sent the data somewhere, to someone or thing that connected my stopping with product desire and through some algorithm, pushed the ad through to me. The level of surveillance and system integration that can make this happen impressed me. But there is nothing unusual about it. So I began to study it."

The man with the blue neckband wiped his mouth with a napkin and folded it back into a square. He placed it next to his plate still filled with a stack of almond cookies. He waved his pale, ice colored hand to the others as if to stop their comments and assume control. He adjusted his shirt and aligned the cuffs of his sleeves to be square with his wrists. His grey hair just brushed the top of the blue band at the back of his neck.

"I read your words. You are not cooperating with the Committee. This is your chance to defend the many words you have written, some very powerful, some rare, but they are full of accusation and implication. All these words came from your viewing an ad? Did you ever consider the words you selected could be read as treason? In this Committee, all words are sacred words. You, however, defied the Rules of the Words. Free speech is not any speech. This is a criminal act."

"I am no criminal. I am a graduate student attempting to finish my degree." Skyla sensed the tone growing darker and that she would have to change her strategy. She grabbed a lock of hair and began to twist it.

"That may be, but you challenged the very ruling order of our society," said the man with the blue neckband as rosy splotches began to erupt on his pale face.

"I did not challenge the ruling order. My aim was to explain it, to show how a non-government power elite reduced a centuries old system of citizen and country to a memory. I hoped to answer how the political leaders, like yourselves, were able to build and spread the mass appeal of your ruling class world view to create the support of fans who follow you." Skyla caught a glimpse of herself in the reflection from a window and stopped twisting her hair just before pulling it into a knot. Her hand dropped to her side.

"Where are you getting these words? Whose words have you taken for your own agenda?" The man with the blue neckband drew back his face and his skin flushed deep red. His eyes bulged as if he had seen a ghost. "These words belong to the dead."

"I did not take words. I did not write an agenda. I wrote my own chapters. So, of course I used lots of words." Skyla kept her answer tight because she began to worry about Tangier. He was supposed to have returned by now. She realized dragging this hearing on was the only way to buy more time. What came next, she didn't know.

"I read your bibliography," said the man with the orange neckband. "I saw references for Gramsci, Mills, Foucault, Greenwald, and Klein. Heady stuff these classics, these writings of dead people who failed to foresee the future. But, take the word "hegemony." Isn't that the real point of your work? You know, wasn't it Marx who said something like the ruling ideas of each era have always been the ideas of its ruling class?"

"Yes, sir." Skyla felt a chill come over her. "Something to that effect."

"But who really comes to mind with that word, hegemony?" he continued. "I read those works too, although very long ago."

"Gramsci. He wrote that if the ruling class can convince the rest of the people that their ideology or rules in your case, are good for all classes, then the ruling class can control all the others, reducing any thought of class struggle or revolution. So, hegemony, rule by a small power elite not only by force but by ideas."

"Are you mixing your theorists? "Power elite," wasn't that Mills?"

"They all contribute to the study," said Skyla.

"You are being coy. You did not just write a travelogue down memory lane, you questioned the righteousness of our very social order. You questioned money power itself and the sacred cult of individualism, of the redemptive pleasure of continuous consumption. And you lumped us all together in the noxious term Big Data." The man with the orange neckband soaked in the nods of agreement from the other members of the committee.

"All this rage came from a push ad on a screen?" asked the chiseled man with black walnut skin wearing the red neckband. "I don't believe that. This study reads like a manifesto, a call to action."

"Sir, it is nothing more than applying social theory to post collapse everyday life. I haven't even written the conclusion. So it's wrong to call my work a manifesto. Plus, the only people who have read it are my professors." She began to pace the length of the table, pausing at the ends now and then to shift her weight. Her legs no longer felt nimble but sluggish and thick.

She brushed her hand against the knot of her shirt, to feel her data stick, where she had saved the conclusion. Jaffa had warned her that the last chapter carried personal risk if discovered by CSA. He had told her that highlighting how the countries were abolished, not by a working-class revolution, but an ideological ruling class takeover by extreme capitalists cut too close for comfort. She knew the risk but stepped into the cyber minefield anyway.

She had reached a point of no return, she had told Jaffa, a point where what she had written so far was damning enough. All she had left was to show how the Affiliations constructed an absolute bureaucracy, a closed loop, with no one person in charge that chugged along in an endless way. The Affiliations, together or separately, had imprisoned the people into eternal consumption and for themselves, eternal profit. This monstrosity need, a name, she told Jaffa. She christened it Big Data.

The scraping of metal tips on the floor shattered her momentary drift from the farce of the moment. She braced herself for the oncoming assault.

The man with the red neckband sat very erect and leaned toward her. "You quote some nonsense from another relic of the past, Simmel, about city life and alienation. You suggested that elements of this can be found in the Periphery and Outlier towns." He focused a cold laser stare at Skyla. "What you fail to understand is that we don't care about people who choose to live there. It is up to each individual to stay in the Core, or earn their way to the Core, or not. Our job is to protect the integrity and safety of the Core for those who worked hard to get there and stay there."

Skyla said nothing, biting her tongue, wishing she could counter his uninspired blather. She wanted to sling back at him, how, aspirational prosperity was not a choice, but the sole method of survival across the world. Endless work for endless consumption, for endless profit by the Affiliations, for Big Data. A lifetime of work in the Periphery would never get anyone to the Core because it wasn't only about spending money units. Following extra special Rules got you there. One wrong move, one mistake, and you are spewed out so fast, you can't even imagine you've landed in an Outlier town, poor as your new destiny. She studied the face of the man with the red neckband, of Affiliation Red, the most powerful of them, the home of CSA and the military apparatus. His shirt neckband reminded her of Tangier's red shirt, the same CSA shade of red. She didn't forget he knew their secret.

The man with the red neckband placed one hand over his heart, and stood up, rigid as a statue. He pounded away with his sermon. "As for surveillance, that is how we keep the rules. That is how we enforce the words approved by this committee. 'Hegemony' is not an approved word. 'Alienation' is not an approved word. 'Revolution' is not an approved word. 'Takeover' is not an approved word. 'Big Data' is not even in our dictionary; therefore, it does not exist. It is, therefore, blasphemy. These words and others you used are outside the approved vocabulary set forth by the Affiliations for the purpose of maintaining markets and consumption and money power. They cannot be part of any presentation, verbal or written." He sat down and placed both sinewy hands, palms down on the table. "Using them, invoking them, is a crime. You should be afraid."

The man with the blue neckband coaxed Skyla with a slight smile and brushed his colleagues off with a wave of his hand. "Before you go all CSA on us, I want to ask the poor girl one more question. I, for one, have enjoyed this sparring. Skyla, tell me what do you think about Foucault? I rather like that old codger. That idea of his about power belonging to the group who controls the words is quite clever. He could have been a member of this very Rules of Words Committee. Wouldn't you agree?"

"His writings showed another way to analyze social power. I wouldn't know if he'd want to be a member of your Committee." She was grateful for the sudden change in tone, from red hot to blue cool, but time was running out. She could stand for a while longer, but with the pastries all but gone and the coffee pot almost empty the Rules of Words Committee would not wait forever. Where was Tangier? She had a creeping sense that something had gone very wrong.

"So, you don't think much of the Committee? You are not scared by our request for you to appear before us?" The man with the yellow neckband sniffed a couple times before digging out a handkerchief to wipe his beak.

"I have been answering your questions."

"Yes, you have. Although, I imagine you do not think much of Affiliation Yellow. After all, we administer the pest control program, the one what sends doctors, like your bleeding-heart boyfriend, to the Outlier towns, to keep a lid on diseases that could spread to the Core."

"I hadn't thought about it one way or the other." Skyla shrugged. She hoped this whole phony hearing would not degenerate into which Affiliation was the best. It didn't matter to her which one was the best. They were each the worst.

"Have you ever heard of Piketty?" The man with the yellow neckband blew his beak again. "Have you?"

"Yes, sir. An early twenty-first century economist."

"And, what was his thesis?"

Skyla thought for a moment. He was not as radical as Polanyi, another theorist she had read, but now was not the time for that debate. She glanced around the room and shrugged. "Trickle down doesn't work."

"There, there you have it." The man with the yellow neckband stood up and pointed at Skyla. "She is not so clever. She still doesn't realize that we don't care! We never intended for anything to trickle down. Nothing about our system has to do with care for anyone. Only the most industrious or clever or beautiful reap the rewards of money power through continuous production and consumption to serve the market, accumulating all the prosperity money power can buy. We don't care if anything trickles down. We are not providing for anyone. Each individual is on his or her own and if he or she doesn't follow the rules, our rules, he or she is out. Fast death by execution or slow death in the Outlier towns. It's a choice. We are not mean. Just tidy."

The empty chair, which meant surrender, the point at which Skyla called a halt to this charade of men posing as thinkers, waited for her. She took a few steps away from it and then back towards it. With a sudden burst of insight, she turned facing the men straight on and said, "You may be the members of the Rules of Words Committee, but you are not in charge. You are just minions of the hidden, truly powerful bosses. They are Big Data. You're just staff."

The man with the yellow neckband choked on his sip of coffee spraying spit and liquid everywhere. The man with the red neckband stood and boomed, "Silence. Mighty brave for a girl who has been abandoned to her fate. Your brother, Tangier, a senior, loyal CSA agent, followed orders and procured you to us. He will get a promotion. We will get rid of you. Life in Cap City will go on and no one will miss you." None of the men moved, frozen in position. The man with the red neckband waved to the black globe hanging in the middle of the room, the POVs lens soaking in these proceedings like it did all human activity around the globe.

A boot pushed open the entry door. Stilton strode in, dressed in a red shirt identical to Tangier's shirt. His steel tipped toes clicked away on the granite floor. "Sir." Stilton stopped in front of the man with the red neckband and saluted.

"Take this miserable turncoat to my personal holding pen. Find any record of her study and destroy it. She is a traitor to the Affiliations and the global order." The man with the red neckband stopped for a moment. "Kill any people associated with her. Find her cat and kill it, too." He turned to Skyla and leaned over the tabletop. "Now, do you still think we are minions? Do you still think we are powerless puppets dancing around to the whim of secret puppet masters?"

"I think you doth protest too much." She scowled at the pretentious men but took note of Stilton, the next threat.

"Where do you get such words?" The man with the green neckband coughed on his own words as he struggled to his feet.

"Shakespeare. Another dead poet from another age," answered the man with the blue neckband. "It's almost a shame; she is so bright, so capable. But, my darling, and you are a darling, you are so deadly to all that we are." He shook his head but extended his hand to the man with red neckband. "You are correct, of course, she and all trace of her must be destroyed."

CSA's top man pointed toward Skyla and shouted, "Senior Agent Stilton. Take her away."

The members of the Rules of Words Committee were all standing like sheep, Skyla thought. She spied the door behind the chair, calculating her odds of running to the chair, using it to block Stilton and run away. There were no odds, she guessed, only luck if it broke her way. She could outrun Stilton, but not outrun a bullet. She sent a burst of love and energy to the boys she loved, wishing them safety and asking Jaguar to become the familiar of Jaffa, in her place. She took a gauge of Stilton's place in the room. Skyla bolted toward the chair, flung it at Stilton catching him in the shin. She found the doorknob and pushed through the door.

Zinc closed the door behind Skyla and bolted it shut. Stilton banged on it and tried to pry it open. They could hear him open fire on the door to break through. Without looking back, the CSA agent grabbed Skyla's arm and pulled her to the left, leading her with running steps to another staircase, used by servants and CSA agents. "Longhouse," she whispered to Skyla, as she shot out any lenses with her gun.

"Where's Tangier," Skyla whispered back.

"Don't know. Don't worry. He survives everything." The agent pulled Skyla to the side and down an exterior path toward the gate. "He improvises the hell out of everything."

They approached the gate and the agents loyal to Tangier. Out of nowhere, half a dozen armed drones flew at close range overhead into sight. Zinc took her rifle and shot at them, knocking them out of the sky like a skeet shooter. She swapped the empty magazine for a new one and opened fire at the gate agents. They fell from Zinc's bullet spray. She entered the code to open the gate. When they were through, she entered it again to close them. By then the guards had sat up and waved her on. "Blanks," said Zinc. "They will have had the POVs video on loop so nothing will show. They are clever bastards."

"What about you? You are done with CSA for good, now," said Skyla.

"I am a plant. I am not CSA. Longhouse. I smuggled in with a food truck that Tangier had arranged. You don't recognize me. Lots of costumes were the order of today. I was the server who brought in the snacks to those buffoons. I saw you in there. You were strong. I heard everything. You need to get to the Keep. That's where the real work will begin."

"The real work?" Skyla cursed herself again for being so insulated. She had been deaf to the sounds of human resistance to Big Data.

"You know from your work that this system cannot last. Big Data will fight to defend it. War will come between Big Data and Longhouse for control of the planet with you leading it from the Keep and Tangier leading from here."

Zinc and Skyla cowered in the shadows as they made their way toward safety. "My work points to the potential of resistance, but I never claimed to be member, much less a leader, of any real resistance." Skyla jumped a wall with Zinc behind her.

"Sometimes destiny comes to you. Call it karma, call it a visitation by the spirits of the ancients. You are only now awakening to your time, your role in Longhouse." Zinc paused to take a long look at her charge. "You and Jaffa are Haudenosaunee. His grandmother, Clan Mother Genesee leads Longhouse. The Keep is our people's home, our land. The Haudenosaunee Confederacy is centuries old. The ways of our people show that societies don't have to live like this. Someday I hope to get to the Keep."

"What are you talking about? Jaffa? Clan Mother Genesee? All I know from Tangier is that we have distant relatives in the Keep." Skyla put her hand on Zinc's arm and held it steady. "I want to get to Jaffa and my cat, Jaguar, like my brother promised. I don't care about anything else. I will go to the Keep but I am not a leader or a teacher. Got it?"

"Yeah." Zinc guided her charge across the boulevard, into a trash alley. She shed her uniform and burned it in a pile of trash. Next came the red-haired wig and a complete face mask. She placed it on the ground and poured water from her canteen over it. A few sizzles and the mask and wig dissolved into the dirt. "Let's go. Poppy is waiting in warehouse row."

Skyla stuck close to Zinc, dressed in tight pants and black sweatshirt with a thin hood. Warehouse row, a criminal's hangout, was haunted by the ghosts of their victims. It bred terror among the Outlier town residents, for the few who ventured into it never returned.

Skyla replayed the hollow statements of the pompous Affiliation leaders over and over in her head. Outrage rose up in her blood heating her core until she could no longer breath. She gasped for air to regain her cool that brought along with it, a reckoning, a reality she could not ignore. She sucked in the new-found grit, and relinquished the comfortable role of innocent student. She embraced a new role as a traitor, an enemy, the nemesis to Big Data. She could weaponize words for a call to action against Big Data, but she would need a place to work far from its all-encompassing reach. Mae Carrington had been right all along; she had to get to the Keep. Skyla ran like the wind, behind Zinc, just as Tangier told her to do. He had never lied to her. Run like the wind.

DISTRACTION

"Of all the god damned times to send me an alert," said Tangier. To him, Riff was an irritating groundhog, who popped up in the most inconvenient times.

"I have to show you something, an irregularity I found," said Riff, sweat pooling at his temples.

"What are you talking about? Why the secrecy? Why didn't you tell Stilton? He's your superior officer, not me" Tangier revved up the van. "We have to go in?"

"Yes, sir. I have to show you at a terminal." Riff felt his heart race but his options were few. He'd hedged his life on Tangier as the better bet for surviving this ordeal.

Tangier drove past the gate, to the plain grey cement block building. Only those with a special access code could get in. Few living people worked there, since everything had been automated a long time ago.

When he reached the front door, he leaned an eye to a retinal scan and it swung open. Riff followed like a lap dog behind its master.

The small entry way was the endpoint for several hallways leading to large conference rooms. The walls were covered with electronic maps of the earth, of solar systems, and rows of computer mainframes. A technician stepped out into the entryway. "CSA? How can I help you?"

"Senior Field Agent Tangier. I need to use a terminal for a classified op." He pointed to an empty room with three monitors.

"Anything you want," said the technician, dressed in a blue jumpsuit including shoe covers.

"Thanks." Tangier stepped into the room and closed the door behind Riff. "Now, spit it out. It better be good."

"Sir, I noticed an anomaly in the satellite path timing and…."

Tangier grabbed Riff by the collar and pulled him close. "What the hell do you do all day? Just troll through every living bit of data for shit on someone? What are you going to do with your little basket of secrets anyway? Blackmail people?" Tangier shoved him away and wiped his hand on his pants leg.

"Sir, I wasn't spying. I think I caused the anomaly." Riff winced at his own words.

"You caused an anomaly? Why were you looking at satellite timing in the first place?" Tangier sat down at a terminal and clicked at the keyboard. He clicked and clicked until he was satisfied that the NOC's one hour offline setup that only he, presumably Jaffa by now, and the few Longhouse leaders knew about was undamaged, and permanent. He spun around in his chair to face Riff.

"I hid a video in the Satellite system," said Riff. All color drained from his face.

"Why would you do that?"

"Sir, it is a video of Senior Agent Stilton executing a member of the board of Affiliation Yellow. A Core member, a member whose father runs the Affiliation."

"Riff. Why would he do that?"

"They argued about something. Stilton shot him in the garage of the CSA headquarters. His name was Swillian." Blood began to flow back into Riff's face, his confidence returning due to Tangier's slow and steady tone of voice.

"Swillian? Why were you in the garage?"

"I was just leaving and heard Swillian's racer car screech to a halt and then loud voices. I turned even though it was not my business, but you know in CSA everything is our business. I looked. Swillian was drunk and armed with a gun. I saw Stilton shoot him stone cold dead."

"What made you record it?"

"Habit. I record everything. But I realized Stilton would edit the surveillance file once he got upstairs. He would get away with murder. Murder of an Affiliation board member. Of course, I hid it far away in an unlikely place."

"The Satellite data bases. That is awfully far from where Stilton would look for it. Did he see you there?"

"He heard something and followed me. He confronted me outside. I swore there was nothing. He never found it."

"Which brings us to today." Tangier sat in the chair with his arms crossed. He listened to every detail even as he began to formulate another plan. Riff could be useful to him.

"I heard Stilton say early this morning that this was his day, that big things for CSA would start soon. He just had to get rid of a big headache for the Affiliations. I worried that he meant get rid of me, even though I am nothing at all. Goes to show you, we all want to be a little bit important. Anyway, I went to check my hidden file and then I detected an unsteadiness in the time sequence. If I did that with my file, I'd get discovered, and I figured it was all over for me."

"Yes. I am getting the sense that this is all about you," said Tangier.

"So, I called you. To tell you that Stilton is a murderer, and I have proof. Second, to make sure that I didn't screw up the Satellites. And the last thing I figured out is that Stilton intends to kill Skyla."

Tangier stood up and pushed the chair back to the desk. "The Satellites are fine. You have a choice to make right now, Riff. You have to choose me or Stilton. No CSA agent should be allowed to murder at will for his or her own motives. Stilton will try to kill Skyla to secure his future and be promoted within the agency. She is my sister, but you knew that, didn't you? I'll stop him. But there is something bigger. He's planning for CSA to launch a takeover of all Affiliations. This we can't let him do. We live with rules now, as unjust as they are, which he would end. Can you imagine the chaos with no rules, and only his and his goons' desires? With your file, you and I can take him down."

Riff stood frozen still. "I already chose you."

Tangier slapped him on the back. "Riff that is the smartest decision you will make in your life. Now, I need to rescue my sister from him." His wrist phone lit up with a signal from Zinc that she had Skyla. The plan was still a go.

Riff opened the door and followed Tangier back out to the CSA van. Tangier sped away from the NOC toward warehouse row, where Poppy had assembled the coven. He regarded the chunky, sweaty Riff as a new asset, an agent with digital skills he could put to good use. It would be a long time if ever that he brought Riff into Longhouse. For now, the safety of that one hour of privacy, set by the lunar calendar, with the satellites acting as guardians was still there. Tangier realized how fragile the setup was, for if Riff could come close to noticing a problem, someone else might too. Technology evolves, he knew, and the safety measures would have to evolve too. He would revisit this situation another day. For now, he turned to the tasks ahead, tricky, dangerous, and with lifelong effects. It would be the last day he would see his sister and Jaffa for many years. The addition of Riff, although unexpected, strengthened his position within CSA. He turned into a trash alley and saw drones flying overhead in formation.

"Out. We go on foot." Tangier jumped out of the van he tucked into a corner. "Armed and alert."

"Yes, sir." Riff drew the gun from his pocket.

They disappeared into the dank, dark, underworld of the Outlier town, their destination, Warehouse Row.

CHAPTER THIRTY-THREE

MASSACRE

Stilton signaled for drones to swarm the skies, confident he would find the phony agent and Skyla. He had to find them and kill them or be executed for incompetence. On his way, back to the room where the Rules of Words Committee members sat stunned and in disarray, he replayed the last week's events. Skyla was Tangier's sister, a possibility that came to him only yesterday. He had dismissed their identical last names as coincidence. He assumed Tangier's last name was an assigned random artifact like his own from the orphanage. Listening in on the proceedings, he had heard the head of the Committee confirm it just now. Stunned by his own incompetence, he could not recall ever seeing her at the orphanage. She had protection, a cover, someone deflecting any attention paid toward her all those years. She had been taught by someone to avoid POVs, any lenses or cyber trails by blending in.

Only because a rat professor finked her out did she become important to the Rules of Words Committee. Riff's little data dumping only confirmed what CSA already knew. She would have been disposed of already if not for Tangier's insistence that he bring her in. He took his lovely time too, Stilton thought, his hand paused on the doorknob of the broken door.

A picture of Swillian flashed in his head, a reminder of the dead body, chemically dissolved, never to be found. Riff, his little fat weak link, could be controlled, he knew, and could not be the CSA traitor. Before he could review anymore, he opened the door. He had to answer the shouts of the men with colored neckbands.

"Do you have her in custody?" The CSA director spoke with the calm of the devil.

"No, sir. She got away. But we'll get her. I have activated a search and destroy mission using all methods. It will not take too much time." Stilton stood very straight.

"Search and rescue, not destroy. I want you to bring her to me. Tonight. Here." The CSA director stood up, so close to Stilton that he breathed his stinky breath into his unflinching face.

"Yes, sir." Stilton turned on his heel and strode out the door. He stopped just before the exit of the building and tapped his wrist screen to search for Riff but he was offline. "You little rat. Where are you? Maybe you are the traitor. Maybe you are working for the traitor."

Cursing himself for being snowed by Tangier, he flung open the door and left without a word. Senior Field Agent

Tangier had been playing him all along just like he would when they lived at the orphanage. For a moment, he envied Tangier and Skyla, the love between these siblings survived the Collapse and the rise of the Affiliations. He, Perdu Stilton, had only an agency and the agents that filled its ranks like clones. But, he had ambition. No brother/sister act could stop his ascent to power.

He jumped into the Phantom and punched at the screen to bring up the latest visual of Tangier's location. The screen showed a white van, abandoned in a trash alley. A field agent stood by the open back door. Empty. Stilton barked the coordinates to the Phantom, which sped off at his command. The location of the van on the edge of the Outlier camp town did little to point the direction Tangier might have taken. As expected, none of the Outlier people saw anything or heard anything.

Stilton pulled up behind the van and stopped. He bolted from the car to an agent standing next to the van. "What have you got?"

"Nothing sir. No one around here saw anything," said the agent.

"Do you think they would tell you if they did? Did you offer them any incentive to talk?"

"Incentive?"

"Yes. Watch and learn." Stilton looked around the alley and located one lens and one monitor box. He shot them to pieces. "Now. Who will talk?"

The people in the alley were silent. A few tried to dis-appear into the shadows. Stilton began to march back and forth. Without a warning, he stopped in front of an old woman who was leaning against a wall. "Did you see who got out of this van?" The woman half opened her eyes and shook her head no. Stilton raised his weapon and shot her point blank in the chest. Her body slumped to the ground. "Who's next?"

He stepped further along the alley only to be met with more silence. Stilton turned to go back to the abandoned van. He shot at anyone unlucky enough to be there along the way.

The pigeons scattered, windows were pulled shut, quiet fell but for the drizzle hitting the metal roofs. The field agent stood by the van, witness to a mass murder he would never dare report.

Stilton paused by the van and faced another direction. He leaned over toward a coughing noise and pulled a scruffy boy, a skinny teenager, out of the shade. He could see a smaller pale child who was wrapped with a filthy blanket. "Did you see who left this van?" he asked the teenager. "I'll help you think." Stilton pointed his pistol at the small child's head.

The teenager raised two fingers. "Two men," he said barely loud enough to be a whisper.

"Men? You sure? Not women?" Stilton kept his gun aimed at the small child.

"Men. Two," said the teenager who pointed in the direction they took away from the van and deep into the Outlier town.

Stilton nodded. He raised his gun and shot the small child first and then the teenager with two swift moves. They fell onto each other in a heap.

He stood and watched the blood ooze from the wounds and soak the blanket, but he felt nothing. They were not his affair, not his assignment. They were irrelevant. Two men were relevant and that was all. He turned to the field agent and said, "Get this van out of here. I am going in alone."

"Yes, sir. But you won't be alone. POVs and CSA are always with you." The field agent jumped into the van, pleased that he remembered to quote the required motto to this senior officer. He wondered when Stilton would come after him, the only witness to his carnage.

Stilton watched the van leave. I should have killed that guy, he thought. He looked around at the bodies slumped into the street. He pulled up his collar and wiped the mud from his steel tipped boots on a cloth from the trunk of the Phantom waiting nearby. The black speedster could not fit in the narrow trash alleys, so Stilton loaded himself with ammo, extra guns, and grenades. Low level weapons were still lethal and effective. He programed the Phantom to return to his garage and sent it off.

He aimed for warehouse row. Stilton craved the coming fight. His most formidable adversary, Tangier, would buckle when he, Senior Agent Stilton, would go after Skyla first. Skyla was Tangier's pet, and pets were always the weak link.

CHAPTER THIRTY-FOUR

DEPARTURE

Jaffa woke to the smell of hot coffee and the clinking of mugs in the kitchen. Grenadine had set them on a table next to a plate of small rolls. His grandmother still slept on the couch, with Jaguar curled up in her legs. Rosario and Genesee stood whispering together in front of the console of monitors and weapons stash. A grey canvas backpack stuffed to the rim with medical supplies leaned against the wall by the door. It did not seem real that today he and Skyla would leave the world they knew forever. It was leave or be killed. It was a life sentence without parole in the Keep. They could never come back.

Jaffa saw Poe perched on Genesee's shoulder. He reached over and stroked Jaguar without waking Zeinab.

"Pretty boy. Pretty boy." Poe's chatter drew Jaguar's attention, who raised and lowered his tail.

"Hush, Poe." Genesee slid her hand down his back. "Good morning, Jaffa."

"Good morning, Genesee. I must ask you a question."

"Of course, anything."

"When will you return back to the Keep?" Jaffa took a cup of coffee from the table.

"Someday. There is work to be done here." Genesee studied his face. "Much work. The day approaches."

"Yes, but what does that mean?"

"There will be war between us and them. It is coming. We are the last civilization that is not controlled by the Affiliations. You will see when you get there. Our people are not backward. They are forward. You will see how life can happen without hurting the earth or each other. You'll see for yourself. You and Skyla know this world and now will learn about a new one. Together you will protect what we hold dear."

"What we hold dear?" asked Jaffa. "Neither Skyla nor I know what you hold dear. How could we?"

"You're right. Let me tell you now." Genesee paused to rub Poe. "What we hold dear is our relationships to each other and Turtle Island, our Mother Earth. We must protect them from all types of POVs lenses, from the culture of money power, and from Big Data. We have survived with Haudenosaunee beliefs and traditions that reject money power, aspiration prosperity, and endless consumption that only strips the planet bare. Big Data brings only starvation and extinction."

"Genesee, does the Keep have a military? How can you speak of war against the Affiliations and their arsenals of chemical, nuclear, and cyber war machines?" Jaffa glanced at Zeinab, his sleeping grandmother. A wave of love welled up inside of him and unspeakable sadness at the thought of leaving her forever, alone in her tiny apartment.

Genesee put her hand on Jaffa's shoulder and pulled him toward the consoles. "We have warriors. We have Longhouse. I speak to the Keep from here all the time. We will speak to each other. Zeinab is too frail to make the trip with you, I fear. The most I can give you is the occasional chat with her."

"No. I'll take her with me. I'll see that she gets there with us. I cannot leave her alone. CSA will kill her. You know that, and I know that. She cannot stay with you. Look around this place. Command central is no place for her. She comes with me or I don't go."

"What will Skyla do? You know her situation."

"We'll work it out. We always do."

Genesee drew Jaffa close and hugged him like a grandmother. "My pretty boy, I watched you from afar. You are like your father. So kind. Always kind." She let him go and turned to Rosario. "Wake Zeinab. Get her ready for a tough trip."

"It is the right thing, Genesee," said Rosario, "It is the right thing.

Grenadine went to Zeinab and sat on the edge of the couch with a steamy cup of coffee. The steam drifted across her face and Zeinab opened her eyes. "Well, aren't you the pretty one, bringing me coffee. What service."

"Get up. Come on. You are going with your grandson to the Keep. You will need to be strong. The trek is long, the last part anyway. You need to wear layers of clothes and boots." Grenadine stood up and looked at Jaguar. "Aren't you the lucky one, Jaguar. You get to go, too."

Zeinab held the coffee cup in her hands and found Jaffa's face. "Jaffa, you don't have to take me with you."

"You are coming with us. There's no discussion. Let's get you ready. Jaguar will ride along with you in a sling. I'll make a cover for it."

"He won't jump out?" Zeinab tapped him on the head.

"He'll stay put. He is used to riding around with Skyla in a sling. My guess is that he knows already he will be seeing her soon."

Before another word was exchanged in the room of brave fighters, the sound of drone swarms filled the air. The screen that monitors the daily soap opera shows and infomercials suddenly switched to a CSA announcement complete with pictures and orders to turn in the suspects shown. Genesee closed the console behind the false wall and all evidence of planning was shoved out of view. Jaffa checked the locks on the paper covered windows and the door to be sure they were secure.

Meanwhile, Rosario stroked Jaguar then placed him in front of two bowls. He slurped up the fish and gulped some water. She put tins of fish into the folds of the sling she had designed for his journey.

Genesee signaled for everyone to be still. The drones swirled past their door and up over the roof. The lens outside on a next door building that was aimed toward the shack continued to show a video loop. "It won't show the drones," whispered Grenadine.

Genesee shrugged. "We must wait. I doubt an agent in CSA headquarters will track them to that degree of precision. The sound will trick them into thinking they see drones."

The sounds grew faint. The regular programming streamed back to life on the screen.

Jaffa knew he needed to speed things up. The sooner they were gone, the safer for Genesee and her posse. He fitted Rosario's sling over Zeinab's head and shoulder, to rest on her side. Her cargo pants were stuffed with extra socks and rolled up t-shirts. He slid a hooded windbreaker over it all, the final top layer over the sling. Jaguar leapt into his arms and nestled into the sling, kneading the folds just the way he did when riding with Skyla. Jaffa zipped up the windbreaker high enough to protect Zeinab and hide Jaguar. He grabbed the stuffed backpack and hoisted it onto his shoulders, ready for battle. He intended to win this one.

He tapped his new Longhouse password, canoe, on the wall and Genesee smiled. She tapped back her reply, canoe home. They embraced as grandmother and grandson, as Clan Mother and warrior. "Now go. Warehouse Row is not so far, but you must move slowly. CSA and POVs will be on high alert."

"My dearest friends." Zeinab could not speak more than this. She followed Jaffa through a trap door that opened to a staircase that led to the tunnels. Jaguar lay still in her protection as she climbed down the stairs.

Genesee secured the door with a lock. She turned to Grenadine and Rosario, who stood in silence. "We have done all we could." Poe alighted on Rosario's out stretched hand. The whirr from the drones swarmed overhead again.

CHAPTER THIRTY-FIVE

WAREHOUSE 54

Zinc and Skyla snuck into the dark corners of the Outlier towns flitting like sparrows from trash heaps to shacks to vast open landfills. The thick stench made it difficult to breathe. The sun had disappeared from view. The darkness gave them cover but also blocked their ability to see ahead. Shapes that moved could be CSA agents. The lenses of POVs did not worry them as much as the squadrons of field agents deployed by CSA headquarters. Skyla pointed toward the row of square buildings that made up the edge of warehouse row. Zinc nodded and with her hand motioned them to go forward.

The rotting concrete and wood buildings once housed grain and livestock from all over the world. The abandoned, empty metal shipping containers stacked nearby, made the perfect hideouts for gangs and thieves. Together or alone, they ruled the underground economy that served the Outlier towns. They trafficked in everything—human, animal or objects—whatever to use in trade. Zinc detested Warehouse Row, but knew that Longhouse could hide here from CSA and Big Data.

"Look. 54." Zinc snaked her way around a trash heap. "We'll go in the back."

Skyla followed Zinc, careful not to let any distance grow between them. She kept watch behind them. They found a manhole cover hidden in part by a stack of wood. Zinc tapped "SOS." A tapping "clear" returned. Together they wrested the heavy metal disc up and away. Skyla climbed down into the shaft while Zinc pulled the cover back over the hole. She followed down behind Skyla to a tunnel. A soft light shone from the end. They stepped as fast as they could toward the opening to a room.

Poppy stood in the cramped room next to a table of guns, knives, and throwing stars covered with sharp points. "You made it." She hugged Zinc. "Skyla, good to see you outside a moving van. Jaffa, the little puppy, has been a demon looking for you."

"I was trying to find Jaffa when all this insanity broke loose. Did you see Jaguar?"

"He's with Jaffa," said Poppy, "you'll see them both soon. They're coming here." Poppy motioned to them to sit on a crate and then she continued to speak. "Once he's here, you'll leave. Zinc will escort you to the edge of the Outlier town. There, you'll find a Longhouse agent with an old hovercraft. It's so old it can't be tracked. You'll be taken deep into the hinterlands, across the dust bowls, the polluted lakes, to the mountains. From there you must go through the mountains on foot. You have only one hour to get to the Keep boundary. Just get to the boundary and the people will receive you. You'll be safe."

"It sounds straight forward, but CSA and POVs will hunt for you as far as the hinterlands," said Zinc. "You won't be safe until inside the Keep." She put her hand on Skyla's arm. "If you are caught, you'll be killed on sight. All of you. Disappeared."

"Then, we better not get caught." Skyla felt the data stick in her shirt knot. "I brought all this down on everyone because I wrote about the Affiliations. I regret it."

"Don't be so pitiful. CSA has been tightening its grip on us all with POVs, the drones, the swarms, and the field agents. You and all of us were bound to stray into its path of destruction. It was a matter of time," said Poppy. "You just do your part from the Keep."

"Yes, but what is my part? I don't know my part." Skyla said.

"Your part?" asked Zinc. "Why, your part is to write, to analyze, to show how the machine of the Affiliations works and what we must do to avoid the paths that led to them. We want to stay true to our own ways You will learn from our old people, study their stories, and help us meet the future. Genesee says it's time for the next great woman, a peacemaker, to come forth."

"What are you talking about? Where is this coming from?" Skyla squinted her eyes as if shutting out the dim light would shut out the panic. "I don't fit any of this."

"You will soon," said Zinc putting her arm around her. "It'll be clear once you are home."

Skyla pulled away and forced a short nod. Poppy looked up from Skyla and held her hand up to silence any talk. She pointed toward the tunnel.

Crouching into the corner out of sight, Zinc put her gun on her knee and stood without a sound. The shuffle of footsteps grew louder. Poppy signaled for Zinc to fire on her command only. The footsteps stopped but the shadows of two people, one tall, one short fell across the door threshold. The tall shadow moved closer until a man filled the doorway.

"Jaffa!" Skyla sprang up from the crate and rushed to him. She flung her arms around him as he lifted her off the ground, her knees wrapping around his hips. Her lips found his and she did not hold back her fierce desire. She needed to breathe with him, to feel his chest rise and fall against her own. All the filth and horror of the last few days melted away as he held her close. She held him as tight as she could.

Jaffa eased her down without a sound, still holding her thick black hair in his hands. He raised her face to his once more and kissed her. He took Skyla's hand and turned her toward the doorway. "Grandma. Come on. It's safe. Come on through." Jaffa reached for Zeinab whose red face and heavy breaths could not disguise her tiredness.

"Zeinab!" Skyla's eyes opened wide above a smile as she stepped toward her. "Jaffa. I love you even more for bringing her."

"Skyla." Zeinab reached for Skyla's hands and pulled them to her waist. "Someone has been missing you fierce." She pulled back the sling exposing the black fur of Skyla's familiar.

"Jaguar, my little boy." Skyla lifted him out of the sling and into her arms. His mighty motor began to hum and he nuzzled his face into hers. She turned to Jaffa. "So much has happened. So many questions. Who are we?"

"A work in progress." Jaffa laughed and kissed her again. He nuzzled Jaguar. "We'll figure it out together."

Skyla lurched to grab Zeinab who listed to the side as she took a step. Jaffa guided her to the crate where she wilted, sitting with her legs splayed out.

"Poppy," Jaffa asked, "what next? Where's Tangier? There is no time to waste. The drones are thick with cameras and agents everywhere. We only managed because we used the tunnels. Where is Tangier?"

"Not here. I don't know what happened. He and his agents were due here by now. You cannot wait for him. You must leave soon in order to reach the mountain range by the rendezvous time. Everything is arranged." Poppy circled the cramped room taking inventory of the travelers slated for the hovercraft. "I did not expect three passengers."

"I would not leave her to die alone in this hell hole. She is the head of my family. Blame me." Jaffa's eyes shifted towards Skyla's.

Skyla sat next to Zeinab and put an arm around her. "Of course, you should be with us. Thank you for bringing Jaguar. He's not a light load in a sling."

"No, your little boy is in fact a big boy." Zeinab plopped her head on Skyla's shoulder. "Maybe it was a mistake for me to come. I just slow you down."

"It was not a mistake. Jaffa was right to bring you. I'll carry Jaguar to make it easier for you." Skyla kissed her forehead. "You'll see."

Skyla left Zeinab to rest and joined the others. She could see the concern in Jaffa's face as he listened to Poppy's plan. Tangier's absence would not prevent them from leaving, but the level of protection fell to zero. There would be no one to run interference, to prevent their discovery by CSA, in the last few lengths above ground.

Poppy could lead with a slight distance from Jaffa, Skyla, and Zeinab. A group of three traveling away from the Cap City toward the boundaries was unusual. POVs would notice a threesome and CSA would read the scene as atypical. They would have to zigzag enough to be ignored. In the end, Skyla doubted that would be enough to protect them.

Tangier's absence weighed on her. The dark, damp room matched her spirit, falling darker, heavier, and sadder. Poppy gave Zeinab a swig of water. Jaguar pushed Skyla's arm with one paw and looked up to her. She reached her hand to his head to feel his soft fur and felt the vibration of his motor. Skyla could wait no longer, the risk of discovery too high. The danger to Zinc and Poppy overwhelmed any reason to wait a little longer for Tangier.

"We should go. Now." Skyla went to Zeinab, and helped her stand. She smoothed the outer layer and freed the hood so it could be lifted without a sound. "Ready, Zeinab? Jaffa and I will never leave you."

"And Jaguar? I have rights to that ball of fur, too."

"He's part of me, a package deal, so it goes without saying. You have us all." Skyla led her to Poppy. "Show us where to go."

Poppy pointed back toward the tunnel. "You will go back past where you first entered the tunnel and take the first left turn. Go about fifty feet and turn right into another tunnel. Don't slip. These are still used to flush out sewage. The next flush is not until tomorrow so there should be no surprises. It will smell, but you'll get used to it. The tunnel will dead-end. You must climb out to the street. This is the most dangerous part. You will still be in the Outlier town, but you will see a hover craft just beyond the barb wire."

"We cut it and jump on the hover craft? The driver expects us, or are we just random passengers?" asked Jaffa.

"He expects you, but only two. You will have to convince him you are not CSA," replied Poppy.

"I will travel with you but stay back to give you cover if something goes wrong." Zinc patted her gun. "Trust me."

Skyla smiled at the well-worn phrase Tangier used for every complication in their lives. "That's what my brother always says to me."

"Me, too." Zinc blushed just enough for Skyla to notice.

"Then we're off." Skyla began to walk toward the doorway. Jaffa followed, holding Zeinab close with locked elbows. Once they made the final turn to the dead-end tunnel, Skyla realized why the tunnels were so neglected by surveillance. As she approached the wall, the vertical ladder came into view. Then, she answered her own question. Anyone in the tunnels must surface some time and be seen in the dull light of day. She assumed the people that use the tunnels would be of little interest to the CSA and Affiliations. Who cared about Outliers? She heard the Affiliation leaders only hours ago declare their total indifference to people outside the Core. With no money power to be earned, no profit to be collected, what was the point of placing expensive surveillance machines in the underground maze? Only the rarest of occasions, like this, did the lack of surveillance in the tunnels challenge CSA. She felt a tinge of pride that she had created a fuss for a system she detested. But, the heavy cost to Tangier, Jaffa, and Zeinab erased any joy from it.

The party of exiles paused for Zeinab to recoup at the base of the vertical ladder. The wide wooden boards showed brown rot due to the sewage flush. Jaffa tested them by stomping on the edges. "Step here," he said and pointed to the firmest wood. He waved his hand in a circle and pointed up.

Skyla tackled the climb first, careful to swing the sling out of the way. Jaguar's motor had stopped a while back. For now, his ears were straight up, alert to everything in his way. She reached the top and popped the cover. Light streamed in through a crack.

"We're through." She slowly slid the cover to the side. Steady drizzle dripped onto her head. She pulled up her hood and took another step higher, to peek out of the rim of the manhole. She locked sight on the steel tips of boots on the edge of the hole. Please be Tangier, she thought to herself. She looked up at the face on the hunched over body.

"Riff?"

"It's me, Skyla. Take my hand and I'll give you a pull." His words froze her in place. "Come on, it's ok. Tangier is with me."

"Tangier? Where?"

"Skyla, you are safe," Tangier called. "Hurry. I am keeping watch. Stilton is on the hunt for us. Hurry."

"It's clear, Jaffa. Hurry." She let Riff pull her out of the hole, but could not say a word. She adjusted the sling so Jaguar would remain covered. He sat low in the sling, somehow sensing to be quiet. She hugged her brother and then let him get back to work. Riff crouched near the edge of the hole and reached down to grasp Zeinab's arms to haul her up. She saw Jaffa pushing her up from behind. "Come on Zeinab. You are almost through," said Skyla.

Zeinab heaved herself toward Riff who caught her shoulders and lifted her out only to let her plop on the ground. "Sorry, Ma'am," he said.

"I'm glad to be out of that stinky tunnel. I'm such an old nuisance. I should have stayed back." She covered her face with her hands.

Jaffa sprung out of the hole, light on his feet, despite the heavy backpack. He stepped toward Tangier and they clapped each other's back.

"There, see that shadow? A long oval mass?" said Tangier.

"Yep. The hovercraft?" replied Jaffa.

Tangier nodded. "You armed?"

"Armed enough. Who's this guy?"

"Riff. He's one of mine," said Tangier. "Riff, this is Jaffa. We're going to get him, his grandmother, and Skyla to safety. To do that, you and I are going to escort them on this hovercraft far into the hinterlands. I will drive, you will cover me, cover us. Return fire at will and make every shot a kill shot."

"Yes, sir." Riff stood straight but did not salute.

"Riff, give Skyla these extra guns. She needs to be armed, too."

Skyla, satisfied that Zeinab was a bit winded but generally ok, left her to join her brother and Jaffa.

"Thanks for these, Riff." Skyla filled the empty pockets of her pants with three Frankenstein guns. She slung a rifle over her shoulder. "Is that the hovercraft?"

Tangier nodded. "Jaffa, you know the timing is non-negotiable. Under no circumstances can you be late." He lowered his voice to a whisper. "Why Zeinab? I can understand not wanting to leave her, but the mission is to get you and Skyla to the Keep. Can she keep up? The trek through the mountain range is not long, but it is rugged. That's what eats up the time. And you have only one hour."

Skyla did not understand Tangier's comment about time. However, the quiet way he addressed it to Jaffa meant he did not want to explain it in front of Riff. It helped that Riff had stepped over to help Zeinab with her outer layer and was out of earshot. She could not fathom how the man she despised so much for all his chattiness and gawking stares at Celebration Wholesale featured in any of this. She understood Riff was with CSA, but his allegiance to Tangier was a surprise.

"Listen." Zeinab pointed to the sky in the direction of the Periphery.

"Drones. They are coming. We must go now." Tangier pointed toward the shadow. "Run, run like the wind."

Skyla and Jaffa each took a side and locked Zeinab in between them. They moved as a unit. Tangier ran out ahead, clearing any trash or obstacles in their path. He reached the barb wire and began to cut it. Riff, in the rear to provide cover, caught up with him and bent the wire back to form a hole. The sound of the drones grew louder. The drizzle turned into a pouring rain, splashing their eyes, and slowing their movements.

Skyla pushed Zeinab through the hole with Jaffa beside her. He pulled her toward the hovercraft and the open door where the pilot stood waiting for them. Skyla turned to Tangier. "How can I thank you?"

Tangier grabbed his sister close, and she buried her head in his shoulder. "Here, I have something for you. Open it when you reach the Keep. I'll be flying escort behind you, for cover. Now go." He pulled a tiny pouch from his pocket and tucked it deep into the sling with Jaguar. He pushed her away toward the hovercraft where Jaffa stood in the doorway, his hand outstretched to her.

Skyla called to Tangier just before she entered the hovercraft, "You are the best big brother a girl could ever have."

"See you soon." Tangier waved them off.

The hovercraft door sealed shut. It lunged forward, picking up speed as the drones arrived overhead.

"Riff, on my count, push the detonator." Tangier and Riff jumped behind piles of trash. Tangier waited until the drones swarmed just above the barbwire fence. "Three, two, one. Now."

Riff pushed the detonator, and the border of the Outlier town and the gateway to the hinterlands lit up with sizzling explosions of fire and light. The radiation interference knocked out the drones' electronic brains, and they began to fall like the raindrops that surrounded them. "That will hold them off for a while." Tangier and Riff snuck toward a tarp covered mound and pulled it off. The nuclear powered two-seat fly-craft, fully loaded with rockets, guns, and electronic weapons gleamed in the pale light.

"How did you get one of these? I thought they were classified," said Riff.

"They are. I am a senior field agent. I get what I want. And I wanted this." Tangier climbed into the pilot's seat. "Come on. You're coming with me."

"Sir? On that? I really don't know what is going on," Riff replied.

"Listen. You chose me over Stilton. That means you are mine. You and I can take down Stilton. What you know is what you need to know. Right now, you need to get your ass on this screaming jet and help me take out the biggest threat to everything we know."

"Yes, sir." Riff jumped into the rear seat, facing all the weapons at his fingertips. He pulled the helmet over his head and adjusted the night vision goggles. This is what he always wanted to do, not sit like the mole he was in some desk job. He joined CSA for the adventures it promised but never delivered to him. He expected to feel his gut start to burn, but it did not.

"Keep alert. Strap yourself in tight. We are going to catch up to the hovercraft. Operation Shield is a go." Tangier locked on his helmet and fired up the shiny fly-craft. Cutting through the thick air like a spear at top speed, he aimed toward the direction of the hovercraft. He took note of the blinks of lights from a similar aircraft racing out toward the hinterlands from another Outlier town. "It's not over yet."

CHAPTER THIRTY-SIX

BATTLE

Stilton stood over the slimy manhole cover near the edge of the Outlier town. He saw finger prints from swiping mud away. A vague trail of footprints, being erased by the drizzle, led away toward the border. That maggot, Tangier. Always crawling around underground. He looked up at the sound of an approaching nuclear fly-craft. The pilot swung it around and edged up to Stilton with short bursts of small power.

Stilton waved his hands over his head and shouted, "Get in the back. I'll drive, agent…."

"Gomez. Agent Gomez, sir."

Stilton grabbed the helmet from the back, slapped it on and locked it with one hand. Gomez jumped to the back seat as Stilton climbed in front, eager to power up and fly. "We are going to intercept them. They'll be surprised to see us. I'll end this shit once and for all." Agent Gomez didn't move. He had been warned to keep silent by other agents who knew Stilton.

The darkness gave them protection, but the steady rain made everything feel slimy to the touch. Stilton knew CSA regulation uniforms were designed for all weather conditions, but he hated to wear gloves. He preferred to feel the smooth, cold metal of the machine on his own skin, no matter how frigid. In the hinterlands, where the air was thin and weak, radiation burned unprotected skin within hours. The open cockpit design of the fly-craft allowed the air to stream past, while its micro-grit scraped any unprotected flesh raw like coarse sandpaper.

The headlight of the fly-craft dispersed light in a wide piercing beam, but the shiny raindrops falling in thick waves clouded his vision. Stilton could not shake the warning from the CSA director to use any method to bring Skyla to him. If he failed, he would be executed. He pressed on.

"Sir, there are lights ahead, two o'clock," said Agent Gomez in the back seat through the audio transmitter between the helmets.

"Copy that." Stilton peered through the rain at the lights and determined they came from a bigger slower vehicle than their own. "It's a hovercraft." He veered toward the lights and shifted from sub nuclear to full nuclear power to achieve maximum speed. "I will strike at you like a bolt of blue lightning."

The agent could hear Stilton's threat but said nothing. His mission was to follow orders, survive, and report everything he witnessed to the CSA Director. He noticed more lights from a drone swarm, swirling in a figure eight at six o'clock, but said nothing. Stilton would not stop until he reached the hovercraft.

Stilton noticed the swarm. "What gives? Didn't you see those drones? What are they doing? Who sent them?"

"It's unclear who ordered them," replied Gomez.

"I did not file a mission plan." Stilton thought for a moment. "Did you log out this vehicle on the official ledger?"

"No, sir. I did not as your request specified classified op."

"Who knows about our recovery mission?" Stilton grew quiet, guiding the fly-craft toward the faint blinking lights of a hover craft. As minutes passed, Stilton began to see a plan set by the CSA director. The unregistered fly-craft could be read as theft. The drones were dispatched by protocol to spy on it all. This subservient Gomez guy, who said nothing, could be serving the director. The simplicity was breathtaking. He, Stilton, was ordered to take Skyla into custody. But the CSA director was setting him up to be killed if he failed. Why? There had to be a deeper, serious threat to the Affiliations beyond Skyla and her fancy words that could not see the light of day.

"Sir?"

"Were you the next agent on the duty roster for sudden ops?"

"No sir. The agent first on the list was assigned to another op."

"Who appointed you to this mission?"

"The director," replied Gomez.

Stilton pulled his gun from his waist turned back toward the young agent. "Screw you and the director." He emptied the bullets into Gomez's body. With his other hand, he pulled the rear seat ejector lever and let the slumped body drop away to nowhere.

He pressed the fly-craft to its limit for speed and could see that he was gaining on the distant lights of the hovercraft. The drones had fallen back and no other craft had appeared. Stilton's hands felt hot and he could see where his knuckles were scraped by the micro-grit in the air. The rain had retreated to a light but steady pour. He figured the time and distance placed him near the mountain range where he had never been before.

The earth beyond the mountain range held no interest for him. Mongrel humans might exist there but nothing like the people of the Core. He had a place in the Core, a purpose in CSA. He would lead the takeover and put the Affiliations under CSA.

Stilton had long dismissed the myths about a green place, a Keep, an old story of quaint people who lived simple, happy lives, as the gossip of the losers. Only losers in the Periphery and Outliers fell for that Longhouse propaganda. Longhouse, a dream for simpleminded folk waiting for a new era, would fade away in time. Stilton knew their time would never come for he would engineer the next version of the post-Collapse world, built with CSA in complete control.

Tangier once accused him of having no imagination. Stilton reviewed the old conversation with his archrival. He searched for a clue he might have missed. He preferred the solid world he could see and feel, but if there really was nothing out there beyond the mountain range, why did the hovercraft go there? Skyla would not survive in the mountains, and Tangier would not allow it. Did his lack of imagination blind him to the unspeakable reality of an alternative society? Could the CSA director know about this?

It dawned on him why he was to be killed off by CSA. He had failed to keep Skyla in custody so the CSA director, without the committee, could grill her again. He must suspect that she knew the secret of another world. She told them as much when she said her work wasn't finished. She hadn't written it down yet, and he needed to know what she'd write.

Stilton knew a good agent doesn't kill a source of information until it has been wrung dry. The CSA director wanted Skyla, a prized source, a little longer. So, a senior agent like him who screws up is a goner. He refused to accept this verdict from the CSA director he despised. Power was close enough to taste and his for the taking if he could survive. He pushed ahead, despite his bleeding hands, closer to the lights of the hovercraft, now in his direct path.

CHAPTER THIRTY-SEVEN

GOOD BYE

The hovercraft skimmed under the limbs of a dead thicket, on the edge of the hinterland next to the steep brown mountains. It idled while the passengers jumped to the ground below. Tangier arrived seconds later. Riff held back, ordered to be ready to fly or shoot, or both, at Tangier's command.

Tangier approached the family he was about to send into exile. He noted the time. In one minute, the one hour window of time would open. For that hour, all the world was private. The goodbyes would have to be quick. He put his hands on his sister's shoulders, face to face. "Skyla. This is it. The path is a narrow, dry riverbed that snakes around the mountains that rise on either side. No sharp turns, only curves, aiming straight ahead. Jaffa, did you get this?"

"Yep. Got it." Jaffa steadied his grandmother.

"The elevation will rise to the point where there once was a waterfall that fed water into the river that flowed down each side of the range. You will climb up for about twenty minutes. The rest of the way is sloped downward. You can pick up speed there." He glanced at Zeinab and whispered, "She will need help, but there is enough time. I am glad she is going with you. She would have been killed tomorrow."

"Tangier. What will happen to you? How will you get out of this mess you're in?" Tears filled Skyla's eyes.

"I'll be fine. I'll always know where you are. We'll see each again. Trust me." He hugged his sister then pushed her away. "Jaffa, Zeinab, this way. Hurry."

"Sir." Riff called from the hovercraft. "Incoming."

The bright headlight from Stilton's fly-craft shined like a spotlight on them. He swung up next to the hover craft. Dust flew into the air and created a thick wave of grainy dirt that gushed over everyone.

Tangier shook the dust away from his face and drew his gun. "Why, Senior Agent Stilton. What brings you out so far away from your little cave in the Core?"

"Just doing my job, you shitty little traitor. I'm going to exterminate a pest, a little girly rat. And look, the rat's boy-friend and his mama. How sweet. Oh, and the brother. I can take out the whole nest." Stilton spit on the ground. "There is probably a cat around here somewhere. too. Oh, maybe in that sling you are wearing?"

"Leave them alone, you scumbag." Skyla stepped forward next to Tangier. "I do remember you now. The tough guy who got off making little kids cry. Still the same."

"Yeah, still the same, you loser."

"You want me, tough guy? Then come get me. The others don't matter and you'll be the hero to your boring, tedious CSA, the lackey to Big Data." She took another step forward, swinging Tangier's arm away.

Jaffa left Zeinab by the hovercraft and sauntered up to Tangier, hands up and open, indicating he was unarmed. "If you want to kill us, do it. My grandmother doesn't like to get soaked in the rain. You should never insult a grandmother."

"I don't think you want to kill too fast, though. You want to know what CSA has hidden from you." Tangier held his gun steady. "Wouldn't you like to know what really exists out there?"

"Shut up, all of you. I don't care what is out there. I care about following my orders."

"What orders?" Tangier shouted, "You make up your own orders as you go. So, what's it going to be? Recapture Skyla? Kill her? Overthrow the Affiliations? Exactly what orders are you about to follow?"

"Shut up, Tangier." Stilton raised his gun toward Skyla.

Before he could fire off a round, Zeinab stood up with a loud sigh. "Do what you want young man. I am too old to get wet in the rain. I'm leaving." She turned toward the mountain range and began to shuffle away.

Stilton turned his gun toward Zeinab and fired. She fell to her side motionless.

"You monster," screamed Skyla who drew her own gun and aimed it at Stilton. "That's the best you have, CSA agent? A little old lady?"

Jaffa ran to his fallen grandmother. Tangier called to Skyla, "Step back. He's mine."

Stilton chuckled. "So it has come to this. Shoot you first or your sister. I believe I'll shoot your sister. It will kill you to know you couldn't protect her from me in the end." He stretched out his arm, took aim at Skyla's head and fired.

Before the bullet reached Skyla, it got trapped, circling through and through Riff's chest. He lay on top of her, a shield against the cruel senior agent he loathed since his first days in CSA. Skyla pushed herself up and took Riff's gun from his hand. She fired it point blank at Stilton until there were no more bullets to fire. She rolled Riff onto his back and knelt beside him. "Riff, Riff, can you hear me?" She patted his head and held his hand. He opened his eyes catching her gaze but said nothing.

"Jaffa, Jaffa, come quick." Skyla looked back at Jaffa huddled over Zeinab. She saw Tangier standing over Stilton's dead body.

"Skyla." Riff spoke with the raspy breath of a soul on the edge of life. "Skyla."

"Riff. You saved me. Oh, Riff," said Skyla, "I was mean to you."

"Yes, you were. But, I deserved it." Shallow coughs overtook his breath. "I loved you. And now I am a hero." His head fell to the side.

"Skyla. Skyla." Tangier pulled her to her feet. "You must go. Now. We have lost time."

"Zeinab?" Skyla watched Jaffa guide Zeinab to her feet.

"She's bruised, but ok. Nothing fatal thanks to all those layers of clothes," yelled Jaffa.

"Skyla, now you must go." Tangier pushed her toward them.

She felt the sling and screamed, "Jaguar's gone. Do you see him? I can't leave without Jaguar!"

"I have him. Hurry up." Zeinab turned to show Jaguar buried in her layers, with only his eyes and nose visible from a deep pocket.

She ran to the grandmother and Jaffa waiting at the bank of the dry riverbed. She turned one last time to catch a memory she would hold for a lifetime. Her big brother stood strong and waved her a kiss. She threw one back to him. With her family and familiar in tow, Skyla vanished into the safe cover of night, unwatched by human eyes, with only the glimmering stars of the Seven Sisters as sentries.

CHAPTER THIRTY-EIGHT

RECORD

The CSA director sat across the table from Tangier in a small windowless room without cameras. The agents nicknamed the room "The Confessional." No one knew what went on inside the only official space known to be free of surveillance. An invitation to this reserved chamber of the CSA director was a fate to avoid.

The CSA director sat board straight in the simple steel chair. His crisp white shirt with red neckband flattered his flawless black skin and gentle eyes. His elbows just graced the top of the table, his fate wielding hands folded together.

"Senior Field Agent Tangier, please explain the events of last night one final time."

"Yes, sir. Per your order, Senior Agent Perdu Stilton was tasked to bring in Skyla Roseau for questioning at the Rules of Words Committee. He, in turn assigned the logistics of her retrieval to me."

"Did you encounter any problems with this," asked the CSA director.

"Yes. The subject was abducted by a porn, organ harvesting outfit in an Outlier town. This abduction delayed my recovery of the subject." Tangier remained motionless in his steel chair.

"Is the abduction relevant to the case in any way other than as a delay?"

"It is relevant to the case. The whole outfit was operated by Swillian, a board member of Affiliation Yellow."

"Go on." The CSA director did not move.

"I was able to rescue Skyla Roseau from Swillian's outfit and put her in a safe house. This enraged Swillian who complained to his CSA contact, Senior Agent Perdu Stilton. A disagreement ensued between the two. Senior Agent Stilton shot the board member Swillian to death and disposed of his body, never to be found."

"How do you know this to be true? You have proof of this?" The CSA director unfolded his big knuckled hands and tapped the table with his fingertips.

"Yes, sir. Agent Riff, a dedicated agent with a talent for data mining, recorded the crime and hid it well. He revealed it to me. He was concerned that Senior Agent Stilton had changed the mission regarding Skyla Roseau from retrieve to execute and had more plans that could threaten the balance of our societies, CSA and the Affiliations. In fact, his words were, 'Stilton is planning a takeover. CSA will control all the Affiliations.'"

"Then you brought Skyla Roseau before the Rules of Words Committee, of course, I was there as head of Affiliation Red." He smiled. "Protocol."

Tangier did not return the smile. "Yes, sir. As you recall, Skyla Roseau escaped. You sir, issued a directive for her to be recaptured."

"Yes, I did. Appropriate for the circumstances."

"Yes, sir, but it played into Senior Agent's Stilton's plan to overthrow the Affiliations using the CSA. Skyla Roseau was found dead, strangled by common criminals, in an Outlier camp town. Senior Agent Stilton did not report this but instead lied to you, saying he was still in pursuit of her. He used this as the excuse to launch his operation."

"This is why he stole a fly craft, to fly to his henchmen in the hinterlands?" The CSA director rubbed his hands together, his eyes staring straight ahead into nothing.

"Yes, sir. Agent Riff alerted me to the stolen fly-craft, and we followed in pursuit to interrupt his takeover attempt. We gave chase and located him and his fly-craft gunman just before the barren dust bowls. He saw us and fired. We fired back. In the end, Senior Agent Stilton and his gunmen were shot dead. Riff died a heroic death, taking a bullet meant for me."

"So, what is your analysis of all this?"

"With your order to bring in Skyla Roseau, I was able to uncover a traitor in CSA, Senior Agent Perdu Stilton. The subject Skyla Roseau has perished, a welcome safeguard to the Affiliations. The criminal agent Stilton has been eliminated. Agent Riff should be awarded a posthumous medal for bravery. I will round up any suspects loyal to Stilton and remove them from CSA."

"Senior Field Agent Tangier, that is quite a story." The CSA director studied Tangier's face and motionless posture. Tangier's steely presence today was no different than the courage of the little boy he had encountered at his parent's home and later the orphanage all those years ago. "There is no evidence of this. No record from any POVs lenses. Yet you speak with conviction."

"Yes. Sir."

"Can you explain this?"

"Sir, Senior Agent Stilton would disable any POVs lenses in the sectors he desired. He programed in a loop of video showing routine life, for the time he anticipated he'd be offline. It was clever, but now we know how he did it and can ensure that it does not happen again."

"I see. When we leave this room, this story becomes fact." The dashing CSA director stood up and Tangier followed suit standing at attention. The director reached out his hand to Tangier. "Congratulations Senior Agent Tangier Roseau. I expect great things from you."

"Thank you, sir." Tangier waited while the CSA director walked out the door. He noted the time and walked out of the confessional.

CHAPTER THIRTY-NINE

HOME

Clan Mother Genesee stood with her arms crossed next to Grenadine in front of their console of monitors. Poe perched on her shoulder. She studied the electronic map, the vague outlines irrelevant to the people of Cap City but sacred to her. "There, Grenadine. Look. There it is." She pointed to a blinking light. "Skyla has put on the earring from Tangier. Our children are home. The Fourth Epoch has begun."

Coming Soon

The Fourth Epoch

The heroic voyage to the Keep was the easy part. Once there, Skyla and Jaffa must scramble to confront the ruthless foes that threaten the future. Internal factions threaten civil war in the Keep. Within days Tangier sends an urgent message they cannot ignore. Can Skyla, Jaffa, and Tangier take down the Affiliations' Big Data? Who will lead the next epoch, Big Data or the Haudenosaunee Confederacy?

ACKNOWLEDGMENTS

When I write, there are many people along for the ride. I wouldn't dare depart down this road without my friend and colleague, Nancy Dinsmore, an expert on familiars, black cats, and just about everything else.

I took along the books of Taiaiake Alfred, Bonnie Freeman, and Barbara Mann. I watched YouTube lectures from Rick Hill and read Kevin White's blog. From all these works, characters emerged for this story and the next.

After reading William Robinson's sharp book on capitalism, he graciously permitted me to quote from it for the epigraph.

As the journey progressed, Kathy Johnson, Kathy Monroe, Mary Sue Baldwin, Rowena Fraser, and Alexis Stutson, provided insightful critiques that kept me on track.

I was lucky to work with editors, Danny Gamble and Nabella Shunnarah, and artist, Chris DeLoach.

Barbara Jerry, my cousin, helped me to find the story of our great grandmother from Montreal, Canada.

I can't write unless my muse, Ava Gardner, a Maine Coon cat, and Cole Porter, a Black cat and my familiar, are nearby. Pete, my husband, inspires, supports, and encourages me.

I am grateful to you all.

BIBLIOGRAPHY

Alfred, Gerald R., *Heeding the Voices of our Ancestors*. Oxford University Press, 1995.

Alfred, Taiaiake. *Wasáse indigenous pathways of action and freedom*. Toronto, University of Toronto Press, 2009.

Freeman, Bonnie M., "The Spirit of Haudenosaunee Youth: The Transformation of Identity and Well-being Through Culture-based Activism" (2015). Theses and Dissertations (Comprehensive). *Wilfrid Laurier University*.

Johansen, Bruce E., with chapters by Donald A. Grinde Jr and Barbara Mann. *Debating Democracy, Native American Legacy of Freedom* Santa Fe: Clear Light Publishers, 1998.

Mann, Barbara Alice. *Iroquoian Women The Gantowisas*. New York: Peter Lang, 2011.

Mann, Barbara A. "The Lynx in Time: Haudenosaunee Women's Traditions and History," *American Indian Quarterly*, Vol 21, #3 (Summer, 1997) pp. 423-449

Marx, Karl. *Capital*. Vol. 1 and 2. Penguin Classics, Reprint edition, 1992.

Orwell, George. *1984* Signet Classic, New York, 1950.

Polanyi, Karl. *The Great Transformation*. Beacon Press, Boston, 2001.

Robinson, William I. *Global Capitalism and the Crisis of Humanity*. Cambridge University Press, 2014.

ABOUT THE AUTHOR

Liza Elliott is a sociologist and teaches at the Sparkman Center for Global Health, the University of Alabama at Birmingham.

www.ingramcontent.com/pod-product-compliance
Lightning Source LLC
Chambersburg PA
CBHW021526250626
47154CB00006BA/1992